£2·50

*About th*

GH00393592

Simon Kettlewell has worked across the world with various organisations, supporting people with mental health issues and educational programs for young people. He has also done quite a lot of other things, but prefers his fictional characters to do the talking. He lives with his family in a surreal community in Devon.

If you would like to know more about Simon Kettlewell and his work, you can find this at: www.simonkettlewell.org or at his literary agency's website: Sheil Land Associates www.sheilland.com

# *Dead Dog Floating*

Derek Jackson, 12 years old, promises his bedridden mother to find his father, Colin, who has absconded from the family home. Mam, his gran and Aunt Mavis all believe that Colin is mentally ill and should be put in a home for his own protection.

Colin had promised Derek to take him on a big adventure to the South Pole but he knew that his father had no intention or the courage to embark on such a journey despite having built a boat with a steel hull to crack the ice. Derek knows the truth of what his father is doing but this is just one more secret he has to keep. He begins to buckle under the increasing responsibility to keep the family secrets and the web of untruths he is expected to tell. He confronts his father living in a back street with Louise Draper and is side-tracked when he sees the object of his dreams – a colour telly as big as the flicks! He is quickly disarmed by his father with two cans of Double Diamond.

Derek returns home, sure that his discovery will kill his mam, and wonders if he should tell just one more lie.

A down-to-earth story of a young boy weighed down with lies to cover family secrets; of a feckless father and a mother unable to confront the truth and the shame that in 1972, ordinary people struggling to make a better life, simply can't have 'the man of the house sneaking away like a thief in the night'.

# Dead Dog Floating

## Simon Kettlewell

*Also By Simon Kettlewell*

*Bread for the Bourgeoisie*

Published by
Peach Publishing

For Ann James

I would also like to dedicate this book to the three lost boys in this story –

Philip Barker, Gary Smedley, and Eagle – to the men they might have been. Also to Derek Jackson and the man I hope he might become.

STAMPED INSIDE THE FRONT COVER OF A
TEXT BOOK –

*'A HISTORY OF WILLIAM SHAKESPEARE'*

**'THE PROPERTY OF DALEMEAD GRAMMER
SCHOOL 1972.'**


'OH WHAT A TANGLED WEB WE WEAVE WHEN
FIRST WE PRACTISE TO DECEIVE!'
*WALTER SCOTT 1808*


WRITTEN IN RED FELT-TIP:

*BUT AFTER WE DONE IT FOR QUITE A BIT
WE GET DEAD GOOD AT IT !!!!!! SHAKSPEERS
A WANKER!!!!!*

*TINA SCOTT IS A SLAPER. RING THIS
NUMBER FOR SEX 2486.*


WRITTEN A YEAR LATER IN BLUE INK:

*TO THE MEMORY OF EAGLE 1960-1972 RIP.*

# Encyclopedia Britannica, Westy's a killer, and God

## On the landing outside me mam's bedroom door
### Now, 1972

In me *Encyclopedia Britannica*, which I've got the full set except for S, it says in the bit about the natural world that babies, when they're born, look like their dads. It's so the dads know the babies are theirs, and they don't piss off or eat them. It says this is all part of *the natural order of things*. So me dad's broken this *natural order of things* cause he's pissed off, and gone to live in Moretonside. He once said to me mam that I looked like the milkman. She told him not to be so *bleedin' cheeky*. Anyway, the milkman's as bald as a coot, so he can't be me dad. I don't think it's the same for starfish or snails, which I'd look up if I'd got the S in me *Encyclopedia Britannica*.

I've got these things running through me head like an express train. I'm down on me hands and knees, and I'm waiting dead silent, like a cat does when it's watching a mouse, ready to pounce and sink it's teeth into it's skinny little neck, like Tom and Jerry. Now, I'm lowering meself down onto the floor dead slow. It's making me arms ache. I've got to crawl on me belly, commando style, me arms out wide like I'm swimming. It's so you don't sink through the mud if you're in the jungle, which I know I'm not, cause I'm on the carpet on the landing. It's the same sort of thing. The carpet's green.

*You've got to be ready*, me granddad always used to say; *you've got to be ready. You never know when they're coming at you. It's when you see the whites of their eyes, and it's too late, and they get you with the cold steel. They run you through.* Me granddad was on the front line in the First World War, in the mud, fighting the Bosh with their pointy helmets. He should know. It was hard for him. But it's hard for me too, cause I've got me parka on and me *docs*, and I can't move me arms very good. It's dead hard to crawl. I want to sneeze. I can't hold it in. If you don't close your eyes, your eyeballs fly out the sockets at ninety miles an hour. Me gran knew someone it happened to. They went right across Harvey Road and down the bank into the old canal. They floated for ages until some crows had them for their dinner.

I know me mam's heard me now I've sneezed. God made me sneeze.

Me mam's got bat ears. All mams and dads have got bat ears. I think she heard me cause the fifth stair creaked when I was coming up. The fifth stair never creaks, but it did this time, cause I know God's watching me, and He's got it in for me. He's touched me with the finger. That's what they say; *The hand of God*. Once He's touched you, you're done for, cause He don't play fair. It's like He's got a gun and I ain't got owt, and He can shoot me whenever He wants. That's why He lets people starve and die in earthquakes, and He let the chip van crash into the wall at the bottom of our street, and crush Mrs Ashby's dog, Tricksy when he were having a crap on Mr West's garden cause he shouts at all the kids. That's Mr West, not Tricksy. He just barked. God does these things to show He's the boss; the big shot in the sky with all them angels and sheep and things. He's flexing his muscles, like he does when there's a storm, and there's hail and everything.

Tricksy's dead cause he knew Mr West's a bastard. Even though Tricksy was a dog, he was dead clever. Tricksy knew Mr West'd killed his wife and buried her in the inspection pit in his garage. He filled it in with this concrete that he had delivered in the middle of the night by his mate who does shifts down the cement works. Mr West made this big thing of telling everybody that he had it filled in cause he was too old to go in the pit. He used to stand by his gate waiting to tell people when they went past with their shopping. He waited to tell them why he'd filled his pit in. It's what criminals do. It's a double bluff. Everybody knows Westy's a killer on the loose. But everybody's scared. No one wants a killer living in the same street. So they don't say owt. Charlie's dad says that these things can affect house prices. Especially puffs. He hates puffs. I ain't ever met one. They do ballet and stuff. Blokes don't do ballet at Dalemead, they'd get their heads kicked in if they did. Anyway, Westy'll get you if he gets half the chance! Once you've murdered one person, you can murder as many as you like. It don't make no difference. Look at *Jack the Ripper*.

Me and Charlie saw Mr West climbing out his pit one day. He had this tape measure and everything. We knew then he was measuring it for Mrs West. She's like a zeppelin. It'd have to be dead wide to get her massive arse in; especially after she's dead, when she's as stiff as a board.

Mr West saw us looking at him. He started yakking, like he does.

– 'er, 'er, 'er … Lads! I'll get bloody-well stuck in there one day and no bugger will 'ear me, and I'll be no more than a skelington when they find me.

He was trying to make us feel sorry for him. He might fool some of the stupid buggers round here with his coloured concrete and his massive onions. Not me and Charlie. We're as sharp as knives. Charlie's going to be a detective with a massive magnifying glass and one of them funny hats when he leaves school.

Mr West did this laugh.

– *Heh, heh, heh.*

If you know what I mean. His teeth are dead long and yellow like a vampire's. He was just trying to throw us kids off the scent. Grown ups think kids are stupid. We see things they can't though. I'll tell you that for nowt. It's all in *The Secret Seven.* They don't listen cause they think they know it all. I tried to tell me mam that me dad's altered the order of things, but she thinks I'm daft. I showed her the *Encyclopedia Britannica,* but she just laughed like she does.

– If it's in the *Encyclopedia Britannica,* then it's right, I said.

– They don't put things in the *Encyclopedia Britannica* for nowt.

She pushed it away. – It doesn't matter. It's just a book.

There's a whole world in the *Encyclopedia Britannica* as long as it don't begin with S.

– Everything matters, I said. – If something happens, then something else happens after that, and it keeps going cause it can't stop. It's like rabbits and why there's so many of them.

Me mam didn't say owt after that cause there was nowt else to say.

Anyway, Tricksy lived next door to Mr West. After Mrs West went, (which was down the pit), Tricksy started doing this whining all the time. He was sniffing under the fence, and scratching in the soil to get under it like a mad dog. So Mr West got the concrete he had left over from filling his pit in, and built this diddly wall to stop Tricksy getting through.

Mr West told everybody that Mrs West was in a home cause she couldn't remember who she was, or anybody else, and they all nodded like them dogs people have on the back shelves of their cars. Mr West started to cry, but me and Charlie knew he was pretending. He was doing what me mam says are crocodile tears. I didn't know crocodiles could cry cause they eat everybody else, then they get made into handbags for the Queen. It's not in the EB, which is what I say for short, as *Encyclopedia Britannica* is a gob full.

– She tells everybody I'm trying to kill her, Mr West kept bleating. – It's a terrible thing. I've never hurt a fly.

This ain't true. He has traps all over the place for mice, and a catapult for the moggies. Me and Charlie just looked at each other.

– She ain't in no 'ome, Charlie said when Westy went inside.

Tricksy just sat on the other side of the fence and looked at us, like he wanted us to help, like *Lassie* or *The Wonder Dog*, or *Skippy* even, cause Tricksy knew that something was up. And he knew that we knew. If you know what I mean. He knew that we knew that Mrs West was down there in that concrete, in that pit like a fossil. One day some bloke with one of them little toffee hammers is going to find her in a million million years time. Then they'll arrest one of Westy's great, great, great, grandchildren for the crime and lock them up.

– And you can bloody well shut up too, Mr West said to Tricksy before he went into his house.

You could see he wished he'd chucked the dog in the pit as well. He hated that dog. Tricksy could smell Mrs West. I mean, she did smell in real life; of fish and cheese, like old people do. Tricksy could smell that haddock and the rotting flesh right through the concrete. Mrs West never did shut up. Not till she was in the pit anyway. Then she didn't say a word.

God don't give a shit. He let Mr West shove her down the pit. He knew she'd never get out cause she's got this hip. So she'd be lying there wedged in this pit while Westy's filling it in, in the middle of the night with concrete. I expect he filled her gob in first to shut her up.

Mr West left. Me and Charlie saw him leave with a woman

to live in the south where they eat salad cause the sun shines all day. I told me mam.

– 'e killed Mrs West!

– People don't just go around killing other people, me mam said.

– Hitler did. 'e killed all them Jews. Jack the Ripper, and there's that Crispin bloke who used to dissolve 'is visitors in a bath of acid.

– It's not the same.

– Why not?

– Because it isn't.

Me mam always laughs when I try to tell her owt serious. That's what adults do. That's what happened with the little boy in *The Emperor's new clothes*. They just laughed at him. The Emperor was in his carriage with all them people watching, and he was stark bollock naked!

New people moved into Mr West's house. Me and Charlie went to see them. Charlie knocked on the door, then he ran up the path, got on his bike, and pissed off. A bloke opened the door and looked at me. He had this massive belly and a beard. If you ask me, he looked like a perv.

– What the hell do you want? The bloke said.

I didn't know what to say. I felt stupid. So I said it. It just came out.

– Mr West buried Mrs West in the inspection pit in the garage.

The bloke rubbed his eyes as if he couldn't see me properly.

– What the fuck are you talking about? What's your name?

– Derek Jackson. I live at number two.

– Well, Derek Jackson, somebody needs to tell you that you ought to mind your own fucking business.

– She's in the pit. I'm telling you. 'e shoved 'er in in the middle of the night. Tricksy the dog next door saw 'im. 'e could smell Mrs West.

I knew what he was thinking. He looked over the fence where Tricksy used to live.

– They ain't got no dog.

– He was run over by the chip van, I told him.

The bloke just looked at me. I didn't tell him it was God. You could tell he wasn't the sort of bloke who believed in God.

– And I'm telling you to piss off and keep your nose out of other people's business.

He was dead angry. I tried to tell him

– She's in there! If you dig it up with one of 'em road drills you'll find 'er!

The bloke started to close the door. He pointed at me. His finger was yellow on the end and smelt of fags.

– Unless she's got a twin sister, she's in *Derby Lodge Nursing Home.*

I didn't know what to say. Then I saw it. I saw that he looked like Mr West. He'd got the nose and the teeth, and his eyes were too close together. Auntie Mavis always says that you can't trust nobody if their eyes are too close together. They're *shifty.* This bloke was Westy's son. He knew. He bloody well knew she was in there, and he was covering for his dad. That's what sons and Dads do. They stick together. It's in the *order of things* cause it says so in me EB. If it says so in me EB then it's right, cause it's written by them blokes with egg heads. Dads defend their kids until they're old enough to look after themselves; even if they've murdered their mams.

Anyway, as I was saying – before I got to the landing outside me mam's bedroom, I got to the top of the stairs. It's the first and the third step, and then the ninth that creak, not the fifth. I knew I was against God then.

– Des! Me mam says.

I'm lying dead still on the carpet now with me face flat down. Me nose's itching again.

– Des! Don't frighten me. I know it's you. Why are you lying on the floor?

I'm lying here dead still and silent. I can slow me heart rate if I want to. I'm highly trained. I'm right outside her bedroom door, and I've got me head pressed up against the crack. I can see her face. There's this massive moon, all lit up like it's day. I can see into the room dead clear. Me mam sniffs and then she blows her nose. It sounds like a foghorn. She's propped up on pillows like me granddad was before he went. It's what they do, so you can see everybody before you pop your clogs. It's also so she can breath in the night cause she says she can't breathe no more, that she's suffocating, that me dad's suffocating her. I don't know how he can do that cause he's not here, but she says he is anyway.

I'm holding me breath and the hammer in me heart's banging against the floor like it's going through the whole house. It sounds like a massive clock. Bang, bang, bang.

– Des!

There she goes again. Me dad says she's like a dog with a bone.

I think about lying here 'til she's gone to sleep, which is never cause me mam don't sleep no more. She say's she can't stop thinking, and then she says I don't think enough. I get up dead slow, so she don't know I've been crawling past, and I stand in the doorway.

– There you are, she says, like she's dead pleased to see me. – You could have been a burglar.

– Why would I be a burglar, I've got a key.

– You could have broken in.

– Like I said, I've got a key. Why would I want to break in if I've got a key?

– Remember that time, she says, – when you climbed up the drain pipe and through the toilet window. You hadn't got a key then. You scuffed your shoes. Me mam's like an Elephant. I don't mean she looks like one, like Mrs West did. Me mam looks like a runner bean, but she never forgets owt, at all!

Me mam's trying to be chatty. It's what adults do. They start chatting about things like the weather and the match and what you do at school, then they catch you out, cause they want to ask you a question that you don't want to answer. But you're answering all these other questions, and you just say it. It's like that game on the telly where they try and make you say yes or no. But I'm not stupid, even though she and Auntie Mavis and me gran and me dad think I am cause I'm twelve. They think that children should be seen and not heard. Everybody has to breathe and fart. It ain't possible not to be heard.

Me mam pats the bed so I can sit down like they do in hospital. But I'm staying here where she can't get me cause she gets me head and rubs it. I hate people touching me head. In the EB it says the first thing people do in an accident or in a fight, is to protect their heads. No one wants no one touching their heads.

– I need to go to bed, I say. – It's school tomorrow. I've got triple maths.

I hate triple maths.

Then she looks at me all pathetic, and starts picking at the sheets like me granddad did just before he died.

– Just tell me, she says. – Did you find him?

I've got to say something.

– I went all over the place. Then me torch broke and me 'ands froze. There was this coloured bloke in the garage and 'e 'ad this map. We looked at it for ages. Then 'e realised it was a map of Leicester, which is no good cause I was in Derby.

– Never mind about the map, Derek. Did you find him?

There's this giant black cloud going in front of the moon. It looks like a dragon with fire coming out its gob, and that someone's putting a blanket over the moon's head. I'm waiting cause I know it's going to happen. Then it goes dead dark and I can't see me mam's face, and that means she can't see mine neither. It's what the commandos do before they attack the guns. I could sneak out right now. I'm as still as a statue, and I'm holding me breath. I can hold it for two minutes in Reginald Street Baths in the deep end when they've skimmed the cockroaches off.

– Come on Derek, don't muck around, she says, even though she can't see me now. – You've been out for hours and hours. You're not telling me you've been riding round and round all this time. It's late. Just tell me what happened.

Her voice starts to sound like she's miles away. She starts off as a person, then she starts getting smaller and smaller until she's this little mouse. All I can hear is this tiny squeak in the dark. She's saying something, squeak, squeak, squeak, like they do in the *Beano* when they've been whacked dead hard and pressed flat. Then I can see this picture. I can see the sea. I love the sea. But we live in Derby and there's no sea, not for a million million miles. I know it's in me head and everything. I'm not like one of them nutters in *Pastures* or owt. But it's always the sea I can see. And the sun's shining dead bright and I could be a million miles away like where the pirates are, and the women in grass skirts like on *Mutiny on the Bounty* with that Martin Brando. I'm only twelve now, but one day I'm going to find that place and live there forever and ever, amen. I know it's real and I'll search until I find it, and be dead happy.

Her voice is getting louder again, and the sea is going away like it's evaporating in the sun and she's coming back. She ain't a mouse no more. I think of the painting me gran has over her gas fire. There's this beach and the sea, and a boat with a blue and white sail, and a shop with a blind over it that's blue and white. People actually live in places like that. They don't just go there on their holidays, they live there. People actually live in Skeggy all the time!

– Derek!

I know I've got to tell her something cause she sent me to find me dad. I let out this big gob of air cause I'm still holding me breath. It's easily three minutes.

I think of what she told me before, so I just say it cause there's no other way. I know God's watching me. He's got it in for me and there's nowt I can do. Me dad used to say *in for a penny*.

# BEFORE

## White lies and black lies

Did you know that there's white lies and black lies? Me mam says a black lie is a proper lie. It's when you look at someone and you tell them the opposite to what's in your head. Me mam says it's like telling someone it's black when it's white, which is obviously where it comes from. Eagle used to tell black lies all the time; even when he had his hand on the bible. He never said it, but I know it's cause he thought God was a git for letting his mam die. And God don't forget. You only have to cross his path once and He's got you in his sights. Everyone says that God has a reason, and we don't have to know what that reason is. So, when Eagle does something, like smash a locker up at school and the teacher says:
– why did you do that Eagle?
He just says:
– Dunno.
Eagle has his reasons, but we don't know why. Eagle still got the cane though. Someone ought to give God the cane, then he wouldn't go around running people over, and so Tricksy would still be alive, and they'd see that Westy killed Mrs West. They'd hang him from a tree like they do in the westerns, and leave him for the vultures so they can peck his knackers. Mind you, they'd be dead small.

Me mam used to say we were Christians. I went to *Twycross*

*Zoo* with the school when I was seven, and you could see the Lions dribbling cause they wanted to eat us. That's what they used to do in Roman times. It's crap being a Christian. Everybody wants to kill you. Mind you, you can't be a Christian if you lie, and they're the biggest liars in the whole wide world cause they say God is good. No one's ever seen him, so how do they know?

Eagle's mam went all the way to Moretonside where the people from Pakistan live. It's where you get the cheap stuff cause they came over to get away from the war, and they opened all these corner shops. Me Gran says that one day they'll run out of corners and they'll run riot. Everybody says they take all the jobs cause the English blokes are too lazy to do them, and they just go on the dole. One of the Pakistan girls in our school gave me one of her sweets. She's dead nice. English kids wouldn't give you one of their sweets. Her dad's a bus driver. He drives all the way to Littleton where there ain't no coloured people, and Auntie Mavis says it's the beginning of the end. She says they're spreading like a rash.

Eagle's mam was carrying her shopping all the way home from Moretonside, cause they didn't have any dough. It's miles. Then this bloke came down Clifton Road in his flash car, and he killed her on the zebra crossing. You can't kill people on Zebra crossings. It's against the law. Eagle's mam looked after old ladies in her street and everything, just like me gran does. Me gran says she was a dead good person. Mind you, me gran was a nurse before she got dead old. She was the first person in the whole wide world to look after this bloke in an iron lung. He had to live in this big metal box all the time until he died. He had to crap in it and everything. Me gran said being a nurse is God's work. But He still killed Eagle's mam even though she was a good person. Charlie says that the vicar at

Eagle's mam's funeral said that God has his reasons for taking Mrs Eagle. Charlie said that Eagle walked right up to the vicar and smacked him in the gob and walked out. Charlie says so anyway. He says he was there, hiding under a pew.

– So God always knows if you tell a lie? I said to me mam.

– He always knows. He knows everything, but it's different with white lies.

– Why?

– You're protecting people. God likes people who do that sort of thing. It's what Christians do. They think of others before themselves.

I know that's bollocks cause Mr West's a Christian and goes to church. He killed his wife! Like I said, God can see everything, and he will have seen Westy stuffing Mrs West in the pit in his garage. So you tell me what that's all about!

– Did you know Jesus was coloured, I said to me mam.

– Don't try and be clever, Derek.

That's what they say: *don't try and be clever, Derek.* It's when they know they're beat.

– No, 'e really was. 'e comes from a dead 'ot country. We painted 'im white.

Me mam just laughed. It's true though. You can't have a coloured person in charge. Charlie's dad says the world would fall apart if that happened. Charlie's dad's a knob head.

Me mam's name's Mary Jackson, and she says white lies are okay, cause they protect the innocent. Me dad used to say you've got to face the facts. He say's that me mam's insane, and me mam say's me dad's insane. They'll probably both end up in *Pastures* in strait jackets, jumping up and down. I'll have to live with me gran, even though she's got an outside toilet, and a pot under the bed. Me dad says some people haven't even got a pot to piss in. Me gran has. She's got three!

When me dad left, me mam said he'd gone mad. Everybody's going mad.

– He should be in *Pastures*. He shouldn't be walking about the streets. You never know what people like that are going to do. They can go off at any time.

– Like a time bomb? I said.

Me mam gave me one of her looks. – If you like, just like a time bomb. You do have a strange way of looking at the world, Derek. She can bloody talk. And she does. All the time!

The mad people go to live in *Pastures*. It's a loony bin. Sometimes they bring them out for the day. They try and grab blokes by the balls. I've seen it on the bus on the way to Derby when they pick them up for their shopping trips. They sit there with hardly any teeth and their hair sticking out all ways and pointing at you with these yellow finger nails, and their horrible big grey tongues hanging out their gobs.

Mr Shaw. He's me mate Charlie's dad, says they should all be shot. He thinks everybody should be shot; the puffs, the coloureds, the women who burn their bras, the strikers, men who touch up little kids, people who don't join the army, Christians and Catholics, which is half our school. Charlie says his dad's a *Nazi,* and he's got a picture of Hitler under the bed. But he's not a *Nazi* cause they all got killed in the war by John Wayne and Richard Widmark. Me dad says that the Americans think they won the war, but they didn't cause they only came in at the end when all the shooting was over. He says they never used a single bullet, and they got all the English women pregnant.

Charlie's dad's a *Jehovah's Witness*. He give's you these little books to read, which nobody does. They use them for bog roll or for lining the boxes where they put the apples in the winter.

Mr Shaw goes to people's houses to brain wash them. If

you look straight in his eyes he's got you, like the snake out the *Jungle Book*. So I never look Mr Shaw in the eyes cause I know he'll have me. He'll make me build one of them Kingdom Halls like a slave. Me dad's a slave. He's Louise Draper's sex slave. She makes him do this stuff in this special room with chains and swings and everything.

# Electric sheets, ships on the sea, and finding Colin Jackson

Tonight, me mam left the light on in the kitchen. I looked through the window to see if the knives are all there cause I forgot to take them with me. There's six and I could see them all hanging from this magnet under the strip light. She left me some sandwiches by the sink for me supper. We've got these cups and plates that never wear out. Everybody's got them. They're made of this stuff called *Melamine* and they're indestructible like *Captain Scarlet*; even if you drop them. It's true, dead honest. I've dropped one out me bedroom window and they still don't break. They just bounce like super balls. They've got this brown stain. Me mam scrubs it off with *Vim* cause it's the only way to get it off. Everything tastes of bleach. Me gran says at least we'll have clean insides. Me gran says nowt lasts forever. She should know cause she's dead old now. She says she's on the last lap like the cars at *Mallory Park*. It was me gran who got us the cups and plates that everybody's got. She got these nylon sheets for the bed that don't need ironing, and queued for yonks in the middle of the night outside *Brentford Nylons* cause they had this midnight sale. Me gran said they made the sheets at the space station in America. Me gran likes shopping even though she's got no dough.

– There's no harm in looking, she says.

Me gran got these special nylon sheets out the packet and held them up.

– It's the modern world, Derek. You can rinse them, hang

them out to dry and they're back on the bed in ten minutes.

– You should be advertising them on the telly, me mam said.

Me gran laughed. Me gran's always laughing except when you mention me dad or me granddad. Then she has this look, which she has when she's got no teeth in, and her chin comes up to her nose. It touches, just like Ena Sharples in *Coronation Street*. I like making her laugh when she ain't got her teeth in, cause she looks just like a little baby. She has to dip her ginger nuts in her tea to make them soft.

Me gran handed me a packet.

– Here, Derek, I've got some green ones for you. They were a bargain!

She loves a bargain, does me gran.

I took them out. They made this funny noise like crunching crisps. Me gran shook one of her sheets. I could see her hair was standing up on end.

– Look at yer 'air! I said.

She went and looked at it in the mirror.

– Why aye, she said, cause she's from Newcastle where the coal comes from. They all say *why aye* all the time. – It'll be the static. They said there'd be static and that it's best to touch some wood or something before you get into bed. It neutralises it.

She started to laugh again like she'd heard a good joke.

– I said they were a bargain! You get free electric! You won't need to turn the light on. Just think of that!

When I went to bed and turned the light out, I rubbed me feet on the sheets. It's dead true; you can see it in the dark, like this glow, and it makes me skin tingle. It's nearly as good as a torch.

– We should have ships on the sea! me gran said.

She always says we should have ships on the sea. I don't know why. We don't live nowhere near the sea.

– Electric sheets! she said, cause me gran repeats herself like me dad does. Her hair was still standing on end like Ken Dodd's and that Frankenstein physics bloke who discovered the meaning of life. – What will they think of next?

Me gran cheers everybody up. Me mam says she's like a ray of sunshine, and keeps everybody going. It was the same with the bloke in the iron lung. She made him laugh every day. It don't work with me mam. She says that she's living in a dark place, and she feels like dying. She says she might as well be dead now me dad's gone.

– It's worse than death, she said.

– 'ow can it be worse than death. Nowt's worse than death. It's the end.

– I'm telling you it is, Derek. Death would be easier to bear.

I don't know how she knows. Nobody knows what death's like until you die.

To stop me mam from stabbing herself in the neck or the heart, which is what mad people do, I take the knives in the kitchen when I go out. I wrap them up in this rag I got from the shed, and put them at the bottom of me Adidas bag.

Sometimes she has this look. It's like she's thinking of a secret.

– Will you do owt stupid? I say. She knows what I mean, and she just laughs like it's a game, which it ain't. She knows the answer. All I want is the answer. – You need to tell me! I wouldn't go out otherwise.

– Of course not, she says.

I don't believe her. You can't trust mad people or turn your back on them or they'll strangle you. The ones they keep in *Pastures* are all in straitjackets lying on the floor so they can't get up and jump up and down all the time. It's what they have to do to stop them. Mr Shaw says they're pure evil. They jump and they jump, like Johnny Watts shakes his head, so that he can feel his brain wobbling like a jelly in a mould. The bloke at the paper shop says they should gas them along with all the kids. Everybody round here thinks everybody else should be shot or gassed or sent to Australia where all the criminals are, in chains. This bloke and his wife from the end of our street went to Australia last year. They told everybody they were going to run a fruit stall by the side of the road. I think they were criminals being sent away.

Everybody's angry with everybody else. Me granddad used to say that what the youth of today needs is a good war, to get it all out their system. All they had to live on was powdered egg, and they were bloody grateful. Me granddad didn't see an orange for ten years! Mind you, he told me he didn't like oranges.

Before she went to bed tonight, me mam just sat in her chair. She always sits in the same chair in the corner of the back room, in the dark. There's a shelf with some books. There's a dictionary with a ripped cover, which me dad said I should read from beginning to end. I said it's just words. Me dad did this dreamy sort of look he does when he thinks you're being a moron, which he does with most people, and he says they've got sludge for brains. If they had sludge for brains it'd dribble out their ears.

– The world's full of words, Des, me dad said. – The world's full of words. It's what sets us apart from the rest of the animal kingdom.

– Parrots can talk, I said, but he wasn't listening. Look at *Doctor Doolittle*. I call him Doctor do fuck all if you get it. Do you get it! You're as thick as a brick if you don't.

There's four *Reader's Digest* books on the shelf that have this *laughter is the best medicine,* which is dead funny. There's a book by Hammond Innes, a Bible, which nobody's read. Me mam just keeps it to stop the devil coming into the house. There's this plastic game of *Solitaire* with a piece missing. I nearly did it once, but it's impossible.

– I don't think I can go on, me mam said tonight. I was doing me homework in the kitchen. It's physics. I hate physics.

– What do you mean you can't go on?

I thought she might have a knife. I went straight back into the kitchen and counted them. She didn't.

– This is killing me.

– What's killing you?

– All of this.

It's cause me dad left. That's what she means. I don't know how it's killing her. She says it is, and she should know.

I stood there for ages. I didn't know what to say.

– I'll go and find 'im, I said.

I didn't really want to cause I'm trying to fix this model. It's a Lancaster bomber, except I put the cockpit on and forgot to put the pilot in and now it's covered in glue, so I smashed it, and felt bad. Now I'm trying to fix it.

Me mam started making this horrible noise that came through her nose and then a big long wet bogey came out. I watched it drip onto her leg. She just left it there like it never happened. It's what mad people do, so I knew me dad was right. Me mam, as he says, is as mad as a March hare, and they're bonkers!

– I'm sorry. It's not your fault, she said.

Me gran sometimes says that me mam should have done more to make me dad stay, and that she should have been a better wife.

– What, like lock the doors? I said.

Me gran laughed and gave me a sweet: *Everton Mints*.
They're stripy with softness in the middle that pulls your teeth
out when they're loose. She always gives me one for later.

– To keep you warm.

They don't keep you warm. But she won't have it. I mean,
how can a mint keep you warm?

I was going to tell me gran about Louise Draper, but I
didn't. I think she knew anyway. Me gran knows things. She
even knew when a bloke down the road was going to die.

– *He looked a funny colour*, she said.

He died! I hope she never tells me I look a funny colour.

Me mam had her head in her hands.

– I'll go on me bike, I said.

It was dark. It was seven o'clock and I've got school
tomorrow.

She didn't say owt for ages. Then she lifted her head and
she looked at me. Her eyes were all bloodshot like something
out of an horror film.

– I think you should go. You need to find him.

– What, you mean now?

– You need to find him. You need to tell him what he's
done. What he's done to both of us. He needs to see, then
he'll know.

– I don't know where 'e lives.

– Yes you do.

– No I don't. I only 'eard what Auntie Mavis said.

– You'll find it. She didn't know that. – It'll be fine. It's
what they say. Sometimes it's not fine. Sometimes it's just
crap. You can't pretend. Face the facts, me dad says, and he's
right; sometimes you've got to face the facts. The fact was, that
I didn't know where he lived.

Auntie Mavis heard someone in the hairdressers talking. Everybody's always talking. Talk, talk talk! Sometimes they whisper and say you mustn't tell a living soul, which means that everybody from here to Edmeston will know in ten minutes flat. Auntie Mavis's always hearing things at the hairdressers. Then she comes straight out with her hair like one of the *Black and White Minstrels*, and starts yapping to the first person she sees on the bus.

At the hairdressers, they put these helmets on you that make you talk all the time and tell your secrets. It's cause you can't hear your own voice. That's where the saying comes from – *I can't hear myself speak*. The alien gas bag women with the helmets said they knew where me dad lived. They say things cause nobody can see their faces. It's like they're under cover. They said that he's rented this house on the other side of Derby. They said that it was on *Conner Street*. That's all they said they knew. They made the rest up about him buying a *Rolls Royce* and getting these colour tellys. I knew it wasn't true, cause he'd promised that we'd get a colour telly. Before tonight I still thought me dad always kept his promises.

– You don't have to take the knives, Des, me mam said.

– I don't take 'em.

– I know you do. When you go out they're gone, and when you come back they're there again.

I left the house, and I could see me mam watching me from the window as I went down to the shed to get me bike. I opened the door and ran back just in case the bloke was in there. He's the bloke who lives in sheds and touched up the little girl at the top of the hill and made her piss her knickers. They say she'll never be right in the head. She goes to *Pastures* sometimes. One day they won't let her out when she starts jumping up and down. They all start jumping up and down in the end. You'll never catch me jumping up and down cause they'll have you before you can say Tina Scott's got crabs!

Me bike hadn't got any lights on cause me dad said he'd put them on when it got dark. He never got round to it. I tied a torch onto the handlebars with a piece of string and tied the back light under the seat so it hung there right under me arse where it lit me crack up.

It was dead cold. I could hear bangers going off down the old canal where Billy Myers and his mates from the tech go smoking fags and drinking *Toby Light*. They don't do homework cause they're stupid. They're only in the school cause they've got this class that can't go nowhere else. Me dad said, they'll end up in *the dirt and grime*. He's always going on about the *dirt and grime*. He says it's where everybody in Derby ends up if they don't work hard at school. They spend their lives up to their necks in filth, and they never get clean. It don't matter how hard they scrub. He says it goes right inside them, and it never comes out. He says they're marked until the day they die, just like the Jews.

– They're like sticks of Blackpool rock, Des. The writing goes all the way through.

He says you can tell what people are like just by looking at the hard skin on their hands, and the dirt under their finger nails. He says you can always tell. I used to think me dad knew everything.

## The gas man and the sellotape, the stick woman, and Annie Gray

One night someone threw a stone at our front window. I knew it was Billy Myers cause he told me.

– Yer dad's shit scared, he said. – That's why 'e won't do owt, cause 'e's a yeller bellied pig. We'll stick a banger in yer letterbox tonight, and a dog turd that stinks.

I got this piece of cardboard and sellotaped it over the hole cause I am scared of Billy Myers now me dad's gone. Your dad's supposed to stay and protect his kids and teach you how to fight. That's what they do in the wild. It says so in me EB. Sometimes, only in the wild, they piss off, which is okay if you're a lion that goes off to eat Christians. Me mam didn't notice I'd sellotaped the letterbox until she found the soggy gas bill on the step. Then she threw it, cause she throws everything that makes her mad. It didn't go very far cause it was wet. It just flopped onto her foot. She dried it out on the boiler and made me post it to me dad's office. That's where she sends all the bills. She says he pays them cause it stops him from going to hell, which is where they go after they've been in *Pastures*.

Me mam uses loads of sellotape. She sticks it on all the cracks on the windows and the grills in the rooms to keep the draught out. I told her it was dangerous. She just laughed.

– We'll get gassed, I said.

She pointed at me like I was stupid or something. She started putting on more of it.

– All the heat's going out through the gaps, she said. – I've got to stop it. It's a waste, and your dad'll only send the bills back.

She started getting these headaches every Saturday when she was watching the telly. The bloke from the gas board came to look at the gas fires cause we'd got this natural gas. The gas board said we had to be inspected.

– I'm an inspector, the bloke said.

Me mam gave him one of her looks.

– You mean you've come to stick your nose into other people's business.

He laughed. – If you like. I've come to inspect.

– Then you'd better get inspecting, me mam said.

He kicked the fire with his metal toecap. It made a mark.

– You need to scrap these, me duck, he said. That's what all the grown-ups call everybody in Derby – quack quack ha ha! – They're buggered. The fireplace is all wrong.

I could see him looking round the room. He saw the sellotape on all the windows. He made this snorting sound like a little pig.

– You'll suffocate, me duck, he said to me mam. He went over to the window and pulled a piece off. It'd gone brown. Me mam snatched it off him and tried to stick it back on. Me mam don't like to waste nowt, just in case there's another war, and they need it to stick up the *black outs*.

– It's the natural gas, me mam said. – And don't call me duck. There was nothing wrong with town gas. You can't smell this new stuff like you could the other.

Me mam thinks cause they're taking the gas from under the north sea that it'll cave in when they've sucked it all out. I think that's bollocks, cause it's gas and when some's sucked it out, it fills up again like farts. If farts didn't come back people'd cave in. You'd see all these blokes crunched up like cans cause they'd farted themselves to death. Me mam also said that she'd read in the *Woman's Realm* that the Russians were diverting all the rivers so that it changed the weather.

– The worlds going mad, she said.

I think she thinks it's me dad's fault.

Me mam went mad with the bloke from the gas board. – When I want your opinion on my fireplace I'll ask for it. Anyway it's a *Marsden*.

The bloke shook his head.

– Room's too small. Whoever sold you this was 'aving you on. You can't put a fireplace like this in a back room of an ordinary 'ouse. It's not bloody Chatsworth!

He tapped the fireplace with his foot again.

– It might not be Chatsworth but we've got fields. It's green belt.

We all looked out the window to the tip, which is getting bigger. There's seagulls that come all the way from Skeggy for the fish and chip papers from the *Crest of the Wave* in Borrington. There were bulldozers running round on the top flattening the rubbish. The bloke pointed.

– You can see that bugger from Edmeston. Bloody eyesore. They'll 'ave 'ouses on that before you can say Woodbine.

He took a packet of fags out his top pocket and sniffed it like they do cigars. It was a *Capstan Extra Strength* cause it had the navy bloke on the front. They make you puke cause they ain't got no filters. Billy Myers smokes them. He don't take it down. Eagle used to. But he'd smoked since he was three, cause his dad gave them to him to keep him quiet.

Me mam snatched the fag off the bloke. It snapped in half. The tobacco hung out the end like they were wires.

– No one smokes in my house unless they're invited!

– I was only going to blow the smoke up the chimney, duck.

Me mam handed it back.

– The man who used to come and clean the chimney before we had these things, she said pointing at the fire, – used a pipe. He was a proper gentleman. He does weddings.

The bloke got another fag out.

– Same thing, duck. Still kills you.

Me mam looked at me and shook her head.

The bloke just winked at me. He lit his fag and sucked it dead hard. He bent down and blew the smoke up the chimney. It came back into the room.

– Yer flue's buggered as well.

The bloke got out this massive sticker and stuck it on the fire. It said *CONDEMNED* in big black letters. *DO NOT USE. RISK OF DEATH*. There was this skull on it. Me mam grabbed the bloke's arm.

– I'll ring the gas board! You can't just come into people's houses and rubbish their fireplaces, and put stickers where the hell you like! How would you like it?

The bloke just shook his head and grinned at me mam.

– I've got 'lectric. It's clean and it's cheap. It's the future. It's progress. Anyway I'm going to work for the 'lectric board. I'm trained.

– They can train monkeys, me mam said.

The bloke looked at me mam and stubbed his fag out on the mantelpiece. Then he tapped her on the top of her head like she was this little dog.

– If that's what you want, me duck. But they'll say the same. I've told you now. If you want to get gassed, then keep them fires and that sticky tape on yer windows, and we'll see you at the pearly gates. He handed me mam a leaflet. – There's loads of fires in there. You should 'ave a look at the showroom in the *Main Centre*.

Me mam threw the leaflet on the ground like she always does when she's mad. Then she stood on it.

– That's where all the drunks go. They're all drunk in the *Main Centre*! me mam said.

The bloke laughed. Then he started to cough. He got out his hanky and gobbed this black stuff into it. He looked at it for ages like it was something dead special.

– Not in the gas board they're not, duck. Not 'til lunchtime anyhow.

He started to laugh and it made him cough again. He opened the back door and went to his van. Me mam ran after him.

He got in and wound his window down.

– I'm going to ring someone high up, me mam said.

Me and the bloke looked up at the sky. I could see a plane. It had these long strings of cotton wool coming out the back. I wished I was on that plane, going somewhere else. I've never been on a plane.

– It's up to you lady. It's a free country. He started up his van and drove off, just like that.

Me mam went straight into the kitchen, got a fish slice out the drawer and scraped the stickers off the fires.

– There's nothing wrong with these fires. What does a jumped up little squirt like him know?

Me mam's going to gas herself and then she'll blame the gas board. I'm thinking of leaving cause I don't want to get gassed. I want to find the place I can see in me head.

There's this bloke who keeps coming round to see me mam. I think he fancies her. His name's Martin. He lives with his mam on London road. He takes us out sometimes on a Sunday to the Peak District. We stop and have these sarnies with the crusts cut off and everything. They're dead small. I could eat the whole plate. But me mam says I've got to be polite cause Martin's just trying to be a friend. Me mam says that he works high up in the council, and that he sorts out the roads. When he was leaving one day after dropping us off, he came out to me. I was cleaning me bike.

– Derek, you need to think about the future, he said.

That's what they say at school, all the time. How can you think about the future when it hasn't happened? Me gran sings this song it goes *que sera sera, the future's not ours to see.*

– You need to get out of here as soon as you can, he said.

He went. He just wants to get rid of me so he can shack up with me mam. I've written this letter and given it to Charlie.

– It's if I get murdered, I said to him.

– What do you mean, if you get murdered?

– Martin. 'e wants to live with me mam. 'e wants me out the way. 'e keeps buying her sarnies with no crusts on in posh cafes. 'e don't want me there cause 'e lives with 'is mam. Me mam looks at me, and then at 'im, and I know what she's thinking. So if I'm found dead, take this to the Police and then they'll know.

Charlie took it, but I don't know what he did with it. He thought it was stupid, but he didn't say owt.

There's this girl in me class. She's twelve too. Her name's Annie Gray. She ran away and went to Blackpool. She was on the telly and everything. She had her picture on the front of the *Derby Evening Telegraph*. It said *MISSING* in these massive letters. I mean, they covered half the page, and her picture right underneath it, which she said was taken in Paris. Annie Gray ain't ever been to Paris. She was famous though. Me Auntie Mavis said she looked like a plain girl, and that she had no business running away like that. Auntie Mavis said she should get the cane, even if she is a girl. Auntie Mavis said she wasted taxpayers' money, but she always says that. Everybody wastes taxpayers' money as far as Auntie Mavis's concerned.

– We own part of that bus, Auntie Mavis said when we went to town.

– Which bit?

Then she gave me one of her looks that means she don't want to talk about it no more cause she don't know. Like the time she said that you can see the sea from her bedroom window. Which is bollocks. It's Markeaton Lake, which is a pond that came when they had a flood and it never went away. They put tench in it, but they died of poisoning. When Auntie Mavis says she can see the sea, Uncle Bob starts singing. *On a clear day I can see forever*, and Mavis goes mad, like she does when he plays *The Sound of Music* at full thrutch cause he's in love with Julie Andrews. Auntie Mavis says Uncle Bob thinks Julie Andrews is in love with him.

Auntie Mavis thinks he's stupid.

– It's because your Uncle Bob thinks Julie Andrews was looking straight at him when we went to the Odeon to watch the film. Do you think Julie Andrews is going to run off with a bloke from the Derby tax office? I don't bloody well think so!

– You never know, Uncle Bob says. – Stranger things happen at sea. He looked at me and he whispered, – of course Mavis'd know that, what with her being able to see it from the bedroom window and all! We laughed dead loud.

– I bloody well heard that! Auntie Mavis said. – And you can. On a clear day you can.

– No, you're right, Mavis. You're right.

Uncle Bob went off singing *on a clear day!*

I asked Annie Gray what it was like in Blackpool, cause she was still talking to people then. She didn't know I was thinking of going as well. Then she stopped talking to no one, which is what famous people do. They had to get this woman in from the special school where all the Educationally Subnormal kids go. She came to make Annie Gray talk by giving her electric shocks through the brain. There's this bloke called Howard Hughes who's in me *Encyclopedia Britannica* next to the *Gastric System* who talks to nobody, cause he's a genius and famous and rich and he's washing his hands all the time cause he says he don't want the filth of humanity on his skin.

Annie Gray never smiles no more, but she did when I asked her about Blackpool.

– It was brill', she said. – There were lights and everything and massive sticks of candy floss. They looked like clouds. There were people all over the place, and they've got loads of money and it's dead posh. There's this massive tower with lights and everything. There were these trams that run on rails all the way by the sea and there were waves coming out onto the road. I was standing on the pier and there was this bloke and woman at the back of this building, doin' it!

I looked at her dead hard cause I thought she was lying

– Really, doin' it? I said.

– They were. Dead 'onest! 'ammer and tongs.

I didn't believe her. There ain't no trams no more; except in the *Crich Tram Museum*. Everybody knows that.

We call Annie Gray's mam *the stick woman*. Her arms and legs are like twigs. She wears these big boots, which I suppose look big cause she's so thin. They make her look like Noddy. Everybody says she's mad. She walks straight past you, dead fast, like she's going somewhere, like she ain't even got the time of day. She's got this shopping bag with string for the handle. People say she's got loads of money stuffed in her pillow. But she always wears this same summer dress with big flowers on it; even in the winter. They're yellow with spiky green leaves. I've seen her in the snow, her arms as red as a beetroot and her hair dripping wet. When she slips over she just gets up again and keeps on going. She's just like a *Cyber man*. Nothing stops her, not even when some of the kids call her names. They shout *stick woman, stick woman, you'd better run when she's comin'*. She just keeps on going until she gets to the bus. Then she's gone. Nobody knows where. She probably goes to *Pastures* for electric shocks, just like Annie does.

Me mam said that Annie Gray's mam was left, and that's why she's like she is.

– She was abandoned by her husband, me mam said – He's a Clive. You can't trust a Clive. He had this little shifty grin that anyone with half an ounce of sense could see wasn't right. He had this boat on top of his car. Never took it down the Derwent. He just drove everywhere with that boat on the top of his car. Speaks volumes. He found a younger woman he worked with. She put a spell on him, like they do.

– You mean she was a witch?

– More like a bitch, me mam said when she was throwing things. – And now they live in a filthy little flat with their filthy little lives in the worst part of Derby where all the coloured people live and everything stinks of curry.

We had a *Vesta Curry* once cause it was what the posh people were eating, and it tasted of the east. How can something taste like the east? It tasted like shit. Me dad wouldn't eat it cause he said that the people who made *Vesta Curry* never washed their hands. Charlie said his dad had one and he had to have his stomach pumped cause it expanded. If they hadn't got it out at the *Derby Royal Infirmary* he would have exploded. He'd only just painted the front room! He said, when they took it out they sent it to make bricks for building one of them mosques.

Me mam went on like she does.

– People like Clive Gray always get what they deserve, me mam said. – Her name was Glenda. You can't trust a Glenda neither. Anybody called Glenda's no good. She was shifty too, and her eyes were too close together.

Me mam made this noise like a little trumpet with her nose. I don't think me mam ever met no one called Glenda.

She still went on though, like she does.

– It'd be better if that Clive Gray was dead, then poor old Alice could get on with her life.

Me mam's got a whole list of names you can't trust. Colin's at the top. That's me dad.

Me mam says it'd be better if me dad was dead too. That's how she says she thinks of him, lying in a coffin six feet under the sod.

– He'd be the sod under the sod! she said.

Annie Gray was a hero while she was away. She nicked some money from her mam's purse and just went. They said that she got a lift with a man she knew who interfered with little girls, and that's why there was this massive police hunt with dogs and everything. She just turned up one day and went home to bed. She ran out of money and came back to school. People ignored her, cause their mam and dad said she was mental and it ran in the family. They said it was a disease. Me mam says me dad's mental, and Auntie Mavis says I'll go off the rails if I'm not careful. I suppose she thinks I've got the disease, which I ain't. Charlie says they've got whole families in *Pastures* who've gone mad. I think he meant people like me mam and dad.

# Eagle and Shakespeare

When I was in the junior school I passed this exam called the 11 plus, even though I was still 10, which is stupid. I told the teacher and he just told me to shut me mouth and get on with answering the questions, which were shapes and things that changed in order. There were some sums, and they made us sit there for ages while the others finished the test. There was this one kid who just looked out the window and didn't write owt other than *I can't answer any of these questions, but I know Mount Everest is the highest mountain in the world*. He didn't spell any of the words right, but the teacher laughed and said that he should be a comedian. There was only three of us who passed it, and they said that we were the cleverest kids in the whole school, which wasn't hard cause the rest of them are a bunch of thickos who are going in the army to get shot by Germans who are clever cause they built the atomic bomb. There was me and Tina Scott and Charlie Shaw who's me best mate. Tina Scott's a slag. We go to Dalemead Grammar School where you have to wear red caps just to show you're cleverer than the others, and posh cause posh people have got big noses and wear top hats like *Lord Snooty* out the *Beano*. But we're not posh cause we haven't got big noses, except for Eagle, and that's why he was called Eagle, even though he said it's cause he could kill owt he wanted.

We take the caps off when we're outside the school or you get your head kicked in by all the others at the tech.

– I'm not wearing no fuckin' cap, Charlie said.

He walked up to the school gate on the first day and the headmaster was waiting. The first thing he did was clip Charlie across the back of his head really hard, even though he didn't know who Charlie was.

– If you don't wear your cap I'll hit you so hard your granddad'll feel it.

– Me granddad's dead sir.

It was dead true. Charlie's such a laugh.

He was killed in the Second World War when he was a home guard. A bread lorry ran over him. I think he got a medal though. Billy Myer's dad said that Charlie's granddad was nicking a loaf so he didn't deserve no medal, seeing as everyone else was getting killed shooting Germans and everything.

The headmaster wears a cloak just like Batman. His name is Stevens. We call him Slug cause his skin's greasy. He slithers round the school clipping boys around the back of the head when they're not looking. They're not allowed to clip girls cause they're nearly women and they're going through the change. You can't do that sort of thing. It's against the law. There was this teacher who did and he's in prison. Me dad knew this bloke in the bank who he went to every time he took money out cause me dad thought he was okay, which he wasn't. This bloke went to prison for nicking loads of money. It was more than two hundred quid.

Charlie told Slug to fuck off under his breath. Slug who's got bat ears heard him say it, cause he called him back and clipped him again. He yelled at his face.

– Look here boy! This is your first week and it could be your last. Give me your name. Charlie looked at the floor. Slug took out his notebook, like a copper's got.

– Name!

– Charlie.

– Surname you little idiot!

– Shaw.

Slug licked the end of his pencil and wrote it down in his little book. Everybody says he's got a diddly willy. All teachers have got diddly willies. That's why they're teachers cause they can't do owt else.

– Detention, my office four o'clock. One hour and you can write four sides on why this school is so fortunate to have a filthy little urchin like you. Now go.

He clipped him again, but Charlie nearly dodged out the way. I thought slug was going to run after him, but he didn't in case he had a heart attack. The headmaster of a school in Derby had a heart attack when he was driving his car. It was in the paper and everything; except a picture. He was hanging out the car door as it was going along and it crashed into a wall. Everybody saw it. I wish Slug was dead and then we could all go home.

Charlie did his four pages. He never told me what he wrote, and slug never caught him without his cap.

On the first day we covered all our books with sticky-back plastic like they use on *Blue Peter*. John Noakes is the best. I wish he was me dad even though he never combs his hair. He makes these models all the time and plays with trains and everything like dads are supposed to. He's always saying *get down Shep*, but it never does. Me mam says he hasn't got no talent like Hughie Greene and all the politicians who run the country, and put people out of work.

Charlie tried to close his book. It just sprang open.

McTavish who is our form teacher clipped him.

– Are you an imbecile, Shaw?

– No sir.

McTavish picked up the book and dropped it on the desk.

– You do a damned bloody good impression you little

twerp. Your parents will have to buy a new one.

McTavish walked away.

Charlie looked like he was going to cry.

He whispered to me – Nobody told us to cover the fuckin' things with the books closed. Me dad'll kill me.

Our English teacher's called Miss Crowe. Charlie looks at her like a dozy love sick girl cause he fancies the pants off her. She laughed when she saw Charlie's book. It was *The History of William Shakespeare*. She ruffled Charlie's hair, which made him go red and sweaty. I know she hates me.

– We'll put it in the library, she said. – I think we've got a spare.

She pointed at Eagle who was mucking about. He'd done the same with his book. She took it off him and looked in the front. I know Eagle had written something cause Miss Crowe laughed when she should have sent him to Slug.

– The spelling's terrible. You can take this to the library and put it with the other Shakespeare books. If I catch you doing this again it's down to the head's office.

Eagle didn't care. She wanted him out the class cause she didn't like telling him off. He was only there cause the school had to have him cause he had problems. Miss Crowe said he was dead clever and he needed help.

– 'e needs 'anging, I said to Charlie. I wished I never did; not after what happened.

Eagle stood outside the door for yonks making faces, spitting and letting it dribble down the glass. He went over to the wall and took out his felt tip pen. He drew a massive dick and a fanny with some words, which I couldn't read. Slug made him rub it off with *Vim* like me gran uses for the cups and saucers and her teeth.

Some of us sat there with books you couldn't close, cause

Charlie was the only idiot to hold his up and show everybody. Tina slaggy Scott and a few other prossers she'd met on her first day sat there singing and pointing at our books cause they'd done theirs right.

– You're a twat Charlie Shaw; you know you are, you know you are! And yer dad'll 'ave to pay for that, and it'll serve you right for living in an 'ouse you can't afford. Now you're fuckin' stuck up like the Queen and Prince Philip, except you don't live in Buckingham Palace!

Charlie's house is called *Shangri La*. Loads of people's houses are called *Shangri La*. It's the place they want to go, but can't unless they win the pools cause it's miles away. You can only go if you catch a plane from *Castle Donnington Airport*.

Charlie's house has got this stone cladding. There's this massive waggon wheel leaning up by the front door. I don't mean the biscuit. It's from a wagon in the *Wild West*, which Charlie said his granddad brought back from America where he was fighting Indians. Their next door neighbour, Frank turned his front garden into this massive pond with big fish cause he said it looked like a stately home. He used to stand outside his front door just looking at it all day long.

– Anybody who's anybody's got a lake in their front garden.

He dug up the *Tarmac* laid by the Irish navvies who'd nicked it off the road, to put it in.

– Looks more like Markeaton pond, Charlie said.

Anyway, one morning the bloke came out his front door. He forgot it was there and fell in. Everybody laughed. He had it concreted over, probably by Westy's mate. After that he painted it green so he don't need no mower. He said one day everybody'll have concrete grass, and that he's started a trend.

I just stuck two fingers up at Tina Scott and the slags. I know Miss Crowe saw me, but she just turned away.

Billy Myers is just a gob. He ain't got owt upstairs. Eagle was the bad apple as McTavish called him. Then they've got the hangers on. There's Johnny Watts who's a coward and only lays into you after you're down. His mam and dad give him owt he wants cause they're shit scared of him. He beats them up if they don't do what he says. Then there's Steve Buxton who's got a moped that he rides on the rec. They're always getting suspended. They go to the flicks and drink *Toby Light*. The teachers are stupid. They give them exactly what they want. Eagle didn't want to come to school. They reckon if he'd worked hard he would've got an apprenticeship at the *carriage-side* cause he wanted a motorbike. They said lots of nice things about Eagle after what happened. Everybody wants an apprenticeship at the *carriage-side*. You get to go free on the train to places like Matlock and Alfreton and Long Eaton whenever you like.

Tina Scott lives near me; except her house is covered in dog shit cause they've got these four Alsatians that crap all over the place. They're wild and they'd kill you if you went in the gate. It's cause they give them raw meat. It gives them the taste for human flesh. They killed a paper boy. There's a rusty car on the front grass. The coppers are always raiding the house cause her two brothers are criminals and they kick people's heads in. I know them so I'm okay. They've had the council round and everything. Mind you they live next door to Mr Oakley. He's not been outside for twenty five years. His son died and he just stays in the house looking at this picture of him when he was in the army. Mind you, he was killed when he and a mate rammed the Post Office wall in Willow Fields with a Ford Escort they nicked from Edmeston. Slaggy says Mr Oakley sleeps in his own piss and that he never changes his clothes. Once, a bloke in a space suit had to go in and spray the whole

house for fleas. They even sprayed the cat! When the bloke
came out he collapsed on the grass outside the house cause
he'd held his breath for five minutes! I think he died cause he
never ever came back, even in his suit.

On the way home on our first day, slaggy Scott was with
two of her new mates. I hate girls.

– Derek Jackson's got a diddly willy, she shouted.

I ignored them cause it's the best thing to do with girls.
Me mam says girls are trouble. She says they just want babies,
and once they've got their claws into you they never let go.
Anyway I haven't got a diddly willy. I wouldn't show it to a
slag like Tina Scott if I had cause you'd get VD and crabs.

The bloke in the paper shop is like a big kid. His name's
Ken and his wife shouts at him all the time cause he stands
there moving all the nudie mags around so he can have a quick
squint at the knockers. We call her the dragon. She stinks of
fags and her fingers are all yellow. Her hair's singed at the
front like it's been on fire. I followed Charlie like I always do.
He's the master thief. Charlie could nick the crown jewels out
the Queen's knickers if he wanted! Not that you'd want to put
your hands down the Queen's knickers cause she's dead old
and so she'll have crabs. That's for deffo. We got an *Aztec* each
and held them out so Ken could see. He was playing with his
*Curly Wurly* badge and pricked his finger so he was sucking
it like a big baby. Charlie had another *Aztec* in his other hand
and slipped it into his pocket. He looked at me. I'm not as
good at nicking as Charlie, but I got a *Milky Way* cause they're
smaller. I had it in me hand. Charlie went to the counter and
put his *Aztec* down. Ken was still sucking his thumb. The
Dragon came through the plastic strips, which they brought
back from the Costa Bravo. They've got some plastic lemons
too, which had ice cream in them. They're hanging on the wall

with a pair of castanets, a tambourine, and a poster of a bull fight with a bloke with a red towel that makes the bull go mental. Me mam says they're just showing off, and you can buy all that sort of stuff on Derby market. They probably went to Skeggy.

– That all? the dragon said.

Charlie stared her out, cool as a cucumber.

– That's all.

– I could search your pockets, Charles Shaw. I know your dad.

Charlie held out his ten pence. They stood there for ages looking at each other. I was sweating like a pig.

Charlie left the shop. I dropped the *Milky Way*. I did it on purpose. I was scared.

Charlie ate his two *Aztecs* slowly as we walked away from the shop.

– You're a fuckin' puff! he said.

– I dropped it.

– You're a fuckin' puff! Fuckin' puff!

He does this little dance.

– And you're a fuckin' ballet puff! I said. Which ain't true cause Charlie's quite hard really. He's got a pair of *hi leg docs* that he wears to the match.

I ain't ever told him, cause he'll think I am a puff, but Charlie's me best mate in the whole wide world.

## The dirt and grime
## When Captain Scott ate his dogs
## The South Pole, and a hull to break the ice

Before me dad went the last time, he was always saying he wanted to live somewhere cold. He said he wanted to go to the place where there's icebergs and everything. It's so cold that your hair freezes. When you go for a piss it's ice before it hits the ground. You can break it off, and you've got this long piece of yellow piss that you can use as a walking stick if you break your leg. I know what he means when he says he wants to live somewhere else, cause like I say, I want to leave. I think about it all the time. I'll go where the sun shines all day long, and there are yellow beaches and ice creams as big as an iceberg.

When me dad was talking about the cold places, he always winked and gave me this look, which meant it was a secret just between him and me. I knew that if he went somewhere cold, it meant me as well. I don't know if it's true no more, what with the lies, and me dad going mad. But you have to believe in something. Me mam says, it's all got to be for a reason, even if we don't know what it is. It's like God; He don't need no reason to do owt. He just does it whenever He feels like it, and never ever says He's sorry.

– You're my second in command, me dad said. – I can see it now. In lights.

He looked up at the sky as if he was looking at something lit up with big bulbs like they have at the *Goose Fair* in Nottingham. This bloke was sick on the roundabout. He sprayed the crowd. They beat him up when he got off. He was in the papers just like Annie Gray. They said he'll never walk again. He has to have his food through a straw. Even his chips!

– Colin and Derek Jackson; father and son, explorers, me dad said.

I always wanted to believe me dad. He had big ideas. You got to have big ideas. I know that. If you have small ideas, then you have a small life. If you have a small life, then you live in a small house without a garage or a car. You'll have to go to work on a bike or a moped.

– We'll go on an expedition, he said one day. – We'll call it *South with Jackson*. What do you think about that?

– Sounds brill'.

We were walking down by the canal. It's all caved in now, and the lock gates are all rotten. The water stinks, but people still swim in it. There's old mattresses, bike frames, shoes, Johnnies and everything, floating. The kids from the tech come to shag under the bridge at night. It stinks of piss. Me dad stopped and he looked at the water. I knew what he was thinking. He was quiet for yonks. He looked at me and still said nowt. I knew he was somewhere else; not in Derby, but a long way away where the snow falls in massive flakes and it's silent. It ain't Derby that's for deffo. It only ever rains in Derby, and people have snotty colds all the time.

I knew why we'd come down to the canal. Me dad had come to tell me the facts of life. He was sweating like a pig.

– You see that dog walking over there, he said, pointing to the other side of the canal. There was this scabby-looking mutt. – How do you think it got there?

I knew what he meant. I know the facts of life. It's in me EB of course!

– I s'pose 'e went over the bridge and down the steps. I said.

Me dad just laughed. He didn't say no more about the facts of life. I don't even think he knew.

A lorry went over the bridge. It made the ground shake like an earthquake. It was only built for horses and carts. One day it'll fall down on all the shaggers.

– You know that Captain Scott got it wrong, me dad said.

You know he's always right when he says things like that, cause he's read the books. I would have looked it up in me EB, but as I said; the S book is missing, and Scott begins with S. So does South Pole.

– What do you mean?

– He took ponies, Des.

He pointed at me, like I'd done something wrong. He had this look. It was because he was serious.

– He took ponies to the South Pole. Only a fool takes ponies to the South Pole. Amundsen took dogs. He came from the north so he knew. He lived in the dark nearly all the time. The dogs were his eyes and ears. He knew when he ran out of food, he could eat the dogs. You've only got to look at the Eskimos. I don't know why we were looking at the Eskimos.

– Amundsen was lucky as well. He had the weather with him. You've got to go fast if you want to make it.

Me dad looked at me really hard. His eyes were wide like a mad man's eyes. I know that now. He gripped me shoulders dead hard and shook me. He made me head wobble. It made me think of the loonies in *Pastures*, but it still felt nice. I was his second in command. I thought about Tricksy. I could never eat a dog.

– You do understand don't you Des?

– Yeah I understand.

I knew then that he was going to do it. You have to be mad to go to the South Pole or climb Everest or go to the moon.

Normal people don't do that sort of thing. That bloke played golf on the moon. Charlie said he was mad. Mr Shaw said it was all a hoax. He said they used the scenery out of *Dr Who*.

– Say it nicely, me dad said. He's like that. – It's 'yes I understand'.
– Yeah, I understand.
– It's with an S, Des.
I laughed.
– I ain't got no S in me Encyclopaedia Britannica.
He didn't take no notice.
– Yessssss!
He sounded like a bloody snake.
Me dad works in an office now where they have to speak proper. He worked in the factory before until he moved from blue collar to white collar. Everybody hated him, or so he says. He says he has to be careful where he goes or they'll get him for deserting the ship.

– It's the suit they hate, he says, – not the person.
– Why don't you wear a blue collar then?
He laughed and patted me on the head like the bloke from the gas board did with me mam. Me dad does that and he grabs me arse to make me jump. He didn't tell me why he didn't wear a blue collar. I don't know how anybody can hate a suit.

He pointed, up over the canal bridge. I knew where he was pointing. It was over at Derby where you can see the floodlights standing out over the top of the *Baseball Ground*, where *Derby County* play.

– They say yeah, Des. All the time. Yeah this and yeah that, and other words that you won't have heard of yet. He means fuck and twat and shit, and words like that. – That's why they are there and we're here. Do you understand me?

– Yeah. I mean yes.

We could see this yellow smoke going up into the sky. There's this noise. It sounds like a train or a storm that never stops. It's the testing beds for the engines at *Rolls Royce*. They're always testing. They never stop testing.

– You know what I'm saying, Des?

He was still pointing over the bridge.

– Yeah.

– It's yes!

– Yes, I said.

We said it together like we always do. Like they do with prayers in church to brainwash you.

– *IT'S THE DIRT AND GRIME!* we said together.

Me dad winked like he does.

– I'm going to build a boat Des.

He started sneezing. It was the summer and there's lots of grass. I sneezed as well. Once someone starts sneezing, everybody starts sneezing. There's this bloke who hasn't stopped sneezing for fifty years. His eyes must have shot out his skull and flown for miles.

– Scott's boat was called the *Terra Nova*, me dad said. – It means new ground. I'm going to call ours *Hay fever* because you don't get hay fever at The South Pole. It's too damned cold.

I knew then that me dad was planning on going to the South Pole. I wished I'd got the S book for me EB.

There was this terrible stink. Me dad looked at me. He thought I'd let one off. That's when we saw it coming out from behind the reeds like it was a living evil monster. It was floating with its massive belly sticking out the water like an island. It was bald and its eyes stuck out like gob stoppers. They were staring everywhere. They looked like were going to burst so that all the jelly would just fly out like the pus out of one of Steve Buxton's spots. He takes these tablets that make his teeth go yellow. He looks like a vampire. Charlie's mam says we should keep away from him or we'll catch them cause it's a disease like being mental. I think I'd rather be mental than have Steve Buxton's spots. He looks like one of them *Hundred and one Dalmatians*.

When it floated over to us, me dad prodded the dog with this stick he'd picked up. He likes a stick does me dad. It's not cause he can't walk or owt. It's cause when he's thinking he swings it and cuts down all the bracken and everything.

– Would you credit that, he said. – Must have fallen in and couldn't get out.

– Dogs can swim, I said.

People get dogs for Christmas cause they're pissed. They buy them down the pub. When they sober up they realise they've got to feed them and get a licence, so they crack them over the head with an empty bottle of *Toby Light*, and sling them in the canal. Me dad changed the subject cause he knew then it'd been murdered. He didn't want a murder on the doorstep. Nobody wants a murder on the doorstep. It might affect the house prices.

– It's about the hull of the boat. It needs to be strong, he said. – Solid. The wood in one piece, sharp as a knife to cut the ice. It's not a job anybody could do.

I knew me dad could do it. He can do things. He can break an apple in half with one hand.

He prodded the dog really hard with his stick. It just burst. It made a bang like a balloon cause it was full of gas. This green stuff sprayed out like a fountain all over the place for ages. It was full of green. Me dad got some on his jacket. He went mad, and started jumping about. He looked at me as if it were me fault.

– Jesus, Des!

– I didn't prod it! You prodded it!

– I know you didn't, but you should have said. The thing's been dead for weeks!

– What should I 'ave said?

– That it was going to explode.

I didn't know it was going to explode. It's supposed to be adults who can see the future. Mind you, Billy Myers gets these straws. He blows air into frogs 'til they're twice the size, and then he shoots them with his air gun. They explode. I didn't tell me dad that.

Me mam says me dad's definitely mental now. Maybe he is cause he's different. It's like someone's changed is brain. He wasn't mental when we went down the canal. I know he wasn't. I know if you have big plans to do something nobody else's done before it can make you go mad, like Van Gogh who we did at school. He cut his ear off cause he was mad. It was cause he couldn't get his colours right, and nobody would listen to him, like nobody listens to me about me dad and Louise. I'm not going to cut me ear off though. Me dad might cause he's like *Van Gogh*. It's got to be right.

– Perfect and pure, he says. – Perfect and pure, like the driven snow.

I was worried that he'd cut his ear off before we went to the South Pole. Mind you, you can lose your ears from frostbite. Then you wouldn't be able to hear it if a Yeti crept up behind you.

Me dad got this book. It's called *South with Scott*, which was good, what with me having the S missing from me EB. (*Encyclopedia Britannica*. I'm not telling you again!) Scott didn't write the book cause he's dead. Someone who was alive wrote it instead. It's all about the expedition, and how they got stuck in the ice. That won't happen to me dad cause he was planning on building this hull made of special wood and a metal strip to cut it. The book's got these pictures of massive snow walls with penguins and everything. It's got a picture of the *Terra Nova* stuck in the ice. Me dad looked at it for ages and ages, so that he understood why it was stuck, and so ours wouldn't.

– This is it, Des, he said. – This is it! He held up the book. – This is our guide. This tells us everything that went wrong, the boat, the ponies, and the base camps. There's a lot to learn. A lot to learn. A lot to learn.

Me dad does that. He repeats himself when it really matters. Says it again and again 'til it sticks. That's what he says you have to do cause people don't listen, like the people who made Van Gogh cut of is ear. Me dad says that people only take in five percent of what they're told. Ninety five percent of everything just evaporates into thin air, and all the words go up into space. There are aliens listening all the time, getting information on everything until they come and take over. Mind you, if they're listening to the shit that comes out of Billy Myers's mouth, they'll miss us by a million miles!

After me dad left the last time, I found the book *South with Scott*. It was at the bottom of his wardrobe, which was empty cause he took all his things. But he'd left the book. He put this piece of paper. It was held on with a laggy band. Me dad always uses a ruler to write as his writing's dead untidy. It said:

*To Des. I know you will want to keep this. Love Dad.*

It's not right when your dad says he loves you. There were three kisses too. And he's a bloke!

Me dad got these plans in the post. He unfolded them on the kitchen table. We looked at them for ages. There were lines and numbers and arrows all over the place. Me dad kept saying hmmm, and right. Me mam stood there just shaking her head, and made us some cheese and onion sarnies. We had some iron brew as well cause the Co-op's selling it at two pence a bottle. It tastes like shit really. If you drink it fast you can't taste the iron. Me mam won't buy pop cause it's too expensive. Sometimes we get that orange juice in a milk bottle, which is dead posh really. We used to leave it on the step so people could see it. We don't get it no more since me dad's gone. Me mam says he's taken the shine off everything. He's taken the orange juice too.

There were loads and loads of plans. I mean sheets and sheets in tubes. Me dad started writing down lists and talking out loud about different types of wood.

– Marine ply, he said. – It's what you need. It's flexible and it gives. It's got to give.

I looked at the plans. – Give what? Me dad laughed.

– It means it moves.

Even though me mam says me dad's mad. He's dead clever and people like that are mad; just like the bloke with the sticky out hair who discovered the meaning of life.

Me mam brought the cheese sarnies and she put them on the plans, which you can't do cause it makes a mark. Me dad said that happened to Christopher Columbus. He's under C in me EB if you want to know.

Someone made a mark on one of Christopher Columbus's maps with a cup. He thought it was a line and he followed it. That's why it took him so long to find America, cause he went round in this massive circle and ended up where he started. He made some of his men walk the plank cause they had to eat their shoes and drink seawater, which made them mad.

Me mam tapped her finger on the plans like she does

when she don't like something. *Tap Tap Tap Tap Tap* with the end of the finger, so that her nail made a mark on the paper. I remembered where it was, cause it might have meant we missed a screw. It could make the boat sink. Every screw counts. Look at the Titanic, which I've got in me EB. We'd have drowned cause only the posh people survived, and me mam says we're upper working class, which is high up, but not posh.

– Where are you going to build this thing then? me mam said.

Me dad looked at her like she was some sort of idiot. He winked at me. He'd got it all worked out.

– Where do you think? He was grinning.

– I wasn't aware we'd become a boatyard. We don't need a boat. We need a new set of cupboards for the kitchen.

Me dad ignored the cupboards. He wasn't interested. You don't build cupboards with marine ply. Everybody knows that. Captain Scott didn't waste his time building cupboards for Mrs Scott.

– In the garage of course!

Me mam just stared at him like she didn't know who he was. – What about the car!

– The drive, me dad said, pointing at the wall. – The drive.

– It'll go rusty. You can't leave a car in the drive, she said. – It's not what people round here do. They put cars in garages, not boats. Boats go on water.

– That's because they haven't got a car or a garage. You've got to think ahead, Mary. If you don't think ahead, things get ahead of you.

Me mam looked at me like I should know something. I just nodded. I didn't know why. I didn't know what it was that gets ahead of you, but I really wanted to build the boat with me dad.

– It's not the point. You can't leave the car in the drive.

They had arguments like that all the time about the things you can and can't do. Me mam says there's rules and they shouldn't be ignored. Me dad says rules are for breaking. That's what I'm going to do, break the rules. I'm always going to break the rules.

Me dad didn't take no notice. He'd made his mind up. When me dad makes his mind up, that's it. The car didn't matter. It was the boat that mattered now. I was dead proud of him. I could hear me mam throwing things about in the kitchen and slamming doors. She always throws things about when she's mad. Then she went out. She slammed the back door so hard it made the whole house shake; which made me dad mad as he was paying for it. He went round the room looking for cracks.

– She's loosened the bloody doorframe! If she bangs it any more it'll just fall out into the drive. He tried to move it. You could see this crack in the plaster. – Can't be worrying about that, Des. We've got a boat to build!

Me dad got out his tape measure. He waved it in the air like a stick. I followed him into the garage. It's made of asbestos, which is dead strong. The bloke down the road saw me dad building it so he started to build one. He fell through the roof cause he's dead fat. He broke his leg. He was just hanging there for yonks with his leg swinging, yelling like a girl. The Fire Brigade had to winch him down in these massive pants and everything. Then he just left the garage in a pile. It's still there going green. He has to park his car on the road, which me mam says makes the place look untidy. I think it probably affects the house prices.

Me dad started clearing the junk at the back of the garage.

We found this dingy from the war with a sail and everything. It's one of them they used in the planes when the pilots jumped out and landed in the sea.

– Check this, Des. We might be able to use it.

I took it out on the lawn and tried to blow it up, but it was full of holes where the moths had eaten it. I put the mast up. It was like a telescope. I sat in it and pretended I was out at sea. We kept it though. You never know. Look what happened to Noah when the rains came.

– Here, me dad said.

He gave me the end of the tape measure and rolled it out to the end of the garage.

– Fourteen feet. He was smiling. – It's going to work.

– 'ow big's the boat?

– Twelve foot six without the rudder.

It sounded massive to me.

– What about the 'ull? I said.

– As solid as steel. As solid as steel, Des.

– For cutting ice?

He looked at me dead funny, like he'd forgotten about the ice. Then he suddenly remembered. – If you like, Des. For cutting ice.

Me dad winked at me. I knew this was just the beginning.

– Des, he said.

– What?

– Don't tell anyone.

I wanted to tell Charlie.

– Why not?

He tapped his nose like he does. – It's our secret.

I didn't want to keep a secret. He made me promise. A promise is a promise. Me dad used to say that your word is all you have in the whole wide world. I haven't chosen me word yet, but I will. When I do I'm going to keep it.

# Que sera sera

Before he went, when me dad started to stand in the garden in the middle of the night in his dressing gown, me mam used to ask him if he loved her. She did it when he was working on the car or then on the boat cause she thought he loved them more than her.

When she asked him, me dad never stopped what he was doing, cause you can't just stop jobs like that and answer stupid questions.

– I don't love anybody, he said.

Once me mam kicked the wheel on the car when he said that. He went mad cause it could have knocked it off centre and killed him.

– You could have killed me, he shouted from underneath the car.

I could see that me mam wouldn't have minded if it had. I bet she wished it had now.

It took me dad a year to build the boat. Me mam told Auntie Mavis, so everybody knew. People kept coming and looking at it in the garage cause they'd heard about it in Edmeston. Even Charlie's dad came. He rubbed his hand on the hull. I could see that me dad was angry with him. Charlie's dad started talking about the bible.

– How do you feel that you're using God's work, Colin?

Me dad winked at me.

– It's not God's work. Des and me have built it all on our own. Haven't we Des.

– But you didn't make the trees.

– No. We didn't make the trees. They grew somewhere in

Scotland.

Charlie's dad knew he wasn't going to get nowhere with me dad cause he's a heathen.

– It's a beautiful thing, Colin, he said. He touched the boat again. Then he left.

Me dad blew on the bit where Charlie's dad had touched it.

– Sweat could weaken the hull because of the salt in the skin.

– What about the salt in the sea? I said.

– Not the same. Entirely different salt. Sweat is full of human filth.

Me dad knows everything about that sort of stuff.

The boat's got no cabin. At the front there's these two holes where you can put your stuff like your anorak and gloves and things. Me dad knew what he was doing. One day he turned it over and did the top. In the summer we pulled it out onto the grass. We put the sail up. We sat in it and ate cheese and onion sarnies. The man from *The Derby Evening Telegraph* came and took a picture, so that we were in the paper and everything, just like Annie Grey. We didn't say owt about the South Pole cause me dad said that people would think we were mad and try to stop us like they tried to stop Christopher Columbus. Also, he said that someone else might try and get there first, like Amundsen.

– Will we take dogs? I asked him.

He tapped his nose.

– Maybe, maybe not.

I knew he'd got a plan.

Me mam came out and laughed cause it's what she does. But I think she thought it was dead good really. She'd never say cause she said it'd make me dad's head as big as a bucket, then he wouldn't fit through the door that she nearly knocked out of its frame.

– So where are you going to sail it then? The sea's a hundred and twenty miles away! Me mam said.

The sea's at Skeggy, but sometimes the sea's so far out you can't see it. But me dad had a plan. One Saturday we took the boat to the River Derwent where you can catch sticklebacks with your hands. This bloke came and filled it with water and it still didn't sink. There was a fish that swam into it. It looked like a tench. The bloke gave me dad a certificate.

The bloke took off his cap.

– Floats like a bugger.

Me dad winked at me.

– So it's good for a long trip? me dad said.

– Ooh God aye. You could sail this bugger down the Amazon.

I know the Amazon's a big river in the jungle cause we've done it at school. It's got crocs and everything, and piranhas that can eat you. They leave you just like a skeleton in ten seconds. They've got spiders too, as big as Mandy Jarvis's arse, which is as big as the Isle of White.

– Can it go to the South Pole? I asked the bloke.

He looked at me and then at me dad.

– Course it could, me duck. If you like.

Then he went. Me and me dad launched the boat.

– Just a minute Des, he said. – I've got to get something. Hold the trolley.

I held it, but it was slipping. I fell on me arse in all this green slime on the concrete slope. Me dad came back. He was holding a full bottle of Iron Brew. He smashed it on the side of the trolley cause he didn't want to break the hull.

– I name this ship, *Hay fever*.

He let it go, and cause of the green slime, the rope slipped out his fingers. It floated out into the middle of the river.

The *River Derwent's* got a strong current. There's a weir at the end near the council houses in Derby. When I was at the junior school there was this kid; Philip Barker who fell off the big black sewage pipe over the river. He was being an idiot and showing off to his mates. He couldn't swim. Sometimes he came to school without any pants cause I saw at games. Sometimes he caught his willy in his zip and he screamed. He had to go to the sick bay to get it out. Philip Barker floated all the way to the council houses. He got his head stuck in the weir and he was dead. All the dinner ladies cried cause they're all dead old and lost sons and husbands in the war.

Me dad started running like mad, shouting at me. He fell over and both his hands went in a cow pat. He got up and carried on running cause the boat was going away. He overtook the boat cause me dad's a dead fast runner, even though he's got a big belly. He just jumped, his arms and legs all over the place, yelling and he went into the water right up to the top of his thighs.

I was still running. I could see him. He was sinking in the mud.

– No, dad! I could see he was up to his waist. – Philip Barker drowned! He got his head stuck in the weir. You'll float down to the Council Houses.

I didn't want me dad to get his head stuck in the weir. The boat floated past him. He couldn't do owt, cause he was stuck in the mud and everything. He wasn't going to float down to the Council Houses. The mud was sucking him down.

– Run after it, Des

I started running. I could feel me stomach turning over like it does when you're dead scared. Me legs felt like jelly cause it was up to me now to save the boat; like it's up to me now to save me mam. I seem to spend all me time saving things.

I saw me dad get out the water. His trousers were black and he'd lost a shoe, but the cow shit had washed off his hands. He started running again. I could hear his shoe squelching behind me.

– Jump in! he shouted.

– What do you mean?

– I mean just jump in! Get the boat. It's a year's work!

– What about Philip Barker?

– He was a bloody little idiot! Just bloody-well jump in!

– But Philip Barker drowned!

I thought of the South Pole and all the things me and me dad had done on the boat. He let me sand the rudder and count the nails and everything. It was what me and me dad had done together. It was our boat. I could see me dad couldn't keep up no more; what with his shoe missing. He fell over again and just sat there with cow shit on his hands. I know he said fuck cause I heard him. Then he started to cry. I'd never seen me dad cry before. I think he thought it was all over. That's what they said when England won the World Cup. *It is now*, the bloke said. But it wasn't over. I knew it wasn't.

– I can't jump in. I'll get stuck in the mud.

Me dad looked up at me.

– Then swim! Just get in the bloody water man! For God's sake we're losing the boat!

I was in front of the boat. It turned just a bit so that I could almost reach it. I tried to get the rope, but me foot slipped on the bank and I fell in. I can swim and I swam dead hard cause I knew if I put me feet down, the mud would suck me in. Charlie says it's a living thing. It sucks you in and you dissolve. It takes ages before you die; if the worms don't eat you first.

I grabbed the rope. Me dad was on the edge now, shouting

at me.

– Climb aboard. You can do it Des!

He was dripping wet and covered in shit. He wiped his hand on his face. That was covered in shit too.

I grabbed the side. It nearly tipped over. I got in, and me dad clapped.

– The tiller! Get the tiller!

I didn't know what the tiller was. Not then.

– What's a tiller?

– The bloody rudder you idiot! The wooden stick thing behind you. Hold it steady.

I grabbed it, and the boat turned. I sat on the seat. I was steering it. The sails were flapping and everything. It was just like the *Onedin Line* that me and me mam watch on a Sunday night when I've had a bath. We sit in front of the gas fires, gassing ourselves. Then this wooden pole swung round and smacked me right in the side of the head. I could see stars. The boat hit the bank and me dad grabbed it. I was the first to sail *Hay fever*! Me dad slapped me on the back, then he kissed me. He stank of shit and he only had one shoe, which he never ever found, cause the mud got it.

– You're my second in command, Des, he said.

I didn't know what to say. Me dad kissed me.

– Hardy kissed Nelson at the battle of Trafalgar when Nelson was dying. It's a naval thing. Men and men, me dad said.

– What, were they 'omos?

Me dad looked at me dead hard. – I don't know where you get some of your rubbish ideas from, Des. It's that music you listen to. Me dad thinks Rod Stewart's a long haired yob. It's because he sang *Maggie May*. He thinks that half the kids in our area don't go back to school cause they're growing their hair and bleaching streaks. It drives Slug mad cause he's as bald as a baby's bum. He could never ever have a duck's arse hair cut at Tommy Swift's.

– Charlie says if blokes kiss each other then they're 'omos.

– You know it's a disease, Des, me dad said. – They can't help themselves.

– Charlie's dad thinks they should be shot, I said.

– Not if they shoot him first!

Me dad don't believe in God. He says if there was a God then Captain Scott would still be alive. He says that George Best would play for Derby County, and that England would win the World Cup against Germany again; what with them killing all the Jews. He says it's only right. Anyway we collected all them coins from the petrol garage, but they didn't win it again. Me dad says that England won't ever win the World Cup ever again. They were just lucky. (*Author's note: I think Derek's dad might be right!*)

We pulled the boat out the river and onto the trailer, which me dad made as well. We put it behind the garage and turned it over. We put this canvas cover over it. Then we left it. Me dad says it's done its job for the time being.

– 'ow long's that then? I asked him when we locked the garage.

He looked at his watch.

– It's getting late, he said. Which it was.

I asked him when we were taking it out proper.

– In time, Des.

Sometimes I look under the canvas and there's this fungus growing on the hull. Some of the varnish is peeling like your skin does when it's burnt. I told him about it when he took me to the footy, and me mam wanted me to get him to come for tea.

– You need to see it. It's spreading like moss. I wanted him to come and look, but he wouldn't.

– It'll have its day, Des. Sometimes you can't have everything you want.

I didn't know if we'd ever get it out again. As me gran says – *the future's not ours to see – que sera sera!*

## Bangers and Bengal matches
## Beating the boy at the bus stop

The first time me dad went, me gran said that I'd be scarred for life cause of what happened.

– I'll never forgive him, she said.

Me and Charlie were coming home from school. It was nearly bonfire night. Bonfire night's brill'. It's the smell of the smoke, bangers and the air bombs I like. There's those roman candles you can hold in your hand, and *Jumping Jacks* that go in people's wellies to make them leap up and down. Old bags don't come out their houses cause they think it's the Germans coming to bomb *Rolls Royce*. Me gran sits under the table in her kitchen now me granddad's dead. Not all the time like; only when there's a storm and it's bonfire night.

– You can't trust the roof, she says. – Not with the council cutbacks and all.

Charlie took out this packet of *Bengal Matches* from his pocket and held it up so I couldn't reach it. He lit one. It made a flash and burned for ages. It went yellow and then blue and then green.

– Fuck! he shouted.

It burnt the end of his finger. He took another packet out. They were bangers. It was already open. He took one out and lit it in his hand. It fizzed and he dropped it down this drain. It made this bang that echoed right down the road. This old bloke saw. He shouted cause Billy Myers dropped an air bomb down a drain last year. It cracked a pipe and hundreds of houses were filled with piss and shit, and other people's used bog roll. The bloke waved his fist like old people do in the cartoons.

– Oi!

We stuck two fingers up at him cause he couldn't see us properly. We ran all the way to the canal bridge.

– I've got a joke, Charlie said. Charlie's always got a joke. – There's this kid called Jimmy at school. – He says – *miss, I shoved a banger up a cat's arse.* The teacher says – *rectum, Jimmy, rectum.* Jimmy says, *yes miss, blew 'em to pieces!*

Charlie just pissed himself laughing cause he always laughs at his own jokes, which makes me laugh even if they're not funny cause Charlie laughs like a hyena.

There was this older kid standing at the bus stop. He goes to the tech school. I'd seen him before. He's got curly hair and he's about fifteen. He'd got this tech drawing tube. That's what they do; they draw all day so they can go and work at *Rolls Royce* and build engines for planes. Me mam says that when they're not testing, nobody does an ordinary job at *Rolls Royce*; that they're all bosses. She says that nobody sweeps up cause it's beneath them. I don't know who sweeps the floor. It'll be them Pakistan people Mr Shaw says.

– The meek shall inherit the earth, he said one day.

What he means is, that the Pakistan people will all take over cause they do the jobs the English blokes won't. Mr Shaw says that's why it's good to be a *Jehovah's Witness* cause they've already got seats in heaven.

– It's like having a season ticket for the *Baseball Ground*, except it's free, he said.

When we went past the kid, he took me cap off me head and threw it in the air. I tried to get it, but I couldn't.

– Give it back.

He started laughing.

– Just give it back!

– Beg! Come on swot, beg and show us 'ow fuckin' clever you really are.

It's not true. If they saw Eagle and Billy Myers and Johnny Watts and Steve Buxton with his crossed eyes and one ear bigger than the other, they'd know we're just like them. McTavish reckons Steve Buxton looks like the *FA Cup* when he's had his hair cut at Tommy Swift's.

We had this kid in our class. He threw a cricket stump at one of the teacher's cause he's a nutter. He should have gone to a special school. The stump had this metal end. It stuck in the back of the teacher's leg. The kid was expelled after that. We never saw him again. His mam and dad were dead rich cause they'd got lots of money from Africa where all the coloured people are slaves.

The kid wouldn't give me me cap.

– Dance, he said.

One day when he's shovelling shit in the *dirt and grime* I'll get him back; if God don't get me first.

– No.

– Then beg.

Charlie tried to reach it, but he's not as tall as me, even though his dad's dead tall. Charlie says Mr Shaw's not his real dad, which I know ain't true. He says his real dad is an explorer who's climbing Mount Everest without any air. He says they don't know if he's dead or alive cause they don't have no phones, which is a lie cause they even had phones on the space rocket. Charlie says he's adopted. Loads of the kids say that cause they hate their dads cause they're always down the pub spending the house keeping. Mr Shaw's deffo Charlie's dad cause they've both got this special shaped nose, which me mam says means they're Jews. I wish I was adopted.

– Give 'im is fuckin' cap back, Charlie shouted.

The kid laughed.

– Mek me.

Charlie started walking away.

– Just leave it, Charlie said. – 'e'll leave it on the wall. No other bugger's going to want a cap with *excellence in all things* on it.

Charlie's right. Shit in all things is what we say.

Charlie stopped. He was pointing to where the shop was.

– I can see yer dad.

Me dad's got a yellow Volvo estate. It's dead old and it's got this rust, which me dad's always painting with this stuff to stop it spreading. Me mam says it's a losing battle.

Me dad started running. He's got this belly, which he says is middle age spread, and it happens to everyone when they get dead old. The kid with me cap tapped me on the head with his technical drawing tube. Me dad was pointing as he ran. His face was bright red and he was shouting. He ran straight past Charlie and didn't even say hello.

– Stop! me dad shouted.

He came flying up to us and had to stop himself by grabbing the bus shelter. He nearly ran out into the road. A car blasted its horn. The bloke wound his window down.

– Twat!

Me dad waved his fist. I thought he was going to run up the road after him.

Me dad snatched the tech drawing tube off the kid.

– Give him his cap back! Me dad shouted.

The kid looked at me dad and handed me cap back to me. The kid tried to get his tech drawing tube back, but me dad held it away. Me dad went right up to the kid and stuck out his chest. The kid was as tall as me dad.

– Why don't you pick on someone your own size? me dad said. The kid backed away against the wall of the canal bridge. You could see he was shit scared.

– I didn't know, the kid said.

Me dad pushed the kid in the shoulder, dead hard.

– Didn't know what? Didn't know what? Didn't know the lad's dad was sitting on the corner?

Me dad was shouting like the kid was deaf. Charlie looked at me, like me dad had finally flipped his lid.

– Fuckin' 'ell, he said. – I'm off!

Charlie started to walk away. I grabbed his jacket. I felt the shoulder rip.

– You fuckin' twat, Charlie said. – You've ripped me jacket. Me dad'll kill me.

– Please don't go. I would have begged him if he'd wanted me to.

– Nah. I'm off.

I watched him legging it up the road. He looked back. I waved, but he kept running. He didn't look back again. I looked at me dad. I wanted to run after Charlie. I nearly did.

– I didn't know, the kid said again.

Me dad gave me cap back to me.

– Didn't know what! Didn't know what! Is that all you can say? Didn't know what!

Me dad put his face dead close to the kid's face. The kid stepped back. Me dad whacked him over the head with his own tech drawing tube. It went flat in the middle like tubes do. Me dad wouldn't stop. Then me dad cracked it over his knee until he ripped it in half. The kid started crying. He had his arms up in the air. He moved along the bridge wall like a crab going sideways. There's this gap where you can walk down to the lock gates. Everybody pisses down it so that your piss goes down the steps like a yellow waterfall. The kid fell backwards. You could see him go like it was in slow motion. I heard his head bang on the wall. He just lay there. I thought he was dead. I think me dad thought he was dead too.

Me dad was breathing like he was going to have a heart attack. The kid opened his eyes. He shouted up at me dad.

– Me dad's goin to fuckin' kill you, yer bastard!

Me dad went down the steps and started whacking the kid again with both hands, holding the ripped tube. I went down after him. It stank of piss. I grabbed the back of me dad's jacket. I heard that rip too. Everybody's jacket was getting ripped.

– Dad! Stop, please stop!

He didn't look up. He just carried on like I wasn't there. The kid was cowering and starting to scream like frogs do when they've been got by Tinker, the stinking, hairy cat from next door. Then me dad stopped. He tried to get up, but he fell forward and landed on the kid. I could hear the air fly out the kid's lungs as me dad's belly crushed him, just like Giant Haystacks does in the wrestling when he drops on Big Daddy's head.

Me dad managed to get up, cause he was crushing the kid's head. He had sweat on his face and he was gasping for air. Me dad looked at the kid who was still lying down on the stairs. I grabbed me dad's jacket. It ripped again. Me dad had this look on his face, like a mad man who can't be stopped until you kill him and drive a wooden stake through his heart, just like Dracula.

– Please! I shouted.

Me dad dropped the two bits of tech tube on the floor and just stared at me. He put his hands on his knees. There was sweat dripping on the pavement. There were people on the other side of the road; some kids from Southfield School. There were some old people too.

Me dad saw them.

– What you looking at? The show's over. You can go now!

Me dad stood up. He started to cry like a little kid. There were tears running down his face and spit coming out the corner of his mouth. It dropped onto the floor in big globs. Two prossers from Dalemead went past and they started to laugh. I knew everybody was going to know. Prossers tell everyone owt. It's what prossers do when they're shagging. They tell you secrets.

The kid started to get up. His blazer was covered in shit from the steps. He picked up his tech drawing tube and he started crying again cause he thought me dad hadn't finished. So, there was me dad and the kid crying on the pavement. Then the kid started to run away up the road. I saw Charlie. He was standing at the end of his road. He didn't wave at me. He just turned and walked away. I thought I might lose me best friend.

The kid kept running. I could still hear him crying. The bus went past him but didn't stop. When he was far enough away so me dad couldn't catch him, the kid stuck two fingers up.

Me dad's fat in the middle cause he drinks this beer he makes at home and puts it in the airing cupboard in this blue plastic dustbin. Me mam says it makes all the towels and the pants stink. She says it's working class, and that me dad's just taking us back where we came from. Me mam and dad bought the house so we're not working class no more cause all me mates live in council houses. Like I said, me dad wears white collars to work. Although usually they have these squares on cause he say's that's what they wear in the country. He gets these letters, which say *esquire* on them. He says it's important, like he's a lord or something.

– I'm the King of my own castle, he said.

Me dad grabbed me hand. I could see the two prossers at the end of our road with their hands over their mouths. One of them was Lyn Slater. She used to be alright, but now she goes out with a bloke from the tech school. He's sixteen and she's gone the wrong way. Tina Scott says Lyn Slater's had the name of her bloke tattooed onto her left tit. Charlie said he asked her if he could have a look. He reckons she showed it to him and everything, but he's a lying git. He's not adopted. Edmund Hilary was the first man to get to the top of Mount Everest. It's in me EB cause I checked it. It said he was dead. McTavish says he's still alive out there on the mountain, a slave to the Yeti. Me dad says anybody who's anybody's dead. That's what make them famous like Captain Scott.

– That's 'im: Edmund 'ilary, Charlie said.

– You're a lying git. That means yer dad's gorra be dead, I said, – And 'e died in nineteen twenty one, so you must be at least fifty! Why aren't you called Charlie 'ilary then?

Charlie didn't say owt about it after that cause there was nowt to say. Charlie's dad couldn't even climb a bleedin' ladder without shitting himself!

Me and me dad walked to the car. I could see he had some cases on the back seat. They were the ones we take on holiday. I knew he was leaving cause he'd got his hi fi magazines on the back shelf. Me dad started to cry again. It was dead embarrassing. Dads aren't supposed to cry.

– Des, I'm sorry.

– Let's go 'ome, I said.

He just got in the driver's seat and started the car. We sat there for ages.

– One day, Des you'll understand all this.

He turned the car round.

– That kid'll kick me 'ead in, I told him.

– No he won't.

Me dad says things like that. I used to believe him. But not no more. He said he wouldn't leave again, but he did. I know that one day the kid'll kick me head in. I'd kick me head in if I was him.

– What do you mean, I'll understand?

Me dad drives like an old bloke cause he don't want to wear the engine out. It took us yonks to get home.

– There are things you don't know, things you don't need to know.

– Is it about you and me?

– Yes, he said. – In a way it is.

– And the boat?

He started to cry again like a blubbering baby.

– Yes it's about the boat.

I think I believed him then. I think I believed that we were going to the South Pole, that women begged their husbands and sons not to go cause they might not come back. But that's how it is; the women have to clean the house. Me mam say she's chained to the kitchen sink, which is bollocks. She couldn't go shopping if she was chained to it. She'd have to take it with her.

We went back into the house. It was all dark and there were no lights on. It was like when the miners went on strike last year. We had to eat our tea with candles. I don't mean eat the tea with the candles, which is dead funny but not true. We used knives and forks for that! It's one of Charlie's jokes.

Me dad stood at the door.

– You go first, he said. He pushed me in the back. – She knows you.

I looked at him. – What do yer mean; she knows me?

– You know. Knows you.

I think me dad was scared of me mam, and that was why he was running away. McTavish said that women are like spiders and in nature; the woman spider eats the boy spider. Slaggy Scott and her mates loved that. McTavish fancies Miss Crow, but you can tell she doesn't fancy him. No one would want to eat McTavish unless you covered him in ketchup.

I could hear me mam in the back room, crying. There was this sniffing sound. She blew her nose and it sounded like a fart. I laughed, even though it wasn't funny and everything was dead serious. I went in and she was sitting in the chair in the corner. She'd got tears running down her face. Me dad walked in and me mam started crying some more. Me dad put his cases down by the door and we all stood in the middle of the room. We put our arms round each other. It was horrible; really horrible. I wanted to die. It was Friday. Me mam says all the bad things happen on a Friday.

# Coronation Street and the moon landing.

I still went to scouts even though me dad tried to leave. I didn't tell Charlie, cause me mam said people didn't need to know, and that they've got wagging tongues. She meant Charlie's mam who talks about everybody whether she knows owt or not. Her name's Eileen and me mam says you can't trust an Eileen. She says you can't trust a Dorothy either cause there was this Dorothy she was at school with, and she did something. I don't know what. There's all these people you can't trust: Clive, Alan, Eileen, Dorothy and tons of others. Now there's me dad; Colin. Oh yes, and there's a Glenda who Annie Gray's dad went off with. Me mam never mentioned Louise. I put her on the list cause you can't trust a Louise, that's for deffo!

I called for Charlie.

– Yer dad's a nutter then, he said.

– No.

– Basket case or pissed?

– 'e was upset.

– Did 'e kill the kid from the tech?

– Nearly.

– Bastard deserved it. Me dad would've shot him. 'e'll kick yer head in. You know that for deffo.

We laughed, and Charlie didn't say owt more. Like I say, he's me best mate, ever.

At scouts we muck about and smoke fags with the ventures and drink *Toby Light*. Our scout leader's called Bob Black. We just call him *Bob the job* cause that's what we have to do every year. The old bags who've got nowt, give you loads of cash and the rich buggers with the cart wheels outside the front of the house and the ponds with fish, give you bugger all. We halve the cash and give the rest to the scouts. I think *Bob the job* takes his cut. The rest goes to the blind, which is okay cause they can't count it!

The scout leaders have all got these dozy names out the *Jungle Book*, like *Sheer Kahn* or *Baloo*, which is a fat bear. There's this old bloke who said he used to be a friend of Baden Powell. He tells us to call him Kim, which is a girl's name. Charlie says he dresses up as a woman at the weekends. His real name's Brewer. He tells us we're a bunch of yobs and makes us do knotting like the Sheep Shank, which always makes Charlie laugh cause he calls it the *Sheep Shag*.

Sometimes we do midnight hikes and go out in the dark in the woods. We sneaked off last time with two other kids; Jonny Wilson and Chris West from the tech. Chris found this pound note on the ground at *Twycross Zoo* when he went on a school trip. He spent it all on fags. We found a hole in this tree and sat in it smoking, but '*Bob the Job*' found us cause he could see the tips of the fags glowing in the dark. He made us give him half the fags. He smoked the buggers himself. When we got back to the hut there was only five of us and *Bob the Job* cause the other soft heads had gone off home to mammy and Ovaltine. We got our sleeping bags out and lay on the floor. Bob got out some bottles of *Toby Light* and said he'd kill us in our sleep if we told anybody. He lit his curly pipe that he got in Switzerland when he was running away from the *Nazis* and passed it round. Charlie went green and chucked up cause he took it down. Chris West told us this story about a bloke and a woman who were shagging in the house when the woman saw a mouse come out the wall. She was so scared that she closed up if you know what I mean. The bloke couldn't pull his willy out, and they had to go to hospital. They had to carry them out on the stretcher still stuck together! She was someone else's wife. We laughed about that all night. Bob said it was bollocks. We didn't believe him, cause he's not allowed to let us talk about stuff like that, what with him being a scout leader and all.

– You're a good boy, me mam said. She gave me an *Aztec*. – It's for bringing your dad back.

– 'e beat this kid up with 'is own tech tube! I could tell she didn't believe me.

– You know he's not well, me mam said. – We might have to call the doctor.

I didn't know why she'd need to call the doctor.

– You can see 'e's different, I said to me mam.

– What do you mean different?

– I dunno, 'e's just different. Like 'e's somewhere else.

Me mam didn't know what I was talking about. She thinks she knows everything. But she don't. She thinks that Polar Bears live in the South Pole, and that me dad and me will get eaten by one before we even start out. They don't live in the South Pole. It's too far for them to swim. Penguin's live in the South Pole and Yetis live on Mount Everest, which is probably the reason why Edmund Hilary never came back.

Me mam knew he was different, even if she said nowt about it. He started combing his hair right across the top of his head, and flattened it down with Brylcream. He sprayed this stuff all over so that he stank like a cream puff.

– Do you think it makes me look younger, Des?

I lied, cause I knew he'd be dead upset if I told him the truth that he looked like a puff. It was only a white lie.

– Course it does.

He bought this set of cravats, which he wore every weekend

and he didn't ask me what I thought of them, cause he knew.

– When we taking the boat out? I asked him.

– Soon, he said.

I could see moss growing on the canvas cover. I tried to scrape it off with a fish slice, but it made this tiny wincey hole and the water started getting in. I put a plaster over it.

In the middle of the night this noise woke me up. I looked out me bedroom window. I could see me dad. He was just standing on the path in his dressing gown. He stood there for ages. I heard him come back in and put the kettle on to make a cup of tea. Old people do that in the middle of the night cause they can't sleep and they have to piss every ten minutes cause their bladders shrivel up.

– It's because of them up the road, me dad said. – They're always banging the doors. They should live on a council estate, not in a private road. The only reason they're here is because there's crime money from Cuba. Their daughter's called Susan Gower. She's twenty and she's beautiful, and she's got a boyfriend called Mickey, and they've gone to live in a prefab in Willow Fields.

– Mickey works at the *Oklahoma*. He wears a velvet suit, which me mam says is no good cause it creases. She says it's better for winter curtains. She says that Mickey must sweat like a pig when he's under the lights doing whatever he does down there. She reckons he hasn't got a job there at all, cause he gets the dole.

– He thinks talent rubs off, and overnight he'll become Ken Dodd, me mam said.

That's impossible cause Mickey's teeth don't stick out like Ken Dodd's. Me mam says he just goes to shake hands with the famous people like Morecambe and Wise, and Tommy Cooper, and Shirley Bassey who Mickey says he's shagged.

Twice!

They were supposed to knock the prefabs down after the war. Me mam's got a friend who lives in one of them with her sister. There's this green stuff growing out the skirting boards like something out of one of them films. Me mam's friend's sister's on oxygen. Me mam's friend says that it's cause all this stuff's leaking into the air. She wears this mask so she can't smoke when she's got it on. She has to take it off to have a fag. The council won't do owt. We don't go and visit them no more. We went there to watch the moon landing cause our telly had broken. Me dad said they were making history even though he didn't believe it was real. I got this Airfix model of the rocket that I didn't finish cause I lost some of the bits.

Me mam's friend's telly broke just as they were going to touch down on the surface of the moon in the space module covered with silver paper.

– It's cause they're interfering with God's world, me mam's friend said. She put her hands together and said the Lord's Prayer. Me mam said it too.

I went outside and stood on this bloke's lawn next door cause I could see his telly through the window. He came out his front door. He was wearing his vest and he had a bottle of *Toby Light* in his hand.

– Why don't you fuck off! he shouted. – Go and watch yer own fuckin' telly. It's my telly, and I'm paying to watch it! If you want to watch some other bugger's telly then fuck off down the *Co op* and stand with all them coloureds and them urchins outside the window.

The bloke slammed the door. I went back to me mam's friend. I hope the green stuff coming out the skirting boards rots his knackers.

Me mam watches *Coronation Street*.

– It's just like watching everybody in Derby living their filthy little lives, me mam said. – I don't understand why people watch it.

Like I say though, she does. She says she needs a sit down and the telly just happens to be on, then she watches it like it's an accident. It's a white lie. I know it is. But who cares if you watch Coronation Street or not. The only programme on the telly that I watch is *Top of the Pops*. I bought me first single. It was fifty pence in the new money, which is ten bob in the old money. It's Rod Stewart singing *Maggie May*. It's about this bloke who's still at school, but he's thinking about leaving and playing pool, which I don't know what it is. But he's thinking of leaving, which is what I'm going to do; just like Annie Grey. I won't go to Blackpool though. I'm going to Devon where I went once on me holidays. The sun shines all the time and they've got these boards with fins on that ride on the waves. Auntie Mavis says she and Uncle Bob are going to retire to Devon and live in a bungalow by the sea.

– I don't know why she wants to go to Devon, Uncle Bob said to me. – What with that spectacular view of the sea she's got from the bedroom window.

– I heard that! Auntie Mavis said. She says she hears everything, like God does. – And I'll bloody well leave your Uncle Bob here with his bloody mam if he's not careful!

Charlie bought *I'd like to teach the world to sing* by the *New Seekers* for his first single. It's really shit. He got it cheap from his cousin, cause it was scratched. He washed it under the tap. It only jumps two times when they sing *it's the real thing*, which they pinched from the advert for *Coke*. It goes thing, thing, thing forever till you flick the needle. Charlie's dad bought this new needle for his record player. On the packet it says that you can play a song three thousand times before it's knackered.

– I'm going to prove it, Charlie said. – If it don't play three thousand times I'm going to take it back and get the dough. Then I can spend it on sweets.

– What about yer dad?

– 'e never plays it.

Charlie's played *I'd like to teach the world to sing* three hundred and fifty seven times so far, so he's got two thousand six hundred and forty three plays to go. His dad says it's driving him mental. I told me mam.

– Then he can keep your dad company, she said. – They can be mental together.

Me mam says we don't need a colour telly cause it's more life like in black and white, and that's how life is anyway. She says it's not full of colours, and people prancing around with sparkly white teeth. Dave Noakes, me mate next door but thirty-seven's got one. It's got this diddly little screen and this massive box, which his mam says she has to dust all the time cause it's like a magnet. She thinks it's going to catch fire. She thinks they'd have to go and live in a prefab with all them people that everybody in our street is trying to get away from. Then they'd be back where they started.

The bloke across the road had a house in Derby that caught fire cause he didn't unplug the telly. There was a spark from the little red light. It set fire to the curtains, the carpet, the furniture and then the doors. The windows and the glass blew out cause it expands. The cat got fried as well. They reckon it looked like a black beef burger when they rescued it. Anyway, it died. Me mam don't like cats. She says they're vermin.

We've got *BBC 2* though. We got it last year, but there aren't many programmes. The first one we watched was *Rowan and Martin's Laugh In*. It's American and me dad says that the

Yanks don't have no sense of humour. We sat and watched it anyway. Nobody laughed.

Auntie Mavis's got a colour telly. It's the biggest one you can get. She has it on dead loud cause Uncle Bob says he's deaf.

– What, he says all the time like Walter in *Nearest and Dearest* when Hilda says *has he been?*

– He's just making it up so he can talk to his mam all day instead of living in the real world, Auntie Mavis said. - There's nothing wrong with his bloody hearing, she says. – He can hear his bloody mam alright, and she's twenty thousand feet up in the air or wherever the daft bugger thinks she is.

Uncle Bob whispered to me after she'd gone.

– It was the bombing, he said. – The mortars and the shells flying over night and day. It leaves a ringing in your ears that never goes away.

Auntie Mavis came back into the room.

– Derek, don't take no notice of your Uncle Bob. It won't surprise you to know that there weren't any mortars or shells in Swanage. And I'm not aware that they sent the *Home Guard* to the front line!

Charlie says you can get this sheet of plastic that covers the screen on the black and white telly, and it makes it colour. He says it only costs a quid, but I can't find one. I've looked everywhere. Anyway, I don't have a quid.

When I get home after being at Auntie Mavis's house our telly looks dead small. It's like this eye that stands in the corner of the room on these black spindly legs. When it breaks down, and the man comes to fix it, I pray that it's knackered. Then we can get a colour telly.

– There's life in this old set yet, he says every time.

It makes me want to slash his tyres.

I dream about having a colour telly. Me mam says that some kids dream about a square meal cause they don't have owt to eat. But I still wish I had a colour telly. It don't make no difference to the skinny kids in Africa. When I don't eat me peas, the teachers at school say that they'll send them to the skinny kids.

– You can't post peas, I said.

The teacher clipped me on the back of me head.

– Don't be so bloody insolent Jackson. It's a metaphor. Not that I'd expect you to know what a metaphor means.

I didn't. I still don't.

## Float like a butterfly, sting like a bee

I know what it was that me dad wouldn't tell me on the day he was leaving, when he hit the kid over the head with the tech tube. He told me on the day when the kid's dad came to see him, and said he'd send for the police. I could tell me dad was scared cause his hands were shaking when the bloke threatened him.

– So how are we going to settle this? me dad said.

He started talking in this voice that I could see annoyed the bloke. He had tattoos on the back of his fingers with LOVE and HATE. Billy Myers has got a tattoo on his wrists. It's a butterfly on one and a bee on the other. It's quite clever really; for Billy Myers anyway. He won't have thought of it himself cause he can hardly write his own name.

*Float like a butterfly, sting like a bee*. It's what Cassius Clay said when he was going to fight. Billy Myers thinks he's Cassius Clay. He's not cause he's not black and Cassius Clay's a genius cause he can dance.

– I'll put you over the fuckin' fence, the bloke said to me dad.

Me dad's voice was shaking. – There's no need to be like that.

– Your lad was attacking my lad. Me dad called me. – Des!

I didn't move. He called me again. I went to the door. The kid's dad was fat. His hands were filthy black. He had a fag on, and his fingers were all yellow. Me dad pushed me in front of the bloke. He was built like a brick shit house.

– See, me dad said. – Look at the size of my lad compared to your lad.

The bloke looked at me and then at me dad. Then he looked at the house and he spat on the floor. His flob was black.

– I should still put you over the fuckin' fence.

I looked at me dad. We didn't have a fence. We had a hedge. Me mam said it was what people with their own houses have. The bloke stepped back and looked up. – It's yer own house then is it?

– Not paid for yet, me dad said.

I didn't know he hadn't paid for it. You shouldn't have something if you haven't paid for it. That's what McTavish says in General Studies.

The bloke pointed at the boat that he could see down the side of the house.

– That the boat you built?

– It is, me dad said.

– I saw it in the paper. Yer a clever bloke then. You use yer brains, not yer fists. I should 'ave worked 'arder when I was at school. I just mucked about. Not me lad though. 'e's almost got a trade. e'll get into Royce's. You want to sell it? I'll give you twenty quid.

I could see that me dad was thinking about it. I nudged him.

– The South Pole, I said. Me dad rested his hand on me head.

– The lad's set on going to the South Pole.

The bloke looked at me dad as if he was mental.

– Wait, me dad said to the bloke.

He went upstairs. When he came down he was carrying two big bottles of his homemade beer.

– Tom Caxton, me dad said, giving the bloke the two bottles.

Me dad didn't sell the boat. Not then. He put his hand out

to shake, but the bloke was holding the bottles.

– So it's settled then? me dad said.

– I'm not 'appy, the bloke said. – I still ought to put you over that fence. But you seem like a nice enough bloke, and me lad can be a bit of a twat. I'll give you that. He looked at me. – They're all the same. You get yerself a trade son and you won't go far wrong.

I looked at his hands again. I knew he worked in *the dirt and grime*. Me dad knew it too. It was a good job he wasn't wearing his white collar.

Me dad patted one of the bottles. I could tell he didn't really want to give them to the bloke.

– Look it was one of those things. I'm sorry it happened. But no harm done eh.

The bloke looked at the beer.

– Twenty quid, he said again. – You let me know if you ain't going to the South Pole.

The bloke winked at me.

Me dad closed the door. I could tell he was pleased the bloke had gone cause he was shaking and he had sweat on his forehead.

– Stick something in their hands. Something they like, and they can't hit you. Blokes like that always talk with their hands. You need to put something in them. You saw his hands, Des. *The dirt and grime*. You can't reason with the people in the *dirt and grime*. Twenty quid. Where's someone like that going to get twenty quid? If they had it they'd put it on the horses or throw it down their necks.

After that, me dad went and got two bottles of his own beer and drank them dead quick.

# Red rent books, loose women, and the St Vitus dance.

Me dad's mam and dad are dead. I never met them. His dad was an engineer and he chewed tobacco all the time. He chopped half his hand off in a milling machine. Me dad said he was never the same after that. He said it was the shock that killed him. Me mam's mam and dad live near us. They're called Alec and Eleanor Winter. They still live in a council house. This bloke comes round to collect the money every week. Me gran keeps the cash in a little brass fly. The wings lift up and it's hollow inside. She's got this little red book. The bloke puts a tick in it and signs his name cause I've seen him do it. After that he goes next door to Mrs Steven's. Mrs Stevens speaks like a bloke, cause her throats all buggered up with the fags. Her chest rattles like me bag of marbles. She's got this budgie called Percy. She's had loads of budgies. They're always blue with black speckles, and they're always called Percy. They lay eggs, but they don't hatch. Mrs Stevens reckons Percy can say hello and how are you. I've never heard it. Me dad says it's called Percy cause that's what her husband was called before he died, but he never got a word in edgeways either. That's why we've never heard the budgie talk cause it's frightened out of its wits. Me dad says that the budgies die of lung cancer cause they smoke Mrs Steven's cigarettes. But I've never seen them do it cause they can't get out of the cage.

Mrs Steven's says that me gran and granddad, that's before he died, are the best neighbours in the world.

– They might have a cold name, but they've got warm

hearts, she said.

When she laughs she starts to cough and she can't stop. If she's standing up we have to get her to sit down so she can gob in this little pot. She puts the lid on like she's saving it.

– For later, she said, patting the top of the pot. Your gran'll do owt for me, she said when me mam went shopping with me gran and left me to talk to Percy. I could hardly see her cause she was in this cloud of smoke.

– What like give you a thousand quid?

She shook her head. She's always shaking her head. Me gran says it's St Vitus Dance. Her head wobbles like the puppets on *Thunderbirds*.

– More like a cup of sugar, she said. – That's what neighbours do.

When the bloke came to beat up me dad but didn't, me dad told me what it was he wouldn't tell me when he tried to leave. It was all about me gran and granddad.

– Your mam's got a sister. She won't tell you, because they're all ashamed. They're covered in shame because it's a shameful thing. Purity. That's the thing, me dad said. – Clean and white like Edelweiss in the *Sound of Music*. It's not hard to keep things pure. Some people have no morals. Do you understand Des? It's vitally important you understand. I didn't. – When you grow up, you watch out for loose women. Your gran was a loose woman. You better know that now. There's no getting away from the fact. She ripped her knickers off like Jack Flash.

– Who's Jack Flash, I asked him.

– It's a figure of speech.

– 'e's not a person?

– Don't be clever Derek.

– What's a loose woman then?

– They run around a lot, chasing after men.

– So I've got an Auntie.

Me dad pointed and started waving his finger.

– I don't want you to mention her name in this house again.

– I don't know her name.

– Marion. Her name's Marion. Now the best thing you can do is forget it.

I haven't forgotten it. You can't forget something you already know. The brain stores everything. It says so in me EB.

I know what a loose woman is cause Billy Myers said it to Tina Scott about her mam, which ain't true cause Mrs Scott's in a wheelchair. She's got this disease where your muscles get eaten away by this worm thing 'til there's nothing left except your head. Mrs Scott can't run nowhere, so she can't be a loose woman.

– Don't tell your mam you know.

– Why not?

– It's driving her mad.

Everybody is going mad.

Me mam said that me dad put me gran and granddad on a pedestal, which is like a small stool, but it's higher than everybody else cause they're more important. We used to go to this field by the river somewhere near Radcliffe Power Station. The blokes who worked there said that cause the water in the lake outside was so warm that a special sort of fish lived in there. They said it was twenty feet long. Charlie said it ate a boy from Nottingham.

Sometimes, the cows are in the river and the place stinks of cow shit. We used to stand in the pancakes. Me mam and dad got cross cause it was all over their shoes. I don't know why they went. We took a picnic and there's this photo of me and me gran and granddad. I'm sitting on a fence. It's a sunny day and the sky is completely blue. Me gran was wearing this funny hat that she takes on holiday and cost her hardly owt to make. I remember it cause everybody was happy. It was before they all started going mad.

Just before me granddad got ill, me mam brought Louise Draper home for tea. I didn't like her from the off. She wears these thick glasses that make her look like Olive out of *On the Buses*. I told me dad. He said that the woman that plays Olive is dead attractive in real life. Anyway, Louise Draper's got a face like a dog's arse.

Me mam works in an office where they fill in forms to do with the council and all that. Mind you, she's not been to work for ages cause she's too thin. Louise was the office manager; even though she's ten years younger than me mam. Me mam says that's what you get for having children. That's what happens to women in Derby. She says they're second-class citizens, which means on the trains as well.

Louise's got these little rat eyes. She started looking at me funny. So did me dad. They didn't think I saw, but I did. I knew then that she'd come for me dad. It was as plain as the nose on your face. Me mam said Louise had a boyfriend, and that he was killed in a car crash. Louise said they were going to get married. They found the engagement ring under the seat, which he was going to give to her. Me dad thinks everything Louise says is true, but it's bollocks. She used to buy me presents, but not no more. She bought me this airfix model of a Spitfire. I started it, but me dad built it when I was asleep cause he didn't want me to bugger it up cause he's showing off to Louise.

– Look what Des and me did, he said, holding up the Spitfire so that Louise could see it.

She was swanning all over the place, and making these noises like the girls in our street did when Westy was doing his multi-coloured concrete. This was before he shoved Mrs West in the pit.

– Me dad did it! I told her.

She didn't listen. She was too busy listening to me dad to listen to me. That's what happened; me dad stopped taking notice when Louise came. I told him that there was a hole in the canvas cover on the boat, and that the paintwork was turning green, but he didn't take no notice. He'd forgotten about the boat, and he'd forgotten about the South Pole. I wanted to gouge Louise Draper's eyes out with a fucking spoon!

Louise's thirty two. She lives with her mam and dad! She don't do owt at the weekends cause she ain't got no boyfriend. It's cause she's too old and too ugly. You have to face facts. That's what me dad says; except when it comes to Louise. Oh no! So one weekend me mam invited her to come on the Sunday picnic with me gran and granddad to the river that stinks of shit. She was dressed like she was going to a party. It was dead embarrassing. She had this short skirt. I could see me gran looking at her. I could tell me gran didn't like her.

I sat next to me gran. I pointed at Louise.

– Please don't point, me dad shouted at me. Me gran put her hand on me arm.

– You point all you like pet.

That's what they say in Newcastle, woof, woof!

– Me dad says she's one of the family, and that she's me mam's boss. He says that you should always keep in with the boss.

Me gran does this thing with her gob and squeezes her lips together when she doesn't like something. Me mam says she looks like she's sucking a wasp.

– She's not one of the family, Des. Now you just remember

that. You can't just muscle into someone else's family. Anyway, the girl's got legs like tree trunks.

We laughed cause it's true. They're like elephant's legs.

– Me dad says I've got to call her Auntie Louise.

– Does he now?

– I don't want to.

– Then don't.

I had to help me gran up as she's got a stiff hip like Mrs West had. I watched her go up to me dad. I could see she was telling him off. He laughed at her and just walked away shaking his head.

Me dad put the blanket down on the grass. I could see this cow pat. It wasn't very big, and it was half under the blanket. I left it there. Louise sat down. I started to laugh cause I knew she'd sat in it. Me dad knew as well, cause he came round and clipped me on the back of the head. He helped Louise up and took her arm and walked her back to the car. There was cow shit all the way up the back of her leg and on her white skirt. I could see that me mam and me gran were trying not to laugh, but me gran went after them anyway cause me gran's like that. She's a good Samaritan. Me granddad just shook his head, cause he was a man of few words. Afterwards, me gran put her arm around me shoulders and gave me a hug. I love me gran. Even though her name is Winter. Mrs Stevens is right; she's got a warm heart and she's the best gran in the whole wide world. I wished I lived with me gran; even though she's got no teeth.

## Black ashes and the 'Terra Nova'

Me Granddad was a soldier in the First World War. He rode a horse and he was there when they played football with the Germans on Christmas Day. I don't know if he scored though. He never said what the score was cause they were all shooting at each other the next day. I looked it all up in me EB. There were loads of battles, and men with *trench foot*. You just rot from the bottom upwards. There's nowt anybody can do. Me granddad wore this silver helmet with this red tail coming out the top. Me mam says that she used to have it, but it got given away, and that people like us give everything away. She says it's why we've got no history; not like all the posh people who keep everything, and that's why they're rich. The Queen keeps everything, but she's got loads of people to look after it in Buckingham Palace. There's seventy two bogs in Buckingham Palace. Seventy two bogs! You could use a different bog every week and still have twenty to spare; if you had the shits that is!

When the First World War finished, which we won, me granddad was going to go to Africa so that he could shoot the blokes there as well, cause they were running riot. But me gran wanted him home. I think she thought he'd done enough shooting, and that he should get a proper job where he didn't have to kill people all the time. Charlie says that loads of the men in the war went mad. So it was a god job me granddad came back cause we've got enough mad people in our family as it is.

Me granddad said to me that there's a war going on somewhere in the world all the time; even now. He also said that one day everything'll be made of plastic and people will just press a button if they want owt at all. He went down the mines and me mam says that he never earned more than ten quid a week in his whole life, and it nearly killed him. Now he's dead, so he never will make more than ten quid!

Me mam said that me dad killed me granddad. It was his fault for leaving, and me granddad couldn't stand the shock. After he died I got his medals. I've got them in this little box with me coins that I collected before it all went decimal. Now we count in tens, which is good cause only eggs come in twelve's.

Me granddad knew then that me dad liked Louise Draper, and that she was at our house every minute of the day. He told me mam, but she didn't listen. I listened through the crack in the door. I'm good at listening through cracks in doors like James Bond does.

– He thinks the grass is greener, Mary. That's what this is about. Me granddad said. I could hear him following me mam round the room. – We should have told you about Marion. We didn't think she'd ever come. I'm really sorry.

Me mam ran out the room, and straight past me. She slammed the door like she does. Me granddad didn't come out for ages.

At Christmas, Louise took me into Derby to see the lights. I didn't want to go, but me dad made me. She bought me a *Bar Six*. I know what she was doing. She was looking at me, testing me out to see if I was a good son that she could adopt after she and me dad went off. Marion, me mam's sister was adopted in nineteen twenty. She was sold for five quid to these people in London.

I was nine when Marion came. Me gran and granddad came up the drive with this woman. Me gran was crying. I'd never seen her cry before. This woman was smiling. I didn't know why then. But it was cause she'd found her mam and dad.

Me dad was on the roof of the garage, putting some asbestos sheets that had been broken by this ivy that had crept right up the side of the garage and gone under the sheets like a snake. It's like the plant out that film *Day of the Triffids* where they come and take over the world. Me dad said it could happen in real life. If ivy was left it'd just keep on growing. It would strangle owt in its way. He says that it'd survive an atomic bomb, and all that would be left in the whole wide world would be the rats and the cockroaches, the ivy on our garage, and probably Mr Shaw who would have shot everyone else. Ooh yeah, and Louise Draper.

– When we're gone, nature will just take over and reclaim what belongs to it. We're just passing through, me dad said. – Everything's borrowed. It's like beer; you only rent it because you piss it out the other end.

I was standing on the ladder passing me dad the tools. There were them little nails with the big heads so they don't go through the asbestos. I waved at me gran and granddad, but only me gran waved back. The woman waved at me though. She said me name. They went in the back door like they always do. We watched them go into the kitchen. Me mam was at the sink. It's the one she says she's chained to.

I handed me dad three nails.

– Who's that then? he said.

– Dunno.

Me dad kept hammering nails in. I think he knew something was wrong, cause he hit this nail dead hard and it broke the sheet. He threw it onto the ground where it broke into a million pieces. Grown ups know when things are wrong, just like kids, but sometimes they don't take no notice. I don't know why. Me granddad says it'll always get you in the end. Whatever IT is.

Me mam came out. I saw her. She had her apron on with the teapot. She took it off and threw it on the ground.

– Colin, she said.

Me mam looked as white as a sheet, and she never calls him by his name. Since he went, she just calls him *the pig* cause she says that people who run out on their families don't deserve to be called by their name. Me dad kept hammering. He doesn't like being stopped when he's doing owt dead important. It was like the boat.

– I just need to get this sheet secured.

Me dad knew that if he moved in the wrong place then he'd fall through the roof. He winked at me. – I don't want to end up like old Morris across the road, falling through the roof. Mr Morris hung there for half a day 'til the Fire Brigade had to come and lift him out.

Me mam came up to the garage.

– You need to come now, Colin.

– Now?

– Yes, now.

Me gran and granddad came out into the drive. Me gran didn't smile at me like she used to, and me granddad didn't wave his fist at me. I can only remember me gran crying once after that day. It was at me granddad's funeral when the coffin went behind the curtain and she never saw him again, which you don't; not as a whole person anyway. You get them back in a pot, which you can sling wherever you want. Auntie Mavis says she's going to sling Uncle Bob over Markeaton Pond with his mam who's now up in the sky.

– You never get the same person, Charlie said, after his gran had died.

Charlie's gran had been in a home for years.

– It's *a blessed relief*, Mr Shaw said.

Charlie said Mr Shaw hated her cause she thought Charlie's mam had married beneath her. I think Mr Shaw does as well, now Eileen's like *Ten Ton Tess*. You wouldn't want to be beneath Eileen cause she'd crush your nuts!

– 'owd you know you don't get the same person? I asked Charlie.

– Just know. Me Uncle Jason was cremated and is wife got this pot. She opened it and she cried cause she knew it wasn't 'im.

– 'ow did she know?

– It was black as the ace of spades.

– Jesus Christ! So what happened to yer Uncle Jason then?

– 'e'll be in some coloured bloke's pot on his way to Moretonside. 'e's probably still sitting there on some shelf in one of them corner shops, looking down at the nudie mags. The jammy bastard!

In the end, me dad came down the ladder. I held it for him cause a bloke up the road fell down his ladder and he never walked again. Mind you he was as pissed as a fart. I followed them to the back door. Me mam stopped me.

– Derek, I need you to stay outside.

Me dad put his hand on me head like he does.

– The lad's alright.

– No! me mam said. – He needs to stay out here. Go on your bike somewhere.

– Where?

– Anywhere.

They closed the door and I stood on the step. I tried to listen. I pressed me ear to the glass, but me mam opened the door and I nearly fell into the kitchen.

– Go!

I went on me bike. I called for Charlie, but he was up the rec, so I went to look for him. He was playing with his cousin. His name's Ant, which is short for Anthony. He's a spoilt brat. Ants are dead clever cause they can build these massive nests and everything, but this Ant's a thicko. He just has to ask his mam for owt he wants and she gives it to him.

– It's cause 'e knows something about is mam or dad, Charlie said.

– What d'you mean?

– 'e knows something secret, and if they don't give 'im what 'e wants then 'e'll split on 'em to the government.

– So what's the secret?

– Ant's dad works for the Russians. 'e's a spy.

– 'e's not a bloody spy. 'e was on the rigs. 'e used to paint 'em.

You have to be dead clever to be a spy. Ant's dad's as thick as a brick. 'e shot himself with an air rifle.

– 'e lived.

– Only cause it was point blank range and the bullet didn't get any speed up.

– There you are then.

– 'e was looking down the fuckin' barrel!

– You don't know what the fuck yer talking about.

I know Ant's dad's not a spy. I could see Ant was crying cause he'd kicked the ball into a garden, and the bloke was shouting at him.

– Anyway, 'e's not on the rigs no more, I said to Charlie. – 'e's in prison.

Ant's dad sends the money so Ant's mam can buy him presents cause she feels bad that his dad's away cause he's a criminal. I reckon the money she gets is from a bank job. Ant's got the biggest *Subutteo* you can get, with floodlights and everything. He's got all the stands and every team in all the divisions. He's even got *Derby County*. Sometimes, when he loses, Charlie says he breaks the heads off the men cause it's their fault. You can't blame a plastic man, though me mam probably would.

So I left the rec. I just watched them in the distance playing footie. Ant's in a footie team where he lives, in Duffield. It's where all the posh people live. He's crap at football, and goal hangs all the time. His granddad paid for the goal posts from the bank jobs. Ant says that if he gets dropped, his granddad'll take the goal posts home, and the corner flags as well. I'd tell him to take his bloody goal posts and shove them where the sun don't shine. You can always use your jumper.

I went up Breedon Hill where you can see right over Leicester. On a clear day you can see London and sometimes the sea at Skeggy if you stare for ages. Charlie says it's a mirage, but it's not, it's deffo Skeggy. Me mam said that me granddad got this motorbike once and they went up Breedon Hill, which is dead steep. He never changed gear all the way until it stopped. He fell off and never rode it again. It sounds a bit like me dad's boat. Me mam says that most men start things and never finish them. Women round here don't like men very much. I don't know why they bother with them.

When I got back home me gran and granddad and the woman had gone. I could hear me dad shouting at me mam through the kitchen window.

– You should have known! me dad shouted dead loud.

– Do you want the neighbours to hear?

– All these years! me dad said. – All these years they've lived a lie. They've lived a lie. How can people do that? They pretend to be decent people when they're not.

Me mam was making this wailing sound.

– They are decent people. People make mistakes. You're saying you never made a mistake, Colin?

Me dad went quiet for ages.

– No, I can't think of any. I didn't have a child with some tart and give it away. But they didn't give it away, did they! Oh no, they made money from it. What was it? Five quid. Blood money! Roll up! Roll up! Baby going cheap! Five quid!

– It was just mam. Dad had gone. They said that. Five years he went for.

– Yes, and I didn't hear him say where he went.

– It's none of your business.

– I know where he was.

– So where then? Go on, you tell me where you think he went. What's your filthy, distorted little mind coming up with now?

– It's obvious, Mary. It's obvious. He was in prison. He was a jailbird.

Me mam screamed. I could hear her hitting me dad. Women can hit men. Did you know that? It's cause they're the weaker sex.

– This wasn't a mistake, me dad shouted. – They couldn't help themselves. They couldn't stop. Now we know. Now we know. Now we know.

Me mam carried on screaming.

– Maybe they loved one another! Something you know nothing about. I can't remember the last time you said you loved me.

Me dad laughed again. – Mary, you don't know the half of it.

I thought he was going to tell her; tell her about Louise, but he didn't.

– When was the last time, Colin? Can you remember? Me

dad didn't say owt. – No, you can't. Neither can I. Not one jot of affection. I marked it in my diary. It's been nearly a year.

– So what am I supposed to do? me dad said. – With this stinking mess. They bring their dirty stinking mess and they drop it on our doorstep like a pile of dog shit. I wash my hands, Mary. They lied. They should have declared this. I had a right to know! Any lawful impediment. What happened then? Where was Marion then? Where was the illegitimate child of these fraudsters then? Huh! Huh! Huh!

Me mam screamed. I could see Mr Morris washing his car. He's always washing his car cause Mrs Morris sends him out cause she can't stand the sight of him. She goes ballroom dancing with this other bloke from Willow Fields cause Mr Morris says dancing is for pansies. Mr Morris was looking and listening cause after he'd dipped his sponge in his bucket he started rubbing it on the wall of the house.

– Marriage isn't some contract for something you buy, me mam said. – This isn't sale or return, Colin. This is the real world. I've got an older sister who I've just met, for the first time! And what about mam and dad?

Me dad spoke in this dead deep voice. He sounded like the devil.

– Fires of hell! They lied, Mary. They lied to me, they lied to you and worst of all, they lied to themselves; until they forgot about it.

I don't know how you can lie to yerself. I mean you'd know the truth. We always know the truth.

– Colin, my parents paid the deposit for this house.

I heard me mam bang on the back door. It made it vibrate.

– We'd be living in Langham Street if they hadn't. We'd be renting that little flat with the ants. What were they? Pharaoh ants that bite you so hard they make you bleed. They gave us all they had. And you took it.

    – I wouldn't if I'd known. It was filthy money!

    – That's utter rubbish! You can't see this for what it is, can you. You can't see that maybe they did this out of love. They did it to give the child a future. This is nineteen seventy two not the twenties!

    – And you think Marion's had a future. She was moved five times, Mary. Five times! A kid shifted from one set of parents who didn't want her, to another, and you call that love. You're as bad as they are. A chip off the old block. You think you'd feel the same if we gave Derek away. Perhaps you'd like to.

    – Since when have you been an expert on love?

    – I know it when I see it.

I think he was talking about Louise. But he has her for sex, so he can *get his end away in half a sparrow's fart* like they say in that song cause he don't want to do it with me mam. You wouldn't want to do it with me mam. No one wants to do it with your mam. It's not normal. Mam's should be like Hydra's that have their babies all by themselves; like trees with buds. But Louise has trapped me dad and he can't get out. It's what women do. It's like the spiders as McTavish says.

    – When you get married, you stick it out – *'til death us do part*, me mam tells me.

I ain't ever getting married. Now me dad's been trapped by Louise and she's got her claws into him, she'll never let him go. He's a dead man. Like I said; I ain't ever getting married. It's like death. It's worse that death. It's like me mam says about me dad going; that it's worse than death. But being married's worse. Then I started dreaming about it. There was this girl, this big fat ugly girl covered in school gravy, which I hate. I had to get married to her so I killed meself. You're not supposed to die in your dreams. It's a dead bad thing. But I did. This man stabbed me with a muliti-coloured Lego sword. I don't know why. I think it was probably God.

I opened the door and saw me mam and dad. They were just yelling. Me dad was leaning on the cooker and me mam was sitting on a chair. Her face was all puffy. I stood in between them.

– Stop! Please stop!

They wouldn't. They just yelled more and louder.

Me mam got up and went out the house. She walked straight past me without looking. She slammed the door. I saw the doorframe move, but me dad didn't say owt.

– Did you hear all that Derek, she shouted from the gate.

I didn't say owt. Me dad didn't say owt after that neither. He just cooked me sausages with crinkly brown chips and peas. Then we sat down and he drank five bottles of his home made beer. I covered me chips with sauce, which me mam don't let me do cause it's what the common people do. Then me dad went to the bog with his hi fi magazines.

Me mam didn't come back 'til it was dark. She slammed some doors and went to bed in the back room. She shouts about the Gowers next door slamming doors all the time, but me mam slams doors all the time as well. I could hear her crying like the cats do by the bins in the night. It was when all the crying started, and it's not stopped. Something happens and people just start crying. Marion started it, then she left, and she never ever came back. She brought us what I call the crying disease.

Me dad sat in the dark drinking more of his beer. His voice was all slurry.

– I've been a fool, Des. Conned. That's what I've been. I put them on a pedestal. Now look what they've done.

He didn't tell me what they'd done. Not then. He looked

out the window, but it was dark. – I'd like to be at the South Pole right now, Des. Wouldn't you?

– Deffo.

– We'll get the boat out tomorrow. Let's call it a prototype.

– What's a prototype?

– It's a sort of first attempt, like a model, before you build the proper thing.

– Will it be bigger?

– Much bigger? Massive. Like the *Terra Nova*. I mean it, Des. You've got to think big. There's a whole world out there. We put a man on the moon. Think what we can do next.

– You said you didn't think they put a man on the moon.

– I've changed my mind, Des. Sometimes you have to change your mind and face the facts.

I thought about him changing his mind.

– We could get a colour telly, I said.

He ruffled me hair.

– We'll see, Des. We'll see. He always says *we'll see*. It means no.

# Burnt fingers, cold steel, and the house of 'shame'.

Me granddad got ill. One minute he was waving his fist at me, the next he was flat on his back looking like a skeleton. Me mam started sleeping at their house. They brought me granddad's bed down into the front room cause he couldn't go upstairs no more.

– He'll never go back upstairs again, me mam said.

I couldn't believe what she said – one day you come downstairs and that's it; you never go back upstairs again.

The doctor said he'd got something wrong with his blood, and that it was full of stuff that shouldn't be there. It was something about pies.

– It's guilt, I heard me dad saying to me mam. – It's eating him from the inside out. That's what happens when you lie.

I nearly said it. I nearly said to me dad that he lied to me mam about Louise. He told her that he was at a meeting when he was being Louise's sex slave cause that's what she was doing. I know she's got these chains and things that she ties me dad up with. She swings around in this room that she's got, shagging him and he can't stop. None of them can stop. They can't stop shouting and screaming at each other, and they can't stop doing things. They can't hear me. They won't stop! They won't fuckin' stop! They just won't fuckin' stop! Now it's okay that I nick from the shops and take dough out me dad's wallet, and I lie cause they do it all the time. They won't stop! And I fuckin' hate them! I'll always fuckin' hate them! I smashed me Spitfire that Louise bought me for Christmas.

I smashed it with one of me dad's hammers into millions of pieces. I smashed the head of the pilot. I pretended it was her. I smashed it until it looked like a little plastic coin. I never cried. I ain't ever going to cry again. It don't matter how much it hurts.

I couldn't go and stay with me gran and granddad after that. Before me granddad got ill, I used to go when me mam and dad went out somewhere. I don't know where. They never told me. Once they went to see *Thunderball* with James Bond. I used to get into bed with me gran and granddad. Me gran didn't have any teeth in. Her face was all caved in like a baby's. We used to eat ginger biscuits. I watched her dip them in her tea to make them soft. In the morning she washed her teeth under the tap cause she soaked them in *Flash* in the night time. She says *nothing cleans them like Flash*. It's what the old bag on the telly says when she's cleaning the floor that looks like a chess board. Me mam says the floor's still black and white even in colour, and that's why a colour telly's a waste of money. I still dream about having a colour telly.

On Saturdays, I went to visit me granddad. He was getting thin like me mam is now. Me mam said I should sit with him, but I couldn't think of owt to say.

So I asked him the big question.

– Did you ever kill a German?

His head was like an alien's, with these big goggly eyes, and little spindly arms that were all blue on the back. They used to have these aliens in TV 21 magazines that me granddad used to bring for me when he worked in the paper factory down Raynesway. He looked just like one of them.

– There's always things, he said in this strange voice. – There's always things that you don't know.

He was in this sort of trance. He gripped me hand, dead

hard. He often gripped me hand dead hard. Sometimes he put his face dead close to mine. He always said the same thing:

– You'll get your fingers burnt. People are always getting their fingers burnt. No matter what you tell 'em.

There was this pilot in the film *Battle of Britain*, which me dad and me went to see at the flicks in Derby. He gets his fingers burnt. Me dad said he wrote a book called *I burnt my fingers*. I don't know if it's true. It wouldn't be a very interesting book anyway; just about his fingers. I cut me thumb, but I'm not going to write a bleeding book about it. That's a joke if you didn't get it!

I don't know what me dad said that was actually true in the end. Me mam said you can't believe owt he says, and that his whole life's been a lie

– He lives a lie, she said.

– You mean 'is name might not be Colin Jackson?

– Who knows? He's a stranger to me. Me mam said daft things like that. – He's not the man I married. I can tell you that.

– Maybe 'e's a spy, like Ant's dad. Which he ain't cause he's in prison.

Me mam looked at me like she was dead cross. – Don't be clever, Derek. I wish he was a spy. It'd be a lot easier. I suggest you leave the jokes to the comedians.

– There was this blade you screwed onto the end of the gun, I said to me granddad.

His eyes went even wider than they already were. If he'd sneezed they'd have gone as far as the Peak District.

– It's called a bayonet, he said.

– I know you use it for stabbing people, I said.

He looked at me dead funny with his wide eyes. They sort of moved in his head on their own like big marbles. He looked like Parker out of *Thunderbirds*. When they stopped rolling about, he looked at me for ages. He spoke dead slowly.

– You drive it home and then you twist it. That's what they tell you to do. That's what all these toffs do with the scrambled egg on their arms. These are men who never saw a day's action in their lives. Soft lily-white hands.

– You can't be in charge if you don't know what to do, I said.

– No, that's right. *The Charge of the Light Brigade*. The biggest military blunder of all time, because some toff told them to charge. Hundreds lost. If not thousands. All them horses. You have to remember that it's another human being on the end of that blade; somebody's father, somebody's husband, somebody's son. Do you understand?

– Yeah.

– Do you understand? Do you understand what it's like to feel the bones of a man's chest break under the weight of the blade, when you're the one pushing it, taking a life? You can hear his breath. He's that close that you can see into his eyes. You know what he's thinking.

– What's 'e thinking?

– He's thinking that he's going to die today. Think about that, Derek Jackson before you twist the blade.

I wasn't thinking about twisting no blade.

Then he fell asleep. He was always falling asleep. I wondered if me granddad was going to die today. I wondered if that's what he was trying to say.

*You'll get your fingers burnt.* It was what he said all the time. It was like he'd got nowt else to say. It's like me dad says *we'll see*, which means no. I say ace, which Auntie Mavis says is a stupid word, and she's sick of me saying it. She says if I can stop saying it for two weeks she'll give me ten pence.

Me granddad died. He died in hospital in Derby. Me mam

said it was once an old workhouse, and none of the old people ever want to go there. It's where they used to put people in the olden days when they had nowhere else to go. Me mam says people don't forget, but me dad says me gran and granddad forgot they had an extra child.

When we went to visit, they'd cut me granddad's hair dead short. When me mam saw him she started crying. It was that bad. He looked like he'd been to Tommy Swift's. Me mam started shouting at the nurse who was standing at the end of the ward. While she was shouting, me mam kept pulling at me granddad's hair like it was a tuft of grass.

– His hair! she shouted. – Have you seen his hair?

The nurse came down the ward. She looked at me granddad. Me granddad looked at me and lifted up his arm. I know he was going to make a fist at me, but he couldn't. I knew that he wasn't going to die yet cause he'd still got some fight in him. He made these words with just his mouth, and no sound coming out. *You'll get your fingers burnt.* I went to the side of the bed.

– Did the bloke die? I asked him. – The one you stuck the bayonet into?

At first, me granddad looked at me as if he didn't know who I was. He said nowt for ages until he remembered.

He whispered. – They all die eventually. It can take hours if you don't hit the spot. There's gallons and gallons of blood in those fields. The Somme, Ypres, all the others. It's where the poppies grow. Everyone is a drop of their blood.

I didn't know what to say.

– You should have seen me skin a rabbit, he said. – Neck broken in a flash. Blade from throat to tail, skin off and gutted. Two minutes. You should see it. It'd toughen you up. You're too soft m'lad. You need to see some death. They should make you stand here when I go. Won't do you any harm.

Me granddad thought me mam was too soft on me, and that she should whack me sometimes. The last time was when I put this plunger thing for cleaning the drains on the wall. I stuck it on and pulled it. This massive piece of plaster came off the wall. Me mam went mad and clipped the back of me head. She sellotaped it back on. I don't mean the back of me head. I mean the wall.

That's why me granddad always made this fist and shook it. He thought I'd be a better boy with a thick ear or the belt. It was cause he was in the army and that's what they did. He said he had a tooth out when he was in the army. This bloke who did the shoes on horses sat him in a chair in the middle of a field. He got these plier things that he used for pulling the nails out of horses' hooves and pulled me granddad's tooth out, without gas or owt.

– His hair! me mam kept saying. – He had beautiful hair and someone's chopped it! I mean chopped it! Someone's used a blunt pair of scissors and just hacked at it like you would if you were cutting a verge of grass.

I could see that me mam wanted to smack the nurse in the chops. Then this old bloke in the bed opposite started laughing. He pulled back the covers. We could see he'd got a stiffy, and then he pissed in the air. It was like a yellow fountain.

– He had nits, the nurse said. – We cut his hair because he had nits. It's the policy. You can't have everybody getting nits.

– Nits! me mam shouted.

– Yes, nits.

– Nits!

They did this for ages, saying nits! Nits! Nits! Me granddad lifted his arm again and tried to make a fist, but he couldn't do it.

– I can tell you, me mam said, – my father's never had nits in his life.

– Well he has now. He came in with them.

I thought me mam was going to go off like one of them rockets. Her face was like a beetroot, and she kept standing up on her toes like she wanted to take off and go into orbit.

They got the old bloke across the way, up out of bed. His pyjama trousers were round his ankles. He looked at me mam and stuck two fingers up at her.

– I'll be back for you love! he said.

We didn't see him again. They probably took him to *Pastures* and put him in a strait jacket.

Me mam got the matron. She likes to speak to someone high up, does me mam. Mind you, she never bothered with the gas board. We just carried on gassing ourselves.

– See what they do then, when we've been gassed, she said.

– But we'll be dead!

– Well that'll serve them right for messing about with things.

– You'll die watching Coronation Street.

– Derek, I've told you before; I don't watch Coronation Street.

We could hear the Matron's shoes clicking on the corridor. She had one of them mats you put under a cake in her hair. She looked like Hattie Jacques. She looked at me granddad's hair.

– Now Alec, the nurse said. – What's the problem?

– It's Mr Winter to you! me mam said.

– He likes us to call him Alec. It's more personal. Isn't it Alec?

– And I want you to call him Mr Winter. He was in the forces, fighting for King and Country. He was in the trenches with his horse. Not like this useless bunch of good for nothings.

Me mam pointed up the ward at two nurses who were playing cards and drinking tea. It was dead embarrassing. I wanted to leave. I don't think they had horses in the trenches. It didn't say so in me EB. I don't know how they would've got them out, what with all that mud.

The nurse patted me granddad's hand. He looked as if he liked it. – What can I do?

– It's his hair! me mam said. She was shouting now. – His hair! Can't you see, woman! Me mam grabbed a bit of me granddad's hair. – This was long and soft. It looks like a toilet brush. He looks like a manual worker, not someone from the forces. He looks like someone from Edmeston.

The nurse looked at me mam and then at me. She had a wart on her chin with a long hair sticking out of it, which you could have pulled out with a pair of tweezers.

The Matron stared at me mam, like she was examining her face for something wrong with it.

– I'm from Edmeston if you didn't know. And I know who you are. You're Mary Winter. I remember you, the nurse said. – They all said you were a bit high and mighty with no cause to be.

– It's Mary Jackson, me mam said. – And I don't remember you.

The matron held me granddad's hand.

– It's okay, Alec. Everyone's upset. I'll get you a nice cup of tea and a biscuit. Then I'll see if we can get your hair out of the bin and stick it back on.

Me granddad laughed dead loud, then he started coughing.

– Now you've made him cough, me mam said. The Matron passed him a glass of water.

– I made him laugh. You should try it. We have a bit of a

laugh around here.

Me mam watched the Matron walk off, but she didn't say owt.

The next week, me mam had me granddad moved back home. A nurse came in every day until she made him go back to hospital again cause me mam and me gran couldn't cope. He couldn't get out of bed for a crap, so they had to lift him up on the plastic potty like a massive baby. Sometimes he missed, and then they had to change the bed with him in it. I hope I never get old. It's horrible. It's just like being a baby. Mr Shaw's right; they should shoot all the old people. Charlie's going to shoot his dad when he's fifty. I think he'll do it sooner. That's if Mr Shaw doesn't hang himself first because of *The New Seekers* and *I'd like to teach the world to sing!*

Me granddad died a week later. Me mam said he died of shame. Then after that she said me dad killed him.

– 'Ow? I wanted to know.

– Mental torture. He knew what he was doing.

– But 'ow did 'e kill him with mental torture. 'e never went to see 'im in hospital.

– Exactly.

So I don't know which one's true, cause me mam says we live in shame now and I say we live in Derby, which is dead funny, but she never laughs. I think she'd only laugh if me dad was dead. She said she'd dance on his grave and sing a little song.

– Which one? I asked.

Me mam had had a couple of sherries, so she laughed. – These boots are made for walking, she said.

Me mam was dead upset when me granddad died. Me dad and her started arguing all the time about who had the best family.

– My parents did everything for you, me mam said.

Me dad used to point his finger dead close to me mam's face.

– You're missing out one vital thing though, Mary. Then me mam started crying cause she knew what he was going to say. So she got in first, like she does.

– And your family's so bloody marvellous. How many children was it? Twelve? Thirteen. Like animals that never left the cave!

That was the day I nearly did the solitaire and me mam tried to sort out the funeral with me gran.

I'd never been to a funeral before.

– Can I go? I said. Me dad patted me head.

– Course you can, son. It'll be an experience. It'll be a bit like Susan Gower's wedding.

– Do you think there'll be a fight?

– More than likely, he said. – More than likely.

# Wrong numbers, funeral blues and 'electric green' socks.

While me granddad was back home and me mam was staying there, me dad went out a lot. Then when he was in, the phone kept ringing. I picked it up and someone put it down at the other end. Sometimes it was dead quiet. I knew there was somebody there cause I could hear them breathing. Me dad took the phone off me and he started talking. I could hear that there was somebody talking back.

– Who was it? I said.

– It was a wrong number, Des.

I just looked at him cause I didn't believe him. You don't talk to someone that's rung a wrong number for half an hour! But me dad's like that now. He tells lies cause he thinks he's protecting me, but he's not.

I got the day off school for me granddad's funeral. I'd never been to a funeral before. I was a bit scared as I'd never seen a dead body. Charlie said that even after they're dead that they can sit up all of a sudden and look at everybody and maybe say something and do this laugh. Me mam said I wouldn't see a dead body, and that me granddad was in a box.

Me mam went to see me granddad after he died, but me dad didn't. He stayed with me and we cooked spam fritters and chips and beans cause me mam won't do it. She says spam's dead common. It's what they had to eat in the war. When me dad cooks his chips they're all exactly the same size. He measures them. He says that cooking's like engineering and you have to follow the rules. He says it's as simple as that.

After the fritters we had treacle pudding out of a tin. Me mam won't do them neither cause she says they'll explode and kill somebody. Me dad says he's never heard of it happening. Me mam knew a bloke who let a rocket off on bonfire night and it went miles into the sky. When it came back down it took his eye out. It went into his brain and it killed him. So me mam said that things can happen. Me dad just laughed. They had an argument cause me mam knew we'd had fritters and me dad had been drinking beer when the vicar had come round.

– It smells like a brewery! she said. Me dad laughed.

– We'll be cast into the fires of hell.

Me mam talks to the vicar. She says he's got good ears. They look like Steve Buxton's to me; like the *FA cup*.

– You spend too much time on your knees, me dad said. – Flopping!

Me dad calls praying, flopping. It's cause when me mam kneels down to pray she looks like she's a rag doll.

– You've got to give yourself to God, she says, – otherwise he can't hear you.

Me mam used to make me go to church and pray. Me dad says that we're heathens. He says that they thought Christopher Columbus was a heathen cause he sailed over the horizon and that he wasn't supposed to. They said that if God wanted us to go to some other place then he wouldn't have put the horizon there. At school the RE teacher asked Charlie what he would give Jesus if he came for tea.

– A can of *Toby Light* and a packet of fags! he said. Charlie got a double detention cleaning the bogs.

– Did Captain Scott believe in God? I asked me dad.

– What do you think?

I didn't know and neither did he.

It rained on the day of me granddad's funeral. Me dad says it always rains on funeral days so it makes people feel miserable.

– People like a bit of misery, he said. – All the wailing and the gnashing of teeth.

I couldn't hear no gnashing of teeth, but the old bags were all crying, even before they went into the church.

Me mam cooked bacon sarnies for breakfast, but she didn't eat any. Me dad and me had double with brown sauce. Me mam just stood and looked at me dad.

– I don't know how you can eat on the day of my father's funeral.

– You made them, me dad said.

– That's not the point.

Bacon sarnies are horrible cold.

– You need to get changed, she said to me dad.

Me dad winked at me.

– Did you hear me, Colin Jackson?

Me dad winked again.

– Please don't tell me! she said. Me dad looked at me and grinned. – Please don't tell me you're thinking of going to my father's funeral dressed like that!

Me dad pointed under the table. He pulled up his trouser legs. He was wearing me electric green socks. He also had one of his cravats on and a blue shirt.

– Someone's got to be cheerful, he said. – Like a flower among the weeds.

Me mam stood in front of him.

– Please tell me this is a joke.

But it wasn't no joke. Me dad meant it.

– I'll wear what I like.

– Do you hate him that much? me mam said.

– I don't hate anybody.

– And you don't love anybody either!

Me mam started to cry.

– It's not my fault, she said. – I didn't know. They did what they thought was best. You might not agree with it. It was all they could do. Everyone has secrets.

Me dad got up and took the last bacon sandwich, took a bite and gave the rest to me. He put on his checked jacket he wears on walks. Me mam threw a book at him. It hit him on the shoulder. Me dad laughed.

Afterwards cause me mam went on and on about it, me dad put on a black tie and a dark jacket. But me mam didn't see the electric green socks 'til we got to the church. It made her cry even more. You could see she wanted to kill him. Then there'd be two dead people.

We drove to me gran's house and there were neighbours standing outside. Me dad said it's cause they're nosy bastards and that people love a tragedy unless it's them. Mrs Steven's didn't come out cause she was upset. Percy her budgie had died too. She said it was cause me granddad had died and that Percy was his spiritual guide. She said that when she went to her special church she would talk to me granddad cause she could find him through Percy; what with Percy taking him through the gates and everything. Mrs Stevens goes to this place where they hold hands and they talk to dead people. The thing is, nobody ever heard Percy say a word when he was alive, so I don't know how he's going to talk to nobody. Me granddad might teach him I suppose. Though I doubt it cause he always called Percy a filthy thing.

When the hearse came, me gran cried. It was the last time I ever saw her cry. She put her head in her hands.

– Oh Alec, she said. She patted me on the head. She

sounded cross that he'd gone and left her. Which I suppose he had really. Like me mam says; *they're better off dead*.

Me granddad weren't there no more. When you think about it, they've gone. When someone dies, you can go all round the world and you can never find them. It's like a Houdini trick except there's no trick. They've gone, and you never ever see them again. I'll never see me granddad again, so I'll never know if he ever did kill anybody with the cold steel. Mrs Stevens will never see Percy; until she gets the next one from the pet shop on London Road.

Me gran said, – sometimes I just look up and I'm sure he's there. Once I said his name and I saw him smile. But I know it was just a dream.

– Uncle Bob can see 'is mam, I said.

– That's not his mam.

– What do you mean? Me gran laughed.

– He's asking God to rescue him from Mavis!

We both had a laugh about that.

It's like when you look at the stars from the mound on the rec, and you try to imagine forever and you can't. I've tried. You just think and think and think and I can see this white line that goes on and on and on and on until you can't go on no more. They say that men have tried and tried and in the end they went mad so that the men in the white coats come and cart them off to the loony bin. Everybody's going to the loony bin.

We got in the hearse. It was a Daimler and it's the biggest car I've ever been in. All me mates were at school, so they didn't see it. We followed the coffin dead slow, so it didn't tip over or fall out onto the road. Billy Myers reckoned that happened in Derby in the middle of the town. The body was just lying there in the road. He said there were women screaming and old people fainting. They had to stuff it back in the coffin dead quick.

They took me granddad's coffin into the church and put it on two decorating stands like me dad's got in the shed. We sang an hymn and said a prayer and me dad nudged me to look at me mam. She was praying.

– Best to be a heathen, he said. – Like me.

Me dad don't seem to care that he'll go to hell no more.

I think Captain Scott believed in God. He talked about God in the book, and that the South Pole was a *Godless place*. That's why he died, cause God was pissed off that Amundsen beat them to the Pole. Me mam says God has *deserted* her and that he ain't listening to her no more. So she don't go to church cause she says there's no point. Which is good cause I don't have to go. She made me go on me own once, but I didn't. I just went and sat on the rec and had a fag with two little kids from the council estate. Their dad's in the clink for nicking loads of money and beating up a bloke in the *Crest of the Wave*. It's cause they gave him yesterday's chips heated up and he was pissed. They always cook yesterday's chips if you go early. We get scratchings from the bottom of the pan for one pence and potato scallops if they're burnt. They're best when they're burnt.

The vicar said me granddad had been a soldier and defended his country. He told everybody that he played football at Flanders and that when we won the World Cup in nineteen Sixty-Six it was God playing his part.

Me dad shook his head and whispered. – God wasn't picked for the team, and he didn't score the winning goal, it was Geoff Hurst.

The vicar said me granddad had seen a lot of action, and that he'd seen the worst things men can do to each other. So

I knew then that me granddad had killed somebody's son, brother, dad or uncle.

We sang another hymn and they took the coffin. We drove to the Crematorium where we sang another hymn. These little blue curtains opened, the coffin went along on these wheels and then it was gone. After all that, they burn it and that's what the chimney's for. They give you the ashes in a little pot that you can throw over something if you want. We stood outside for ages. It was freezing and then we went back to me gran's house and ate some sandwiches. I got a gulp of me mam's sherry.

Me mam and dad didn't speak for four days after me granddad's funeral.

Me dad went on and on about me granddad after the funeral, like he couldn't let it go.

– He was in the *dirt and grime*, Des. That's why it's important you don't go in there. You look what happens to them all. They go there, to the factories, day in and day out, day in and day out, day in and day out. They work all the night, stoking the furnaces. They look like a bunch of coloureds, their bodies glistening with sweat. You can hear the testing beds all night long. They're pounding metal, stripped to the waists. Their bodies are black with soot. It gets in your lungs, Des and in the end it kills you. For what? You tell me. For what?

Me dad always asks a question and then he answers it.

– For nothing. They retire, have all their teeth out and do nothing. Because, Des, they can't do anything. They're finished. They don't have anything left. They're knackered. Is that what you want, Des? Is that what you want?

– No, I said. – It ain't what I want.

– It's isn't! People in the 'dirt and grime' say ain't.

Everybody round here says ain't. It's only right. If you didn't say ain't you'd get your head kicked in. That's fair.

# Liquid Nitrogen, Ballet, and the RB211 engine

In the morning the siren goes off. It's the one they used in the war when the Germans were coming over in their bombers to drop bombs on *Rolls Royce*. They had these big balloons. Me gran had one outside her house. One day it took off and this bloke was hanging onto the rope and it took him right up into the sky until he fell off and was strawberry jam. After the siren's gone off, all these mopeds start up and it's like bees buzzing from all the roads. They're like a swarm at the traffic lights. They're all going to *Rolls Royce* and the *carriage-side* where they're building this train that leans over when it goes round corners. It's called the APT. One day the siren didn't go off. *Rolls Royce* went bust and the testing beds went all quiet. Nobody could get to sleep no more cause people used to say that the testing beds were like music and it put people to sleep. They said they couldn't stand the silence.

– It's the sound of poverty, me dad said. – All you can hear is the sound of grown men crying into their beer.

I couldn't hear them.

There were fights at the dole office. Blokes went down to Moretonside to beat up the people from Pakistan cause they said it was all their fault, cause they'd come over and taken the jobs. Charlie said there was this axe fight in the street and there was blood flowing in the gutters where they'd hacked heads off and everything. Billy Myers said his dad was there with this axe that Billy made in metal work, which was bollocks cause we all made one and they were toffee hammers.

You couldn't kill no one with a toffee hammer.

Some of the blokes who didn't have jobs still went to work. Me dad said it was cause *Rolls Royce* had turned them into robots, and they didn't know owt else. They just stood outside the gates with these massive mental eyes and lit fires in bins with holes in the sides. People killed themselves. There's this place in Dovedale called *lovers leap* where men and women killed themselves cause they were in love and me mam says it's an illness. These men jumped off and their heads were smashed to pieces on the rocks.

Me mam did a bad thing to Dave Noakes and his mam and dad. They're Christians, and one Sunday before I started at Dalemead Grammer, me mam said I should go to church with Dave to keep him company. I said I'd go cause I fancied this girl, even though she was a Christian. But the bad thing me mam did was cause I passed me eleven plus and Dave didn't. Me mam made me put me Dalemead uniform on.

– I don't want to. It's stupid. It's for school.

– You'll do as I say, she said.

– I ain't wearing me cap.

I went round to Dave's. He came to the door. He was putting his coat on.

– Yer only coming cause of Glenda Newbold, he said.

– That's bollocks. It's cause I want to talk to God. He laughed.

His teeth are all crooked. One day they'll take them all out like his dad, and they'll bleed for yonks. He'll probably die.

Mrs Noakes came to the door. She looked at me and made this noise that adults make when they can't think of no words. She pointed at me and she opened and closed her gob just like a goldfish. I could see that her finger was shaking.

– I don't know, she said. She was shaking her head like she'd got the St Vitus dance like Mrs Stevens. – I don't know how you've got the nerve! she said. – Coming here!

– I've come for Dave.

Dave had got his coat on. He came outside. He shook his head twice to feel his brain wobble. Then his mam grabbed him by the collar of his coat and oiked him backwards. He nearly fell over. His face was going purple.

– Mam! What yer doin'? he shouted.

Mrs Noakes pointed at me again like a witch.

– He's damned-well not going. Not with you. I take it this is your mother, Derek?

I knew it was the uniform and the badge and everything. I knew it was what me mam wanted to do. She wanted to rub her face in it cause me dad left. She wanted to get her back.

– She made me.

– You didn't have to do it. You've got a mind of your own.

– But me mam said.

– Your mam's a first class bitch!

Mrs Noakes slammed the door dead hard, and the glass cracked. I could hear her shouting. She clipped Dave cause it was his fault for not passing the eleven plus. Everybody's glass was cracking cause of the door slamming. Dave was crying. He ain't spoke to me since, and he was one of me best friends. He gave me a penknife from Scarborough, which said *Shirley* on it. I don't know why. I didn't go to church. Glenda Newbold's got crabs anyway.

The government gave *Rolls Royce* all this cash, and they got a contract for the *RB211 engine* so everybody went back to work. Me dad said it was from Russia and now they're all spies and sending plans back to Moscow so that they can make more bombs.

– That's the problem, me dad said.

He always says there's a problem. He says the world's full of problems, and all we do all the time, is solve other people's problems. If there weren't no problems we'd have nowt to do. I think he's right.

Captain Scott kept a diary. When they found him with the others in the tent they were frozen stiff like fish fingers in the shop fridge. But the diary was okay, cause you can't freeze paper. But you can freeze other things. This bloke with an egg head came into school. Most people won't come into school cause they're shit scared. He had this pot of steaming liquid, which he said was really a gas. Billy Myers and his mates: Johnny Watts, Steve Buxton and Eagle were mucking about and farting.

– That's a gas, Eagle said. – If it's a liquid it's a liquid.

– What's your name? the bloke asked him. Eagle didn't say owt.

– Did you hear me boy?

– Oh la di da! Slaggy Scott said at the back of the class.

The bloke folded his arms.

– I said, what's your name?

– Eagle.

– That's a bird. I want your name.

– Eagle.

– Don't be stupid. Your real name.

– Eagle. Me dad changed it on me birth certificate.

The bloke gave up. Eagle really believed he was Eagle.

– All right then, Eagle; if that's what you want to be called. You speak when you're spoken to. Do you understand? Oh and by the way, I'm the Prince of Wales.

Only slaggy Scott laughed. Eagle didn't know what the bloke was on about. He was having a laugh.

Eagle always sat with his legs apart. The women teachers

were always on at him about it cause he was feeling himself so he'd get a stiffy. He thought it was funny cause he liked to act as if he was Educationally Sub-Normal, which is what they call the mongs. It was so he could go to one of them special schools that go in those blue buses to *Riber Castle*.

Eagle stood up and just stared at the bloke like he does, cause he thought he was an Eagle. He really did, and he thought he was going to swoop down and rip the bloke's face off with his claws. Except he bit his nails.

Eagle spoke, dead quiet like.

– You want to mek somet' of it then? cause that's how he spoke, dead slow like Clint Eastwood out the Dirty whatever.

The bloke just laughed. – I'm a black belt. Then he span round and he kicked the metal chair right across the room, which anybody could do. He walked over to Eagle. – So you still want to make something of it? Not even Billy Myers moved.

The bloke lifted his hand to scratch his head, and he made Eagle flinch. Everybody laughed. I sort of felt sorry for Eagle then, which I'm glad I did cause I hated him really.

– Me dad'll kick yer fuckin'ead in, Eagle said to the bloke.

The bloke was so fast you couldn't see his arm move. He had Eagle on the floor with his arm right up his back in a half Nelson as quick as slaggy Scott can drop her knickers. I've seen it on the telly; not slaggy Scott dropping her knickers like. It was with the wrestling on a Saturday afternoon when *Giant Haystacks* drops on *Big Daddy's* head. Me dad says they're just acting and that they're mates really. But me dad don't know everything.

The bloke marched Eagle to the door.

– I'll be five minutes, the bloke said to us. – You don't move any of you or you'll all get the same.

No one moved a muscle except for Tina Scott the 'slag heap' who strutted around the classroom with two of her mates; Mandy Crawford the bike and Julie Beale. Charlie reckons they'll have a bun in the oven by the end of next year, and then they'll get a flat and live on the dole.

When the bloke came back, he took the lid off this pot.

– This is liquid Nitrogen. It becomes a liquid at minus 196 degrees Centigrade and can freeze your balls off. Which he's not supposed to say, but he wanted us to forget about Eagle and make us laugh, which he did. He put this stick of rhubarb in. When he took it out he smashed it on the edge of the desk. It shattered into a million pieces. Captain Scott died of frostbite. I reckon when he fell off his chair he would have broken into a trillion pieces and they had to pick them all up so that they could take him home in a bag.

Billy Myers said he'd got some liquid Nitrogen at home under his bed. He said that his dad got it cause he's a scientist working for the government. But he ain't a scientist cause I've seen him outside the dole office with his mates having a fag. Billy says it's just a cover for all the secret work he does. But it's bollocks. Billy's dad's as thick as he is.

All the kids in the remedial class reckon they're going to be Astronauts and fighter pilots and racing drivers or pop stars or owt they want. Mickey Tate even reckons he can speak German. He just mixes his words up and he thinks he's talking German. He's so stupid, that he actually thinks he is. He says that German people would understand him instead of shooting him.

– Hanza, oyez, strazumberg, wizdumbuder. He's a complete wanker.

Captain Scott's diary's in a museum where you can look at it. They were eleven miles from their next camp, but they couldn't go on. Me mam kept a diary, but she don't write in it no more. The last thing she wrote in it was on the Friday when me dad left the last time. She called it *Black Friday*. She says it was when her life ended.

Me dad waited six-months before he went again. I knew he was going cause he bought loads of new pants and vests. He got this new suitcase and hid it at the back of his wardrobe with these nudy mags. I nicked one. It was *Men Only*. I'd never seen a fanny before. I told Charlie.

– Yer dad's a perv. You don't look at fannies when yer dead old.

Charlie says he's seen loads. He says everybody's seen Tina Scott's and that if you give her a B*lack Jack* she'll let you touch it.

– I won't, I said. – You'll get crabs.

Me mam changed her job to another office, but she's not been to work now for ages cause she's too thin to go. She still works for the council; something to do with traffic lights. There's this bloke in the office who me mam says lives with his mam and he's got a massive train set in his bedroom like a big kid. Their office is right next to a church. He keeps a black tie in his drawer and every time there's a stiff he goes to the funeral and sings the hymns and cries. He's definitely a perv!

On the day me dad left, it was dead cold. *Granddad* was number one by the bloke out of *Dad's Army*. He was the one who kept saying *don't panic, don't panic!* I knew all the words and when I sang it, it made me think of me granddad, which made me sad. Me mam said that he was singing it just for us cause he sings *just because you're far away*. Me gran says that me mam needs to think he is otherwise she couldn't cope.

– How far d'you think it is to 'eaven then? I asked me gran.

– Oh a long way away.

– Past the moon?

– Further than that.

She needs to think it is or she'd go mad.

In the afternoon on the day me dad went, this bloke came to the school to talk about dancing, which none of us do, cause you look like a puff. The bloke had this fuzzy hair and a scarf round his neck, which he kept flicking.

– Dance is an expression of the spirit, he said.

Billy Myers copied him.

– Dense is an ixprission eff the spirit.

Eagle was rubbing his balls like he does.

The bloke showed us some ballet on the screen. Billy Myers stood up. We were all watching him. He pointed at the screen.

– I ain't watching no fuckin' puffs, he said. – Me dad says it's a fuckin' disease, which you can catch.

He started walking to the door. The bloke went to stop him, but Billy opened it.

– I ain't watching no puffs in tights and you can't fuckin' mek me.

The bloke blocked the door.

- Oh yes I jolly well can young man! The Education Authority demands that you go to school. Do you want a job when you leave?

– Not as no fuckin' noncy ballet dancer! I'm joining the army. They shoot people like you.

– Your dad'd like that, I whispered to Charlie – shooting puffs.

– Billy's goin' to clean their boots! slaggy Scott shouted dead loud.

The bloke pushed Billy in the chest dead hard and he fell back and banged his head on the wall. Then Billy barged the bloke and got out the door.

– Me dad's goin' to kick yer fuckin' head in. Yer bastard!

The bloke let him go. We watched the rest of the film, which was crap.

When he pulled up the blinds, we could see out across the playground and there was Billy Myers with his dad coming across it. I poked Charlie in the ribs.

– Fuckin' 'ell! he said. – That's Billy's dad. He's rock hard. Killed a bloke down the *Framley Arms*.

Billy's dad kicked the classroom door open like John Wayne in a cowboy film. He just stood there with Billy behind him. He's got this big belly like he's got a cushion stuffed up his shirt. He looks like he's going to drop a sprog. His trousers kept slipping down and he kept oiking them up.

He went right up to the bloke. Billy was sniggering cause he'd got his dad with him.

– Me lad tells me you've been making 'im watch a bunch of nancy boys prancing around in women's knickers.

The bloke looked at Billy's dad for ages, like he was going to deck him with a kick.

– It's part of the curriculum.

Billy's dad made this face and did this posh voice.

– Oh it's on the nancy boy curriculum is it? Well, you listen 'ere, you fuckin' shirt lifter. You don't spread yer filthy ideas with these kids.

The bloke shook his head. – I'll teach them what they need.

Billy's dad grabbed the bloke by his scarf and pulled his face dead close.

– Me lad says you belted him!

The bloke was going red in the face and trying to get his scarf loose.

– I tried to stop him because he was trying to leave.

Billy's dad pulled the scarf tighter, and then he let it go and the bloke fell back. He pointed at Billy's dad.

– I'll call the Police if you don't go.

Billy's dad grabbed him again, and then he smacked him one. We all heard the crack. He broke the bloke's nose. Then he grabbed Billy.

– We're going, he said.

The bloke stayed down for ages. Billy Myers counted him out at ten. We watched Billy and his dad walk back across the playground like nothing had happened.

Charlie turned to me. – This one's not got a black belt.

– Only in puffin' about, I said.

– You know, Charlie said. – I don't think Billy's dad works for the government.

– Well of course 'e don't work for the fuckin' government, you dickhead. 'e's a scrounger. 'e's unemployed.

– I mean, Charlie said – if 'e worked for the government e'd wear a uniform.

Charlie can be a real idiot sometimes. I don't know how he passed the eleven plus. Dave Noakes's mam said they picked the names out of an hat and we were just the ones they picked. It's bollocks and me mam say's she's just bitter. She says 'there's nothing worse than a bitter woman'.

On the way home the arm fell off me coat. There was this piece of cotton and I pulled it. It just kept coming and coming until the arm just fell off like Nelson at the battle of Trafalgar. Me gran said she'd sew it back on.

Charlie laughed. – At least you're 'armless. I tried to stuff the arm in his mouth.

– Ha fuckin' ha! So I walked home with one arm off.

Just before me dad went the second time there was this weekend when he went mad. I mean he went completely bonkers. Me mam made this cake and it didn't come out right.

Me mam blamed the natural gas, like she does, and then goes on and on about it. Auntie Mavis said she was wrong, and Uncle Bob agreed. Auntie Mavis also told her (cause she's got a *National Geographic* magazine cause her uncle was an explorer in the jungle) that cause homos put their dicks into other homos' arses, they get this disease. They've found it in monkeys cause some of them must be homos' too. So Billy Myers dad was right, even though he is in prison for breaking that bloke's nose. Billy's back at school now, but he's got a social worker with him all the time in case he gets violent, then he'll go to prison with his dad.

– You see! Charlie said. – Billy's dad does work for the government now sewing mail bags!

*An engineer's point of view*
*Mam on a cloud*
*Gary Smedley's dead*
*I am Joe 90*

The cake me mam made had nuts and currants and everything. It came out dead flat. Me dad got hold of the cake and kept looking at it. He kept picking it up then putting it down again.

– From an engineer's point of view, me dad said. – From an engineer's point of view.

He kept saying *from an engineer's point of view* even though he's not an engineer. He did build a boat though.

– From an engineer's point of view! What the hell's an engineer got to do with a damned cake? me mam said.

– Everything. From an engineer's point of view it's about heat and density and depth and circumference and the even heat in the oven. Did you have it on the right heat?

Me dad talks like that. He knows a lot about heat and stuff.

Me mam took off her apron and threw it on top of the cooker. It started to burn cause she was boiling me dad's handkerchiefs to get the snot out. That's what wives have to do as well as scraping all the crap off their pants and things like that. It must be an horrible job being a wife. In the end you've got snot soup, which tastes salty cause me and Charlie gave some to this little girl up the road. Her mam said that we were filthy little boys. It was dead funny cause the little girl said it was nice. I'm glad I'm not a woman.

– It's snot soup, I said.

– Yes it is, she said.

– Oh no it's not! Charlie started to laugh cause it's a clever joke.

Me dad was going mad. He had this look in his eyes. They were wide open like he'd seen a ghost. He started crying and shouting at the same time. Me mam said it was a sign that he was going mad. She sent me to get Auntie Mavis. Auntie Mavis ain't got no kids. She had one but it died, which is very very sad.

– I see you as a son, Derek, Auntie Mavis said.

Uncle Bob was in the garden. He calls me *the prince*. He does a lot of weeding so he can talk to his mam. Auntie Mavis gets dead mad with Uncle Bob.

– Just look at him, Derek. Just look at him! Lives in a world of his own. It's obviously a better place than number five Wellington Avenue.

They live in a semi that they bought off the man that invented *cats eyes*. He lives in this massive mansion now, somewhere up north with a million cats that shit everywhere. You can get these worms from cat shit and they dig their way into your eyes and then you go blind, which is brill' for the man who invented *cat's eyes* cause it's made him dead rich.

Uncle Bob always agrees with owt Auntie Mavis says, so she can't tell him off. *You're right*, he says. Auntie Mavis likes being right. She said that chewing gum wraps around your heart if you swallow it. It's bollocks. And that Welsh people can talk to sheep.

When Uncle Bob's in the garden, he always wears this army jacket, which he had in the war. It's brown and there aren't any badges on it. Me dad says he did National Service in Swanage, which is where we went on holiday once and I got stung by a bee on me big toe. It hurt like hell. Me dad says that Uncle

Bob just had to look out for an invasion, and that he wears the jacket to remind him of the best time of his life when he had wine, women and song. Now he's got Auntie Mavis as a punishment. Me mam says you always have to pay in the end. She means me dad.

I went to Auntie Mavis's on me bike. I bought half of it from me paper round. Me dad gave me the other half. It's a racing bike and it's got chrome forks. The rest is light blue and it's got yellow rings on the down tube. It's got no mudguards so you get this line of crap up your back when it's raining. I love me bike.

Auntie Mavis was painting her kitchen. Uncle Bob's crap at DIY, so she don't let him do it cause he'll botch it up. He can't even knock a nail in straight. Me dad says he does it on purpose so he don't have to do owt.

– It's a good strategy, me dad says, whatever that is.

Auntie Mavis had got paint in her hair.

I was standing behind her.

– Me dad's going mad! I said.

She carried on painting. She's dead small, so she has to stand on a chair to do everything. She'd painted over the light switch.

– You've painted over the light switch, I said.

– White spirit, she said. I didn't even know she knew I was there.

– You'll get electrocuted.

– Don't try and be clever, Derek. A hello would have been nice. Everybody knows electricity doesn't flow through white spirit.

She tries to talk dead posh, but she keeps dropping her h's. Me dad says she drops so many that the council ought to make her pick them up.

– No, I mean it, me dad's really gone mad. 'e's shouting and crying and everything. Me mam's apron caught fire!

Auntie Mavis put her paint brush back in the pot.

There was this patch up in the corner near the grill.

– You missed a bit.

She leant back on the chair and wobbled. She nearly fell off.

– It's the light, she said.

Auntie Mavis is never wrong. It wasn't the light. She missed a bit.

Uncle Bob was sitting in a chair on the grass. Auntie Mavis calls it a lawn. Me dad says it's only people who play croquet who have lawns. Uncle Bob was reading the *News of the World*. He only gets it for the knockers. Auntie Mavis makes the paper boy fold it inside the *Sunday Express* so nobody sees. There's a bloke on London Road who has *Mayfair* and we all rubber neck it before he gets it. He complained that the pages were all creased.

– Put that thing away! Auntie Mavis shouted. – There's an emergency at Colin and Mary's. Make sure you put it in the shed. Bloody filth!

Uncle Bob closed his paper cause he didn't want her to see what he was looking at. He shoved it under his chair. The dog grabbed it and ran off down the garden. He's called Bob, which is dead confusing, but Auntie Mavis gets names mixed up all the time, so it's easier for Bob and Bob to have the same names. She sometimes calls me Colin.

Auntie Mavis waved her arm at Uncle Bob. – Get changed. They need us now!

Uncle Bob looked at me. He winked like all the old blokes do. He put his hand in his pocket and he gave me ten pence even though I hadn't walked the dog. Then he did what he always does, even though I was there watching him. He twisted his head and he looked up at the sky for ages. He smiled and he said something like he always does, but you can never quite hear what it is. He looked back up again and that was it. Everybody, even Auntie Mavis says it's cause he's talking to his mam who's dead, and that he's promising that one day they can be together on a cloud. I think he misses his mam. I bet it's only a two person cloud for just him and his mam. Imagine being on a cloud for ever and ever with Auntie Mavis being right all the time. You'd rather be in hell.

– I'm sorry about your dad, he said. – You say he's gone mad, I hear. He always puts his hand behind his ear when he says *I hear*.

– Yeah. Completely bonkers.

– I'm really sorry to hear (hand behind his ear again) about that, prince. Give him my best wishes.

He didn't even get out of his chair.

Auntie Mavis came round the corner. She'd painted her face and everything, and she smelt like a cream puff's parlour. She'd got her sheepskin coat on, which she got from Devon cause they've got lots of sheep. It looks massive on her.

– I want you to come, she said to Uncle Bob.

Uncle Bob got out of his chair and pointed.

– The dog. The dog was being sick on the path. They feed it too much chocolate, and it looks like a furry barrel. – The dog's being sick.

Auntie Mavis shook her head like she does. I knew what she was thinking cause me mam told me. She was thinking she'd rather have married the bloke she knew in the war who ran off with a woman in one of the bomb factories.

– He left her standing at the altar, me mam said like it was funny.

I don't know how long for. I think it was ages.

– You'd better stay with the dog then.

Uncle Bob looked up at the sky and smiled like he was saying thank you to his mam. It was cause she'd made the dog sick, so he didn't have to come and see me dad going mad.

– You follow me, Des, Auntie Mavis said. She's like a Sergeant Major. Uncle Bob saluted her behind her back.

– Yesss sir!

Auntie Mavis got in the car. It's an Austin Maxi. It's for the dog and it's massive. She drove dead fast to the end of her street and she was gone. I could hear the gears grinding right up Jubilee Road. She has a new clutch every six-months cause she can't reach the pedals. Uncle Bob has to put these wooden blocks on them so she can reach.

Me dad was in the front room where nobody goes apart from special people like the vicar and people from me dad's work, oh and Louise Draper, of course. I hadn't seen her for ages. I was hoping she'd pissed off to whatever slag heap she came from. Me gran was there. She was talking to me dad, but he wasn't listening cause he was staring at the fire. It was the same one that's slowly gassing me and me mam if you didn't know. When he saw me he started to cry. He grabbed me hand and pulled me over. Then he kissed me.

– I'm sorry Des.

– S'okay.

I wiped his spit off me cheek.

– It's just one of those things.

I thought then that it wasn't just one of them things. People don't just go mad in their own front rooms for no reason, and sit there crying like a baby.

I looked at his eyes. They say you can tell from looking at their eyes.

– Are you going mad?

Me dad laughed and looked at me gran.

– I wish I was, Des. I wish I was.

– Why would you want to go mad?

– So I can disappear.

– You mean go into *Pastures?*

– At least they'd leave me alone to get on with it.

– Going mad?

– Going mad.

– They'll make you wear a straitjacket.

– It doesn't matter to me. He tapped his forehead with his finger. – It doesn't change what's going on in here. It doesn't change the things you think about.

Me mam came in and sent me out. I went out the back and rode around on me bike for ages. Charlie turned up.

– What's going on? I asked him.

– Gary Smedley's dead.

– Gary Smedley?

– Gary Smedley.

– Dead? You mean croaked?

– Dead, you thick git! Brown Bread.

Charlie likes the Cockney slang.

He says *dog and bone* for phone. He's got one of them *trim phones*. He's always taking it apart to see how it works. It drives his dad mad, just like *The New Seekers* and *I'd like to teach the world to sing, sing, sing*; when it sticks.

– 'is dog pulled 'im into the road at six o'clock in the morning. It was on London Road. On the bend. 'e was looking both ways, and this bloke came round the bend at an 'undred miles an 'our and bang! The dog pulled him out, and Gaz was strawberry jam.

– Fuckin''ell! I said.

I don't know what strawberry jam rhymes with in Cockney.

– 'e was dead before they got 'im to the DRI. 'e broke every bone in 'is body, Charlie said.

– 'ow do you know that?

– Me mam saw your Auntie Mavis at the 'airdressers last night.

We sat on the grass without saying owt, then Charlie started to laugh.

– Sos, he said.

– Gaz Smedley's dead and yer laughing! You'll go to 'ell

He was stuffing his hand into his mouth and biting it dead hard.

– I know, but me dad'll be in 'eaven, so I don't want to go there with 'im and his team of twats.

– Then stop laughing. It ain't funny. Gary Smedley's dead.

– Sos. I always laugh when someone dies. It was the same with me gran. I couldn't 'elp it. I just blurted it out and they 'ad to take me out the church. Me mam says it's a nervous reaction cause it wasn't funny. I just couldn't 'elp it. They reckon I might need tablets if it don't stop.

– What sort of tablets?

– Tablets that stop you laughing when yer not s'posed to.

– That's bollocks. Yer can't get tablets to stop you laughing.

– You can get 'em to stop you farting.

– That's different.

– Not if you talk out yer arse it ain't.

Charlie went all quiet. Then he looked at me.

– You know what this fuckin' well means don't you.

– What?

– It means Des, that we won't be going to the footy for Gaz's party.

– It's Man U. George Best, Nobby Stiles, Dennis Law.

They'll have the tickets and everything What they going to do with the tickets? They'll 'ave a spare!

– They're not going to still 'ave the party if 'e's dead, yer silly twat. Not with the birthday boy on some slab.

– But there's all those tickets.

Charlie thought about this.

– S'pose yer right.

– Nah. You've got to do the right thing when someone's dead. Out of respect.

Charlie started laughing again, and I did too. Me gran came out and told us both to belt up.

– The doctor's here, she said. – You need to be quiet.

Charlie looked at me.

– 'as yer dad kicked the bucket then? We started laughing again.

– No, I said. – 'e's gone mad. We laughed for ages until me gran came out again. She sent Charlie home with a flea in his ear, which is Cockney slang for *bugger off*.

When the doctor was going, he stopped in the drive and looked at me. He's as bald as a coot, so he couldn't be me dad neither. Fancy having a doctor as a dad. He'd always be examining you.

– Hello Derek.

I didn't know what to say, him being a doctor and all, cause me mam says they're the most important people in the world along with vicars and the Queen. Then he winked at me. Everybody was winking at me like they'd got that St Vitus's dance. That's all he said. He went. He's got this big Jag. It's bright red with two exhausts and a big silver Jaguar on the front. It's got leather seats and it takes a whole day to fill it with petrol. It only does two miles to the gallon.

I looked through the back window of the house and I could

see me mam and Auntie Mavis and me Gran drinking tea from the best tea cups. They're *Crown Derby*. Me mam said that one day they'll be mine. I'm not allowed to sell them as I've got to hand them to me kids. Not that I'm having any. When me mam and dad are dead I'll sell them in the *Derby Evening Telegraph*.

Me gran waved at me, so I went to put me bike back in the shed. It was getting dark. I closed the door. I used to have a mouse called 'mouse' as I couldn't think of a name for it. I kept it in the shed. It ate all the hairs off a massive paintbrush and then it died. Charlie and me cremated it in the garden just like me granddad. We said a prayer, not that it'll help. I don't think there's a mouse heaven.

I haven't got no brother's or sisters. Charlie's got an older brother call Kev. He's a right tit. He's into electronics. He builds things that can tell you if something's wet or not. You might as well stick your finger in it! He converts these old tellys into computers that have wavy lines on them that mean bugger all. Mind you, he did do this thing where he got this rat's leg and he put electricity through it. It moved just like in Frankenstein. His mam says he's going to Oxford. Charlie says he's more likely to go to hell for mucking about with God's work.

I'd like a brother. Then I wouldn't have to do all this crap with me mam and dad. It'd be better if there was more than one of us. But I can go to these places in me head. Any time, any place, anywhere; just like the *Martini* advert. I wish I was in the *Martini* advert in real life. But I'm *Joe 90*. He's not on the telly no more. But he's got these glasses that give him super powers. He can do owt. I sit in the chair in the shed and I'm *Joe 90*. I can save the world. *Joe 90's* dad does all the special stuff, cause that's what dad's are supposed to do. They're not supposed to keep pissing off cause they want to be with some slag called Louise Draper in her sex room, chained up for hours and hours, sweating and shagging.

Me gran knocked on the door of the shed. I didn't open it.

– Derek, I know you're in there love. Open the door.

– 'e's not 'ere. It's *Joe 90*. I'm just off on a mission, and I can't stop. I've got to save the planet from mad people.

– It's not funny, Derek. I need to talk to you.

– Like I said; I'm off to save the planet from the loonies.

– Well, before you do that, I want you to open the door.

I opened the door.

– What are you doing sitting in the dark?

– I didn't want to go in the 'ouse cause me dad's gone mad and I was scared.

Me gran ruffled me hair, which I hate. But I don't tell her cause she's known me since I was a baby.

– I wish I was *Joe 90*, I said.

I'm not really him. I used to think I was, but not no more. I used to think you could do anything, but it ain't true.

– I wish you were *Joe 90*. Then you could save us all.

Me gran came in. I stood up so she could sit on the chair.

Me gran knows about *Joe 90* cause she used to watch it with me when she came to baby sit, even though I'm not a baby, which is stupid. It should be called 'boy sitting'. We watched *Stingray* and *Fire Ball XL5*. Me favourite was *Captain Scarlet* cause he's indestructible and he always comes alive. But the best of all, which is better than me favourite, is *Batman*. No one knows who he is.

– You're dad's been very ill, Derek. I mean very ill. The doctor's been to see him. He's got to stay in bed for a few weeks.

– A few weeks! Is 'e tired?

– You can go and see him if you want.

– 'e can't stay in bed for a few weeks.

– Well that's what he's going to do.

I didn't know how to tell her, so it just all came out at once.

– 'e was going to leave, I said. – 'e beat this kid up on the bridge with is tech drawing tube and 'is dad came round to beat me dad up. But me dad gave 'im two bottles of is 'ome made beer and 'e went away. 'e wanted to buy the boat. But we're going to need it.

– I know, she said.

– No you don't. I've only just told you.

– It's all right, Derek.

It wasn't all right. Even me gran wasn't listening to me no more.

Me gran tried to get out the chair. I had to pull her out cause she's gone all stiff now she's dead old. That's what happens when you're old. It's called rigor-mortis. It happens when you're close to dying. Her arm cracked. I thought I'd broken it.

– Old bones, she said.

I wondered if she was going to die then, cause she closed her eyes and I thought of me mam and the knives. You never know what grown-ups are going to do. I didn't want her to die though. Me mam couldn't cope if me gran died.

– You and your imagination, Derek.

I helped her down the steps cause her knees were stiff too. Rigor-mortis creeps like a disease through your bones until your whole body's completely full of it, and then you just fall over, dead.

Me mam didn't tell me gran that me dad tried to leave. Not then anyway. Me gran didn't know. It was a lie to protect her cause it might kill her, what with me granddad dying and everything. She thought I was just making it up cause I wanted to be *Joe 90.*

When we got to the house, me mam and Auntie Mavis were pouring me dad's dustbin of beer down the drain. It was running all over the drive. Me mam was smiling cause she'd always wanted to get rid of his beer.

– It's liquid evil. Only men in back streets drink beer, me mam said – We need to start drinking wine.

Me dad'd never drink wine. It's for puffs.

Me mam nodded like everything was okay. It was like a sign that grown-ups make to say that everything's back to normal. I knew it wasn't. Sometimes grown-ups just want to believe it's okay when it ain't, so they don't listen to nobody.

I nearly said her name, but I didn't, not out loud anyway. I said it right inside me head where I live nearly all the time. When you're not supposed to say things like someone's as ugly as an arse, you still think them. The vicar said if you think it then it's real, and it's what you mean, and it's as bad as saying it. I can't control what I think. It just comes into me head. I thought Louise Draper. Then I thought, she's a bitch, which I know she is. I made me mind up to send her a ton of gravel, which Billy Myers did to 'slug' our headmaster. He couldn't get his car out his drive for two weeks. I think he thought it was Eagle. Everybody thought everything was Eagle. If there was owt missing then it was Eagle, or if someone had drawn a dick and some balls on a wall, it was Eagle. Sometimes it wasn't Eagle. Sometimes he wasn't even there. They still blamed him. Charlie says he was the whipping boy.

– You don't have to be there, laddie, Mctavish shouted at Eagle when someone crapped in the urinal in the boys bogs.

– But I wasn't there, sir. I was bunkin' off!

– Laddie, you just have to think it and it's done. Double

detention for bunking and double detention for defecating in the boy's urinal.

Charlie didn't like what McTavish was saying.

– Sir, you can't give Eagle double detention for deefy whatever, and double detention for bunkin' off, cause 'e can't 'ave done both.

McTavish stared at Charlie for ages. He looked like he wanted to kill him.

– What's defecating, sir? Eagle asked.

– Shitting, laddie. It's shitting! It's that material that falls out of your mouth and your arse on a regular basis.

McTavish walked over and clipped Charlie round the back of the head.

– That's for trying to be clever, Shaw. That'll be double detention for trying to be clever when you don't have the raw materials.

Sometimes, Eagle just went off across the fields and sat on a fence for ages, hacking at a piece of wood with his knife. He was thinking about doing stuff. He was always thinking about doing stuff. He used to get pizzas sent to people's houses. He once rang this old bloke and told him he was the gas board. He said there was a gas leak, and that the bloke had to open all his doors and windows. The bloke did it. Eagle didn't ring him back, and the bloke got hyper-something where you get cold and go all stiff like me gran. After that, you go blue and your blood freezes, then you die like Captain Scott. They had to take him away in an ambulance and everything. Charlie says he's dead, but Charlie says everybody's dead when they're not. He told Miss Crowe that his dad was dead once cause he hadn't done his English homework.

– 'e was crushed, Miss.

– Oh Charles. She always calls him Charles. – I'm so sorry.

– Yes Miss. 'e was reading the Sun. It was 'is break and this forklift backed 'im against the wall. They couldn't tell who 'e was cause 'e was like strawberry jam.

Billy Myers started laughing.

– 'is dad's not dead miss. I saw 'im today on is moped going to work.

Charlie looked worried, but he carried on.

– They couldn't tell miss, it was such an 'orrible mess. Four doctors passed out.

Miss Crowe looked at Billy Myers who she likes cause he writes about cowboys and Indians, and it makes her laugh. Then she looked at Charlie dead hard, like.

– So he's not dead then, Charles?

Charlie started doing this thing he does when he knows he's been found out. It was such a stupid thing to do. He started clicking his teeth with his nails.

– No one knows. Me mam's broke up about it.

Everybody started laughing. Even me.

– Billy seems to know. He says he saw your dad on his moped going to work.

– 'e was injured dead bad. They thought 'e was dead. They got the coffin and everything.

- But 'e was on his moped. Billy said.

– 'e normally walks, but 'e couldn't cause 'e's been crushed.

Charlie looked at me. I put me head in me hands.

– We 'ad to 'elp 'im on the moped; what with the plaster cast and everything. They'll 'ave to 'elp 'im off when 'e gets to work. That's if they know who 'e is, cause 'e looks like a mummy. We 'ad to tie a label on 'is toe like they do in *Ironside*.

Miss Crowe started to laugh. You could see her teeth. She's got beautiful teeth. She ruffled Charlie's hair. He went bright red. She ruffles the hair of the kids she likes. I wouldn't mind if she ruffled me hair.

– It's a great story, Charles. Nine out of ten and a house point. You can write it up tonight and give it to me in the morning in your neatest handwriting.

– Miss!

– Tall stories, Charles. Oh what a tangled web we weave.

Then Eagle said. – If you practice to deceive. But after you done it for quite a bit. You do get dead good at it.

Miss Crowe started clapping.

– Bravo! Three 'ouse points for Eagle! Eagle stood up and danced around the room like a monkey with his arms hanging down.

– Bravo! he shouted. – Three 'ouse points for Eagle!

They were the only house points he ever got.

## Derby County – 4 Man' U – 1
## Smarties, and good beer down the drain

Gaz Smedley's dead and God didn't save him. They reckon the driver'll go to clink cause he was driving too fast. Everybody knows that Gaz's dog would never pull him into the road. It's mam's a guide dog for blind people. They always look before they cross. They have to learn this *Green Cross Code*. Me mam joined me in the *Tufty Club* when I was little so I didn't get run over.

Cause of Gaz getting run over, we never went to the footy. Me dad couldn't take us, cause he was on these tablets and the doctor said he couldn't get out of bed. Even if he did, me mam said he couldn't go cause he was mad, and mad people don't go to the football match. That ain't true. They take some of the nutters from *Pastures*. They chain them together so they don't run onto the pitch. Mind you, they let them go when it was Leeds United. Everybody hates Leeds United. There's always a scrap.

– He couldn't cope with the crowds, me mam said.

– But 'e's got a season ticket.

– What's that got to do with it?

– 'e's got to go. It's Man U.

– I don't care who it is. He's not going.

– Nobby Stiles takes 'is teeth out, just like me gran.

– Your gran's not Nobby Stiles, and I don't care if he takes his head off, Derek. Your father's not going.

When Auntie Mavis went home and me gran as well, I went up to see me dad. He was in bed. I don't know why they make mad people go to bed when they go mad. He was sitting up having a cup of tea. There was this massive jar of coloured tablets that looked just like smarties on the table. He wasn't in a strait jacket or owt.

– 'ave you got to take all of 'em?

Me dad winked. – Not if I can help it.

– They look like smarties.

I looked at him for ages. He was looking at the wall. We've got this picture of a flower that's red. He kept staring at it. I wanted to ask him the question.

– Dad, I said.

He kept staring at the flower like it was doing something that I couldn't see.

– Yes.

He said it like he was a robot.

– Do you want to jump up and down? He stopped looking at the picture.

– Why would I want to jump up and down?

– 'cause when you've got things wrong, I pointed at me head. – They say that you want to jump up and down cause it makes yer brain wobble.

– No, he said. – I don't want to jump up and down.

– That's dead good.

– Is it?

– Yeah. It means yer not mad and you won't 'ave to go to *Pastures*. Everybody in *Pastures* jumps up and down.

Me mam came into the room. I could see that me dad wanted her to go. She took one of the tablets out the jar and gave it to him. I don't think he took it cause I knew he wasn't mad then. If you take them and you're not, then they can kill you or make you mad anyway. I reckon he put it under his pillow.

– Your dad's got to take them until he feels better, me mam said.

Me dad's eyes looked all funny like Tom out of *Tom and Jerry* when he's been smacked over the head with a frying pan. There were these little veins like twigs coming out all over the whites of his eyes.

Me dad got the book out: *South with Scott*. There's this picture of the *Terra Nova*. It's going into the pack ice and all the blokes are standing on the front of the ship looking at it.

– If you go at the right time, me dad said, – the ice cracks. There are these gulleys that you can get through. In the winter they seal up again like a giant scar.

In the book there's these icebergs that look just like pancakes. That's what they call them. The penguins lie on them in the sun.

Me dad always turns to the last pages of the book where they all die. There's this thing that the bloke who wrote the book tells you what they were like when they found them. You could stand them up like cardboard cut outs cause they were all stiff. But they weren't old like me gran. That's what she'll be like. She'll just be standing there one day and stop cause she's as stiff as Captain Scott. It'll probably happen at the shops. She's always at the shops.

When he was feeling better, me dad came down stairs and watched the telly.

– We should get a colour, Des. Me mam shook her head cause she wanted a new washing machine. She said she couldn't wash clothes in a telly, which is a stupid thing to say cause we know.

We watched *Star Soccer* and they had the match with Derby and Man U. We won 4-1. I wrapped me black and white scarf round the telly, but me mam made me take it off cause she said it would set it on fire.

– I'll have a glass of beer, me dad said.

I looked at me mam and you could see that she was nervous. She hadn't told him what she, me gran and Auntie Mavis had done; that they'd poured it down the drain.

– I don't think that's a good idea, she said, – what with the tablets and all.

The adverts came on. They have this advert for *Davenports Beer* and there's this little bottle that dances on the words so you can sing it. Me dad started singing it. Me mam turned the telly off. He kept on singing it anyway.

– We poured it away! she said.

Me dad just looked at her like she was a nutter. He looked at me and laughed. He nudged me dead hard.

– What do you mean, poured it away?

– Mam (she means me gran, cause me mam calls her mam, mam!) and me and Mavis, poured it down the drain because the doctor said it was making you ill.

Me dad sort of snorted like a pig. He does that when he's getting angry. He hit the arm of the chair dead hard with his fist. It made this cracking sound. It's *Ercol*. Me mam said only the top people have *Ercol*.

– Jesus! me dad shouted.

He made me jump.

– Des, you'd better go, me mam said.

Me mam handed me dad his bottle of tablets. He threw them on the floor. The bottle bounced even though it was glass.

– You need to do what the doctor says.

Me dad snorted again. He just stared at her like he wanted to kill her.

– He didn't say that. He drinks ten times what I drink! Tell me it isn't true. Look at the colour of his nose! He's got eyes like piss holes in the snow!

Me mam picked up the bottle of tablets. I'm telling you, Colin, it'll react with these.

– I'm not taking the bloody tablets, Mary! Me dad kicked the jar dead hard and it smashed against the skirting board. – Tell me for crying out loud, you haven't poured fifty pints of perfectly good beer down the drain!

Me mam laughed and handed him one of the tablets off the carpet.

– Take one of these. It'll calm you down.

– I'm perfectly calm. You had no right! Me dad stood up. – You had no right. He looked like he was going to cry. – I'm a prisoner. He looked at me. – Don't listen to this, Des. Close your ears.

It ain't possible to close yer ears.

Me dad pointed his finger at me mam. It was the one with the end bit missing that he lost in a machine when he worked at *Rolls Royce*.

– No! You and your mam, and that nosey bitch Mavis, decided. It was nothing to do with the doctor. He's got more damned sense. You and your mam. You had no bloody right! You think you know best. You should take a look at yourselves before you start accusing other people. Your family aren't in any position to criticise anybody else. Look what they've got hiding in their cupboards!

Me dad took the tablet from me mam and threw it across the room. It landed in a vase and sank to the bottom dead slow like the plastic man in the bottle.

– I'm not taking these tablets so you can brainwash me.

Me dad turned the telly back on.

The *Davenports* advert had finished. The film had started.

We knew what it was going to be. It was *Scott of the Antarctic* with John Mills.

Me mam left the room. She slammed the door. I could hear her banging cupboards. I think she was looking for the things me dad said she had in them.

– This is a classic, me dad said. He says that about all the old films with these actors who are all dead. – I mean a classic. They don't make them like this any more. Look, he said pointing at the screen. – The wind bites into your skin like a knife. The snow's so hard you couldn't even break it with a pick axe. Nebraska, he said. He talks like this. It's hard to keep up. But I'm used to it. – That's another place. It's just wilderness, nothing between you and the end of the world. Men who go to Nebraska don't come back. I don't know why. Sometimes when you go, you just can't come back. Do you understand me Des?

I didn't even know where Nebraska was. I was going to look it up in me EB, but I never have.

– When the box is open, Des, you can't ever close it again; not when you've looked inside and walked around.

– It's a big box then.

– You know what I mean. Don't get silly.

I didn't. Not then. I asked me gran.

She said, – it's like when you get your fingers burnt. When you open the box there's no closing it. Because you've opened it, you have to take everything out and face it. It's like a can of worms.

– Worms in a can?

– Take them out and you can't ever get them back in. It's like *Pandora's Box*. Same thing.

I didn't know what *Pandora's Box* was. I still don't. I ought to look it up in me EB.

I heard me mam slam the back door. We saw her walk past the house and up the street. It was raining, but she hadn't got a coat. She didn't look as if she cared, just like Annie Gray's mam. I think it was the beginning of the end.

Me dad got out of his chair.

– Come with me son.

He picked up the tablets and the glass and put them in the bin. Then he went into the kitchen. I followed him into the pantry. He got out this big bar of Cadbury's chocolate and gave it to me. It was the one grown-ups have when the children have gone to bed. He reached up to the top shelf where me mam can't reach, and took down this box. Inside there were hundreds of tins of *Double Diamond*.

– Know thine enemy, he said. – Don't tell your mam. He whispered like she was still there.

I never did tell her, which was a lie really if you think about it.

I knew me dad wasn't ill. I just knew. He still had that look in his eyes that had nothing to do with the tablets. They were like devil eyes. The black dots in the middle were dead, dead tiny, just like black heads. Inside them I knew there was hell.

Me dad was on his third can of *Double Diamond*.

– Remember, Des, what I told you. He looked out the window and even though we could only see the fence next door, he still pointed. – If you were a crow and you flew in a straight line you'd end up flying through the smoke and over the factories.

That's what me dad says; that crows can go anywhere. He says we don't realise how clever crows are or rats or cockroaches, that you can't kill unless you drop a ton block on their head and keep it there for five days!

Me dad kept pointing, like he does with his funny finger.

He used to make me look at it, like me granddad used to hold his fist right up close to me nose so I wouldn't forget that it was there.

– They're out there now, me dad said. – Up to their armpits in grime, shovelling it, breathing it, taking it into their lungs. On a Sunday! If that's what you want it's up to you. There comes a time when you've got to stand up and be counted; face the world like a man. You'll be on your own soon, Des.

I didn't understand him then. But I do now. He meant I'd be on me own proper. And I am.

# The land under the bog and the gravy-boat girl

We didn't go to Gaz Smedley's funeral, but Slug made us do a minute's silence in assembly. Mark Harris did a silent but deadly and there was a big circle in the middle of the hall where everybody moved out the way.

– It's a fuckin' living thing! Harris said.

Harris farts all the time and Charlie says something's crawled up his arse and died. Harris's dad's got a pub in Edmeston. It gets smashed up every Friday night and they have to put these boards on the windows to stop people robbing the place.

McTavish walked into the middle of the circle. He's Scotch and he's got a face like a beetroot cause he drinks too much whiskey. Me mam says that Scotch people are mean cause it's the north and it's so cold they can't afford to give owt away, and that their hands will freeze if they take them out of their pockets. But it can't be right cause they say, which I don't believe, that Father Christmas lives at the North Pole and he's always giving stuff away. Ha ha ha!

McTavish stood right in the middle of the circle.

– Right! Who's made this God awful stink?

Everybody pointed at Harris. He went up to Harris and put his face dead close. McTavish fancies Miss Flint, the girls' PE teacher, as well as Miss Crowe. But Miss Flint's got big knockers and Charlie says you're either a big knocker or a small knocker bloke. They said that they did it on the tennis courts when it was dark. But it's a lie cause they lock the tennis courts at six o'clock, cause otherwise they get vandalised.

McTavish pushed Harris. – Right, you flatulent little oik, you can scrub the showers out this lunch time and then one hundred lines – I shall not emit noxious gases in assembly.

Harris smirked, like he does cause he don't give a shit.

– That's two hundred!

– What's noxious, sir?

McTavish clipped the back of Harris's head. It made a hollow sound cause he's got no brain.

– Look it up in a dictionary! It's a book with words if you didn't know. There's one in the library, ten years old and looks like new. You can't miss it. It's under D for dunce.

Slug said a few words about Gaz. He said he was a good lad, had lots of mates and that he was going to be twelve. He said that some of us were going to the match with him and his dad. At half time we'd have a pie. He didn't say the thing about the pie, I'm just telling you about that. Gaz's dad always has a pie. Me dad won't let me have one cause he says it's horse meat, and it's what the Frogs eat. He says that they nearly lost us the war. I don't know if it was to do with the horse meat.

*The Rams* (that's what they call Derby County, but I don't know why. Billy Myers says it's cause they're a load of sheep shaggers) won four one.

– I think Gaz Smedley was spurring them on, Slug said.

Charlie kicked me shin dead hard.

– That's bollocks. What the fuck does 'e know? He supports Cardiff City. They're deffo a bunch of sheep shaggers.

Derby County are the best. We won the *Texaco* and the *League Cup*. It'd got nowt to do with Gaz Smedley. He was crap at football. He just made us miss the match. I've never seen George Best or Bobby Charlton or Nobby Stiles or all the others. I don't suppose I ever will.

Me dad wanted to leave. It's hard to explain really. But he just didn't want to be there, if you know what I mean. It was like he'd gone somewhere in his head and wasn't ever going to come back. It's like I do. If you go in to our bog and sit there for ages, the floor opens up. Underneath it there's this massive cave with stalactites and stalagmites and underground lakes. There's this lift that goes down from our bog and you can go for miles. No one knows about it except for me. If you walk down one of the tunnels you come out next to the sea, and it's only at the bottom of our garden really. No one; not even Charlie knows it's there. As well as that, I can close me eyes and I can go to the place that I think about whenever I want. Soon I'll be able to fly. It's just mind over matter. You've got to believe. That's what *Peter Pan* says. Me gran says I live in a world of imagination, and that I'll have to leave it one day. I ain't ever leaving. It's the best place in the whole wide world. If I leave, I'll go mad like everybody else.

We'd started back at school for the second year. I hated it. It was when me dad left home the second time. He'd still got the devil eyes. I kept out of his way. He started making the beer again. I nicked a bottle and took it to the rec with Charlie. It's dead strong and we were pissed. I puked on me bike and had to wash it off at the petrol station. Charlie nicked two *Mars* bars and a *Milky Way*.

We went home the back way, and got some conkers from a tree at the end of Charlie's street. We could hear Charlie's dad singing cause he's happy all of the time. He's got God you see; like Uncle Bob's got his mam. Charlie's Dad talks to God all the time. God tells him how wonderful everything is, and that he's going to look after him in the kingdom of heaven with all them other people who go round knocking on doors and telling everyone what sinners they are.

We watched Charlie's dad leave. He was going knocking on doors again. His name's Cyril. He was carrying this little briefcase with the bible in it and these magazines that they hand out. When he'd gone, Charlie and me went through the hedge and sat in the field at the end of his street. Its *green belt*. Everybody's obsessed *green belt*, cause it keeps the common people away. I'd got a headache from the beer. It was banging like a hammer at the front of me head.

Charlie got up and pointed across the field.

– Look, it's yer dad! he said.

I could see this bloke on the other side of the field. I knew it was him. I could feel the sick at the back of me throat.

– Don't be so fuckin' stupid, I said. – Let's go. I didn't want to be there. I wanted to be anywhere except there.

– It is! he said. – It is! I knew it was.

Charlie's got this squeaky voice when he's excited. He sounds like a girl.

I felt me stomach turn over. I thought I was going to puke. I knew it was me dad straight away. I saw him before Charlie did. I just didn't want it to be. I wished and I wished as hard as I could that he'd disappear. He'd got a stick like he does, and he was swinging it like a mad man, which me mam thinks he is anyway. He was whacking this bracken and chopping it down all along the edge of the field. He was walking dead fast like he was in a hurry.

Charlie was standing up. – See! It is yer dad! 'e's chopping all the grass down!

I grabbed Charlie's arm.

– Get down, I said. I was trying to pretend it was a game. – 'e mustn't see us. 'e's a German.

– It's yer dad.

– It's not. 'e's a German.

– I can see it's yer dad.

Charlie just wouldn't shut up, so I whacked him on the back of the head, then he whacked me. I pushed him, and he fell over.

Then I saw her. She came out of the bushes and put on her coat. It was Louise Draper. She fell over, cause it's a field and you can't walk in big heels in a field. Me dad didn't even turn round and wait for her.

I heard Louise shout at me dad.

– Colin Jackson! Just come back!

Me dad didn't even turn round, he just kept on going. She started to chase him. She fell over again. Charlie laughed dead loud.

– She's chasing yer dad!

Me dad turned when he heard Charlie's voice. He was looking straight at us. I dropped down on me belly, but the grass wasn't long enough to hide in. Red Indians could do it or Commandos, but me and Charlie are only in the scouts, and we tie bloody knots all the time. I was thinking of leaving cause I don't want to do any more sheep shags. It's piss boring. But me dad said we'd need them for the South Pole, so it was the only reason I carried on. Me dad always said in life you have to do things you don't like. I didn't know it'd be every bloody thing!

I knew me dad had seen us. Louise shouted something and fell over again. It was the third time, and she stayed where she was. If you drop a book in McTavish's class he says *leave it laddie! The thing can't fall any further if you leave it on the floor!* I hoped Louise had broken her leg, or even her neck.

I grabbed Charlie by his T-shirt. It ripped.

– You fucker! You ripped me Alan 'inton.

It had number eleven on the back, which is where Alan

Hinton plays. He can score from a corner. I've seen him do it from the boy's end at the *Baseball Ground*. It's like he bends the air. He wears these white boots, which me mam can't afford. But Charlie's got some to go with his shirt.

Me dad started running.

– Yer dad's running! Charlie shouted.

I could bloody-well see that. I didn't need Charlie to commentate, like he does when there's a football match and you can't hear what they're saying.

– We'll just wait for him, Charlie said. – He'll give us some dough to keep our gobs shut cause he's been doin' it in the bushes. I can't believe it; yer dad's been doin' it in the bushes!

I grabbed his shirt again. It made a hole in the arm.

– Leave it! We need to go.

Charlie was more interested in his shirt.

– You twat. He said. – When 'e gets 'ere, yer dad can pay for this and all!

– Please! I'm begging you, I said. – You can ride me bike for two 'ours.

I can't believe I begged him. I would have done owt to get out of that field.

– You promise? Make it three 'ours.

Charlie can be a selfish bastard. – It's a promise. You can 'ave it for the whole day. Now come on!

– That's the whole day then?

– Yes, yes! The whole fuckin' day. We've got to go!

We started to run. We went through the hedge. I scratched me legs and arms and twisted me ankle on a bike frame in the ditch. We ran along the street and at the corner I looked back. I could see me dad looking over the top of the hedge. I heard Louise shouting at him.

– Colin! Colin!

So I knew it was me dad. I don't think Charlie heard.

When we got to Charlie's, we went into his shed and locked the door. Charlie got out a bottle of *Iron Bru* from his secret stash under the bench. He gave me first swig, cause I needed it. I pretended it was Gin like Auntie Mavis drinks with tonic to make her look posh. She says it soothes her nerves, living with Uncle Bob. She says she'll get her reward in heaven. I think she'll meet his mam again.

– Jesus! Charlie said. – Did you see that? I mean that was yer dad in the bushes with some tart. I mean that's fuckin' brill'! Yer dad's got a tart. Me dad'd love a tart.

– No it's not.

– Who is she?

– I dunno.

– Yes you do.

– I said I dunno.

– Don't believe you.

– Then don't believe me then.

– Do you want to nick some *Aztecs*?

I just wanted to go. I didn't want to talk about me dad.

– Okay then.

We went to the garage up the main Derby Road. The bloke went out to serve somebody, and we went in. I could see him looking back cause he knew we were nicking, but he didn't say owt. I nicked two *Aztecs* and a *Walnut Whip*, which me gran likes. She has one on a Friday night as a special treat. She licks all the cream out first, eats the chocolate and saves the walnut until last. I hate walnuts.

Charlie nicked a *Mars Bar*. That was all. I was chuffed. I was always scared of nicking before, cause you can go to borstal. Me gran says it's the thin end of the wedge. She's got a wedge with a little tiny mouse on that goes under her kitchen door to stop it slamming when it's windy.

I tried to tell me mam about me dad in the field. I wanted to tell her. She needed to know. She was cooking tea. It was a *Fray Bentos* steak and kidney pie. I have brown sauce with it, and it makes me tongue tingle. Sometimes we have chips, but we were having mashed potatoes which is okay as long as it don't have no lumps in it. I don't like gravy. We have it at school in these massive jugs. One day this girl called Helen Cope who's our table monitor, knocked it over. It was like a big brown lake. It crept to the edge of the table. We all had to jump out the way. McTavish ran over and started yelling.

– What the hell do you think you're doing?

– She knocked the gravy over, I said.

The gravy was dripping on the floor like diarrhoea. Then Helen put her hands in. It went right up to her wrists. She started crying. The tears were running down her face and into the gravy.

McTavish started shouting and pointing at Helen Cope.

– It's always you!

He was going red in the face. He is a nutter. They're all mad in Scotland. It's the cold.

She took her hands out of the gravy and put her head in them. She looked like one of them mud men. Then she ran off. That's what she did when she swallowed a ten pence piece and locked herself in the bogs until it came out the other end. I don't eat gravy no more. I never will. I can't get it out of me head.

– I saw me dad. He was in the field at the back of Charlie's 'ouse, I said to me mam.

She carried on mashing the spuds as hard as she could. She didn't look at me.

– I said I saw me dad in the field at the back of Charlie's

'ouse.

— Wash your hands.

— I've washed 'em.

— Wash them again.

— Why?

— Because I say so.

I washed them again and came back into the kitchen. Me mam took the pie out the oven.

— Here.

She gave me the knives and forks.

I heard me dad's car. He came in the kitchen. He gave me mam a bunch of flowers and a box of *Quality Street* and went upstairs for ages. We started eating our tea, but I wasn't hungry no more. It's hard when it's your favourite food and you can smell it and everything, but I couldn't stop thinking about Helen Cope and the gravy on her hands and then on her face. Me dad came downstairs. He sat at the end of the table, his hair slicked back with *Brylcream*. He just looked at me. He was talking with his eyes. He was telling me to keep me mouth shut, and not say owt. He just started eating his tea. Just like that.

Me mam tapped me hand.

— Thank your dad for the flowers and the chocolates.

I looked at him and he shook his head.

— 'e didn't give 'em to me, I said.

Then I knew. She wasn't talking to him. That's what they did. Or at least me mam did until it drove me dad mad. It's what she was doing on the day he went mad after he shouted at her about the flat cake. They call it the silent treatment. It's what the Nazis did in the war when they were in their submarines. They didn't have no women on board cause they can't keep their gobs shut.

Me dad put his knife and fork down dead loud.

– 'e can 'ear you, mam, I said. – There's nothing wrong with is ears.

– Just tell him.

But 'e's not deaf. Thanks for the flowers and the chocolates, I said.

Me dad got up from the table and he left the room. He went up the stairs and shut the bedroom door. Me mam carried on eating her tea like nothing happened. I'd had enough. So had me dad. He left. He left me with me mam. I hate him for that.

*Charlie's conker,*
*Out of body,*
*Formica (Golden Peach),*
*and the dead boy*

Me dad wasn't waiting at the shops. I knew he'd gone. I think I read his mind. I could see what he was thinking. It was the end of October. All the leaves were falling off the trees, except for Christmas trees that is. They don't lose their needles cause they're carnivorous and they come from cold countries where the trees keep their leaves to keep them warm.

We'd got conkers. Charlie had this one, which he said was a sixtier. It had a big crack down one side. I knew he'd put it in vinegar and then baked it in the oven. He said it was still a conker. I had a tenner. I knew I could smash his.

Charlie wouldn't take it out.

– It's retired, he said. – It's stopping at the top of its game.

– Conkers can't retire. You 'ave to carry on 'til they get smashed. Then you start all over again. That's 'ow it is with conkers.

– I'm keeping this for me kids.

– What, the ones yer 'aving with Tina slaggy knickers.

– Don't be a twat, Des.

– Then get yer fuckin' conker out you div.

– You'll smash it.

– Yeah. If you don't get it out then I win. Then yer conker will be retiring at the bottom.

– That's bollocks.

– Refusing to play means I win. It's the rules.

– Whose rules?

– Rules made by *William the Conqueror*. It's obvious. Don't you know owt?

Charlie laughed at that one.

Charlie got his conker out. It looked like a wrinkly prune with this split down one side. You could see the string and all the yellow insides. It looked like a sad conker.

– See, he said. – It don't stand a chance. I thought we were mates. Now you want to smash me conker. It'll be like 'itting yer gran.

I got me conker ready to wack it.

– We are mates, but this is conkering. It's not the same thing. It's got nowt to do with being mates. This is war. It's like in the civil war when brother fights brother. Then they go 'ome for their tea.

– What if I tell me mam about yer dad in the field with that slag?

I didn't tell him that she wasn't no slag, and that she worked in the same office as me dad now. Me dad got her a better job. I didn't tell him that she'd never had a boyfriend and that she was pure, which was what me dad wanted. *Pure and perfect*, Des. *Pure and perfect*. I understood then. It was cause we were all diseased cause of me gran and me granddad. I didn't tell Charlie that Louise and me dad shagged all the time in this massive room with machines and things. I didn't tell him I wanted to go and live at his house; even though his dad's a religious maniac.

– Don't tell yer mam, I said.

I didn't really care, but me mam might hear in the hairdressers, and it'd kill her.

He had this smirk on his face. I could have smacked him

one. I never ever wanted to hit Charlie cause he's me mate. But I hated him then cause he could've told his mam. He was still holding his conker.

I swung me conker even though he wasn't ready. It hit his with this crack, and it split it into a million pieces. All he had hanging there was his piece of string with a knot in the end. Then I felt bad.

– You bastard! Now I'm deffo telling me mam and me dad.

He ran off. I didn't go after him. There was no point. Even though his mam still asks me where me dad is, even though she knows. I don't think Charlie ever told her. He's got a new conker now. He says it's a hundreder. I don't believe him. Charlie's full of shit.

I walked across the fields from school. The slug says we're not supposed to, but he's never stopped us. I was looking at the leaves. There were a million colours. They were all dying. I think they look better dead. When the trees are completely bald they look like someone stuck them upside down in the ground and it's the roots sticking out until the summer comes, then they turn them the right way up again.

We live on Grace Road and all me other friends live on streets. Streets are more common than roads. They don't have roads on the council estates cause roads are more expensive. I still call it our street like Charlie calls his house our shack. His dad goes mad cause he says he paid for it with blood sweat and tears, which I don't believe cause you can't buy an house with blood sweat and tears. He says that he hasn't worked all his life to end up living in a street. Me mam and me dad go mad if I call it our street.

It was nearly dark when I got home. I knew he'd gone. I have this thing where I know things. The voice in me head tells me. I know that only mad people have voices in their heads. I can hear me mam and dad talking all the time about me being a good boy. They say you mustn't do this or do that. If it's not them, it's me granddad behind them, waving his fist and saying *you'll get your fingers burnt*. Then there's this other voice that says, *whose little boy are you?* It's what me mam and dad used to say to me cause they think it's funny, and they wouldn't stop. It started driving me mad cause I just kept saying I'm yours, but now I ain't bothered. I don't want to be theirs; not no more. I wish Auntie Mavis and Uncle Bob were me mam and dad. I wish I was the baby they had who died, except I wouldn't want to be dead. I've told you that I go to this sunny place, a long way away. It makes me feel sleepy and warm. I can't hear the yakking bastards no more.

There were no lights on in the house, except for this little strip light under the cupboard, which flickers. It has moths stuck to it that smoke when it's on. It lights up the knives and I counted them. Auntie Mavis says that I'm a strange boy, and that I'll go as mad as me dad. I'm not as strange as Uncle Bob. I don't talk to stiffies in the sky every day.

I put me key in the door, but it was open. I didn't want it to be, but it was. I was wishing hard, cause sometimes if you wish hard then things aren't like you think they're going to be. Me gran says that while you're wishing, you forget how bad you thought it was going to be before. If you know what I mean. But it was worse. Me mam was in her chair. She had the lantern light on. I could see the wet on her face. I didn't want to be there. I wanted to be somewhere else like Devon or Swanage where Uncle Bob was shooting Germans, or even Blackpool. I knew then why Annie Gray went to Blackpool. I can't say it in words, but like I said, I know these things. You just do. Me mam looked at me. I knew what she was going to say. I can do things like that. When I was four I died. Nobody believes me, but I've read about it in me EB. It says it's *an out of body experience*.

I told Charlie. He looked at me and laughed.

– That's bollocks! Who do you think you are? Fuckin' Jesus H Christ!

– What's the H for?

– Don't you know owt? It's 'erald. You know 'ark the 'erald Angels Sing.

– It was Peter O'Toole, I said. – 'e said it in a film. *Murphy's War*. You 'eard it in that film. He said Jesus H Christ.

– It's 'erald, he said.

– All right Charlie. It's 'erald. Sometimes Charlie just won't be told.

I had peritonitis. It's appendix gone mouldy. Me dad said he'd sue the doctor for making a mistake, cause she said it was something else. I knew me dad thought that women have no right being doctors. It's a bloke's job. Women are nurses.

They took me to the City Hospital in an ambulance with the blue light flashing and the bell ringing and everything. I was unconscious, but I know I saw it. Me mam was there. She said that me dad had gone to a party cause he'd been invited, and the people were dead posh. He said if he didn't go then they wouldn't ask him again. He said it was important to shake hands with the right people.

There was this boy lying on this white trolley with all these machines, and this man and woman in white coats. They went inside this telephone box thing and closed a door. The boy didn't have no clothes. His knees where curled up like a baby does when it's asleep. I knew the boy was me, cause he had this mole on his neck just like me. I was high up. I was looking down on me. It's dead true. Dead honest! I was at the end of this tube thing. It was like a tunnel. It was dead bright. There was this light not far away. After that, I can't remember owt else. I'm sorry about that. I woke up the next day with this slit in me belly and some metal things holding the slit together. There was this pipe coming out that went into a bag.

I was only four. I didn't know then. But I was dying.

– I died, I told me mam and dad when we were having dinner. It was Sunday. We were having roast beef, roast potatoes and Yorkshire pudding with onion gravy.

– You died? me dad said.

– When I 'ad peritonitis. I was going to 'eaven.

– You got better.

– But I still died. He looked at me mam.

– You will if you let your dinner go cold, he said.

Me mam just smiled at me. – Des, you didn't die. You were very poorly. But you didn't die.

I know I did. They just hear what they want. Kids don't lie until they're told to. I died. It don't matter how many times they say it. I died!

When I got home and she was sitting in the dark, I didn't know what to do with me mam. She just sat there like this frightened bird. I did feel sorry for her, like I felt sorry for Charlie when I smashed his daft little conker.

– I'll ring me gran.

Me mam shouted. – No! It'll kill her.

– What about Auntie Mavis, I said.

I could hardly tell what she was saying.

– She's got Uncle Bob. You know what he's like.

What she meant is; that they think Uncle Bob's going mad as well. He said he couldn't use his legs properly.

I heard Auntie Mavis going on about him to me mam once.

– It's because he's bone idle. He doesn't want to get off his back side, she said. - He's too busy talking to his bloody mother all the time. If he spent as much time talking to me as he does to his bloody mother, things'd be better than they are. I don't know if he's noticed, but I'm a bloody woman! You lose the use of your bloody legs if you don't move them.

Auntie Mavis started shouting. I could hear her in the garden.

– And that counts for everything else as well!

I know she means his willy. You can't blame him. Who'd want to use their willy on Auntie Mavis! I'd rather have crabs.

If you ask me, but nobody does, I think Uncle Bob's got some sort of disease, cause he falls on the stairs like he's drunk. Auntie Mavis says it's cause he's looking up at his mam. You shouldn't look up when you're coming downstairs. That's a rule that is.

Sometimes, I look at the sky to see if I can see owt, cause Uncle Bob can see his mam up there. Me mam says it's just a habit. I think it might be to do with his legs going funny. Everything's connected. They say people don't go mad for no reason. There's a reason for everything. God knows all about that.

I didn't know what to do with me mam. I didn't know what to say or owt. I could feel me stomach in me mouth.

– Maybe 'e's gone to see Louise, I said.

I couldn't believe I said it. It just came out cause I was thinking it. I was thinking of seeing him in the fields. I knew he was with her.

Me mam just stared at me.

– Louise! Louise!

– I was just saying. 'e goes to fix 'er car.

– Don't be stupid, Des. We've not seen Louise for ages.

I didn't say owt about the field again.

I went out to the phone. It's green. Me gran's never had a

phone. She says it's the beginning of the end, and everyone'll be listening to everybody else's business all the time, cause you can't turn them off.

I rang Auntie Mavis, but she didn't answer.

I went on me bike. I found her in the shed trying to cut some *Formica* with this massive saw. She looked even smaller than she actually is. She looked like this miniature person; like *Thumbelina*.

I stood behind her for ages. She was going mad with this *Formica*. She was shouting at it and everything.

– I can do that, I said.

She looked at me and didn't say owt for ages.

– Derek Jackson, don't you ever creep up behind me like that again! I'm using a saw. I could have taken me hand off.

Uncle Bob was standing behind me. We were like in this queue, with me first and him behind me.

– Isn't that so, Bob?

Uncle Bob winked at me. – You're right, Mavis. You're right.

I think Uncle Bob was wishing it was her head.

– If you pour boiling water on it, it'll make it soft, I said. – Then you can cut it like plastic.

– Don't be so stupid, Derek. Where did you hear that rubbish? This is *Formica*. Do you hear? *Formica*!

– *Blue Peter*. John Noakes was making a base for the train set. That's what 'e did.

When I told her it was John Noakes, I think she believed me.

– Right! Bob, boil the kettle.

Auntie Mavis pulled the big sheet out into the back yard, and put it on the floor. She got this Stanley knife out. I thought of me mam and the knives in the kitchen. I hadn't got them with me, again.

– Me dad's gone, I said.

Uncle Bob came out with the kettle and just stood there. Auntie Mavis banged him on the leg.

– Just in case you've forgotten your uncle Bob's losing the use of his legs. Convenient. Don't you think, Derek?

She always says these things when he's standing there, like he's invisible.

– Me dad's gone, I said again.

– Give me the bloody kettle! Auntie Mavis yelled. Uncle Bob gave her the kettle. – Gone where?

She poured the water over the *Formica* and some of it ran onto her foot.

– For God's sake, Bob. I'll be scalded alive! This water's boiling hot.

– Sorry. You did say boil the kettle.

– It's a figure of speech, Bob. A figure of speech.

– A figure of speech, Mavis, he said. – I'll remember that for next time.

– This better work, Derek. *Formica's* expensive. Not everybody's got *Formica* worktops. Not this colour anyway. It's *golden peach*.

It didn't look like peach to me. It looked orange.

– I mean me dad's gone off, I said again.

Auntie Mavis laughed. – What, like meat?

– No. Not that sort of gone off.

She held the Stanley knife up like it was a sword.

– Silence! I'm going to make an incision! She put it on the *Formica* and started to cut it. I couldn't remember if it was *Formica* on *Blue Peter*. It was too late to see if there was anything in me EB. It might have been plastic. It was working all the same. I was dead pleased. Auntie Mavis don't like it when someone else's right and she ain't.

Auntie Mavis stopped cutting, and looked up at Uncle Bob. He was looking up at the sky. I suppose he was staring at his mam. I couldn't see owt.

– See, Bob. Even a twelve-year-old boy's more useful than you are! And stop looking at your mam! She knows as much as you about *Formica*. Lord, she said. – Now I'm even bloody well talking to the woman!

I know Uncle Bob's a bit daft sometimes and maybe his legs are okay cause he's had lots of things before. He said he had a chill once, but Auntie Mavis said that only the Royal Family get chills. She's a bit mean to Uncle Bob. Women can be mean sometimes. It's like the women spiders when they eat the blokes.

Auntie Mavis finished cutting the *Formica*. It looked good; for Auntie Mavis anyway.

– So where's your dad gone? She got the *Formica* and started staggering with it cause it was as big as she is. I followed her into the kitchen. She put the *Formica* onto the wood where she was going to glue it.

– 'e's left 'ome. Auntie Mavis turned round dead fast.

– Left home! She grabbed me by the shoulders and she shook me dead hard. I could feel me brain wobbling.

– For God's sake why didn't you tell me?

– I did. I tried to tell you.

– You should speak up when it's something as serious as this; something that's life and death.

– 'e's not dead. 'e's just left.

There was this cracking noise. I could see it happening behind her. It didn't do that on *Blue Peter*. Nothing ever happened like that on *Blue Peter*. They always said *this is one I made earlier*, which meant some other bugger had made it for them. I never could make owt they made on *Blue Peter*.

Mine was always crap. The mountains I made for me train set looked like piles of shit, except they were green. Even me mam said that me Christmas candle holder made out of coat hangers looked like it'd been sat on. Mams' are supposed to say it's brill' whatever you do. Then it caught fire, and she said that we'd be burnt to a cinder like the pilot in the *Battle of Britain*. Mind you he wrote a book.

Auntie Mavis let go of me and grabbed the *Formica*. It was buckling like the front wheel of Charlie's bike when his dad ran over it in his car. She grabbed the hot bit, and she yelled then dropped it on the floor. It cracked into loads of pieces just like glass. We just looked at it for ages like it was going to glue itself back together, which it didn't. Then Auntie Mavis stamped on it and it cracked some more.

– It cost the bloody earth!

She thumped Uncle Bob right on the shoulder. – Must be something wrong with it, she said. – It can't be the proper stuff. Trust you to get the wrong stuff, Bob! The Pickards have got *Formica*, all over the place. But they didn't have to fit it themselves. Oh no! They got someone from the *Institute of Tradesmen* to do it. Here I am doing it myself, Bob!

She thumped him on the shoulder again, dead hard. – How do you feel about that?

I could see that Uncle Bob wanted to talk to his mam, cause he kept turning his head. He rubbed his shoulder.

– You're right, Mavis. You're right.

– Which bit am I right about, Bob?

Uncle Bob looked worried. He didn't know which bit it was she was right about cause he don't listen to her yakking.

– All of it, he said. – All of it. I'll get a dust pan and brush.

Auntie Mavis got her coat.

– You can leave your bike, Derek. Time is of the essence.

– Is Uncle Bob coming? I asked.

He started rubbing his leg.

– Does it 'urt? I asked him cause his face was all screwed up.

He pointed at his army jacket. I looked at it. He was talking about the war. He leaned over and whispered in me ear.

– It's shrapnel. Don't tell Mavis. It's best she doesn't know. They couldn't get it out.

– Where is it then?

– It moves all the time. You can't be sure. They took a picture of it, opened me up, and it was gone.

– Where did it go to?

– Other leg.

– 'ow'd you get it then?

He looked up at the sky. I thought he was asking his mam, but he didn't say owt. Then he looked at me

– Messerschmitt. It came down under fire. Killed half of us stone dead.

Auntie Mavis pulled me arm.

– Come on Derek, there's no point in waiting for this one, she said pointing at Uncle Bob. – He'll be paralysed by the time we bloody well get there! Then she ran up the path.

Uncle Bob put his hand on me head.

– It'll be okay, prince, he said. I think he calls me *the prince* cause his son's dead, which is sad. He only lived for seven days. He had some sort of disease. I like it when he calls me *the prince*.

– Your dad'll come back.

I don't think he knew that, but he looked up at his mam anyway. He smiled like he knew something. He saw me looking at him.

– Messerschmitt, he said. – You can't get out the habit of looking. You never know.

– The war ended ages ago, I said.

– You can't trust the Gerrys. They'll have a stash somewhere. If there's ever something they don't like, they'll be over. You can rest assured we'll be mobilised; what's left of us anyway. Shrapnel or not.

He touched his army jacket. I left him in the kitchen, thinking about Messerschmitts.

Charlie says he had an uncle with a piece of metal he got in his knee. It got into his blood stream, and it made him blind. Then he died. Not cause of the metal though. He walked out in front of a car when he didn't have his white stick. It just ran him over. He was dead old. He was at least fifty three.

Auntie Mavis started the car.

– Come on, Derek. You haven't got time to talk to Uncle Bob. God knows what we'll find when we get there.

Uncle Bob hobbled out onto the pavement. I wondered if he'd changed his mind, but he'd still got his slippers on with the dog on the front. They were from *Marks and Spencer* cause Auntie Mavis leaves the tags on, so people know.

– Bloody useless, Auntie Mavis said. – Bloody useless.

All grown-ups say things twice. It's cause they think every other bugger's stupid.

– Maybe 'e's still talking to is mam, I said. – Or looking for enemy planes. She laughed.

– Enemy planes! Enemy bloody planes! It's his mam. He don't have to stay at home to talk to her. Mavis crashed the gears like she does. – Oh no, when we go out he brings his bloody mam with him!

– Maybe it's not 'is mam.

Auntie Mavis looked at me dead funny like I was stupid.

– What do you mean, not his mam?

I wish I hadn't said owt.

– What I mean is that it might not be 'is mam that Uncle Bob looks at when 'e looks at the sky.

– Don't be stupid, Derek of course it's his mam. He started doing it the day after she died. She was still washing his smalls after he married me. I only found out because I caught her sneaking them into his drawer. Bloody weird if you ask me. What sort of woman irons her sons underpants when he's thirty seven, and he's got a wife? So who else do you think he's talking to?

I didn't say owt cause I know now that sometimes it's better to keep your gob shut.

– I dunno.

I did though. I thought he might've been talking to his dead little boy.

# Spontaneous combustion, and the murder of Susan Gower

Me mam says Auntie Mavis loves a drama, as long as it's somebody else's. She drove like a mad person all the way to our house.

– This'll kill your mam. You do realise that don't you, Derek.
I didn't think it'd kill her. Not then.

– Me dad's got this friend, I said.

Auntie Mavis stopped the car at the end of Jubilee Road to let the trolley bus go past. It was sparking like mad on the wires. It looked like lightening flashing off into the sky. There was this bloke who got stuck on one of the wires when he was working on it. He got fried like a crispy piece of bacon. They left him hanging there for days cause anyone trying to get him down would have been fried as well. You can't have rows of fried people hanging like it's a Monday wash day. People like Auntie Mavis would be writing to the paper.

I like her, but Auntie Mavis is fat. She's got short legs. She looks like a little kid's picture with a mini head, her arms sticking out like a snowman's do. She wears these big coats that make her look like a sheep. She's better than me mam though. I'll be sorry if she catches fire, which fat people do. They can't stop their piss when they get old. I think I read it in me EB: There's this acid in the piss that when it dries into crystals in their knickers they rub together and make a spark like on the trolley bus wires. They catch fire. They burn cause of all the fat. Auntie Mavis'd burn for yonks. I don't think Uncle Bob'd call the Fire Brigade either. I'm never getting fat.

I don't want me knackers to catch fire.

– We've left me bike. I should get me bike, I told her.

Auntie Mavis's not for telling. It's Uncle Bob's fault. Me mam says that if he told her she was wrong sometimes, then she'd stop being right. I don't know how that works.

– Leave it, Derek.

– It's not got a lock on it! It'll get nicked! I didn't want someone to nick me bike.

– You need to know, she said. – People don't steal things in Wellington Street.

She was doing this funny voice like she's got something stuck in her gob. She thinks she sounds like the Queen, but me dad says she sounds like *Hinge and Bracket*.

– We like to think we're a better class of people here in Fradley Lock. It isn't Edmeston, you know.

I'm fed up with people saying bad things about Edmeston.

– There's nowt wrong with Edmeston. Loads of me friends live in Edmeston.

I don't know what it is with Edmeston. Me mam's always going on about Edmeston. She went to school in Edmeston.

Auntie Mavis crashed the gears again.

– It's because of the murder, Derek. You know that- Susan Gower.

Auntie Mavis always says *you know that* when you don't. But you can't know everything. Even Auntie Mavis can't know everything, even though she's got *National Geographic* on her shelf next to this massive bible. She told me about Marion. The full story, cause she's a gobby cow as me dad says.

– I don't know about no murder.

– Course you do. It was in all the papers.

– I don't read the papers.

– *Derby Evening Telegraph* front page. Big print. You know,

Derek, you must know. You deliver the damned things. Not that kids of your age should be listening to such filth. Landlord killed her. Stabbed her in her own front room. In her own front room it was! The paper said he came from Fradley Lock. I wrote to them. I told them that we don't have people like that in Fradley Lock; not people that go around stabbing other people dead in their own front rooms. It was Edmeston I said. You should get your facts right.

– Susan Gower's dead?

– Dead as a Dodo.

– That's a mythical bird. It's in me EB.

– Don't try and be clever, Derek.

I couldn't believe it; Auntie Mavis said Susan Gower's dead. Susan Gower, dead. Beautiful Susan Gower. I only said it in me head. I'd never tell no one that I fancied Susan Gower. I think I might have loved her. Me first secret girlfriend was dead.

– What 'appened to that bloke?

– Clink. Got life.

– That's a long time, I said.

– That's Edmeston, Derek.

– She lives in Willow Fields.

– Derek! There you go again. It's rudeness, arguing. It was Edmeston.

– It was Willow Fields. I know it was.

– Derek!

– Susan Gower came to see 'er mam at the weekend. She ain't dead. Auntie Mavis didn't say owt.

– Never mind the dregs of Edmeston. Your dad's gone. That's the matter in hand.

– There's this woman. It's Louise, I said. – Me dad knows 'er.

– And?

– I think it's 'er. I think he's gone to 'er.

Auntie Mavis stopped the car outside our house.

– Derek, I suggest you keep your silly little ideas to yourself. Your father's mentally ill. He needs help. Your mother's on the verge. They'll be both in *Pastures* before you can say knife. Then what? They never come out you know.

– On the verge of what?

– A nervous breakdown.

– What 'appens?

– They just stop and stare into space. The nerves in the brain just pack up and they look like one of them tailor's dummies you see in *Dunn's* on the Spot in Derby. Or those waxworks in *Madame Two Swords*.

– So she'll just stop dead still?

– More or less.

– 'ow do you know?

– Derek, I did *First Aid*. I'm the first point of contact at work. Not anyone can be the first point of contact.

– What do I do with 'er?

– Call the doctor.

– Shall I lean her up against the wall in case she falls over?

Auntie Mavis shook her head.

– Sometimes, Derek Jackson I wonder about you.

– Wonder what?

– If you're not alright in the head.

Auntie Mavis put the kettle on in the dark. They always put the kettle on. It's like when women are having babies in the films, and the men have to boil some water.

– Shall I put the light on? I said.

– No! We don't want to cause any shock.

– It won't cause no shock.

– Derek!

I looked through the crack in the door. Me mam was still in her chair. I waited for ages until she moved. I knew she hadn't had a nervous breakdown and become one of them tailor's dummies.

Auntie Mavis pushed me out the way, like she does Uncle Bob. She tiptoed across the room. Auntie Mavis can't do anything quiet. She's like an elephant. Me mam was looking straight at her. Auntie Mavis got a chair.

– Bob and me have been to the brink, she said. – You know that, Mary. It's not always been easy. Not with David's death.

Me mam didn't look at her. She just looked at me.

– He'll be back, Mary, she said.

Me mam made this noise like an owl.

– I don't know what I've done. It's not like there's anything wrong. You know.

Auntie Mavis put her hand on top of me mam's.

– I know, Mary.

Auntie Mavis sat down on the chair.

– It's an illness, Mary. He's not been well. Think of the pills he's been taking for his nerves. They can do long-lasting damage. There'll be something in his brain that's not working. It might never work. We have to accept that if it's true. Mind you, they can do wonders these days what with the electrical treatment.

– 'e didn't take the pills. 'e flushed 'em down the bog, I said.

Auntie Mavis waved her arm.

– Shut up Derek! It's lavatory.

Me mam put her head in her hands.

– He's taken the car. You know that. He's taken everything. Every stitch of clothing. Everything!

I sneaked out and went down to the shed. His tools were

gone. All the stuff he used to make the boat. I wondered if he was going to make another one with Louise, and take her to the South Pole. I hope he bloody well leaves her there.

It was just after me dad went that God started on Eagle. God's a bastard. I know you're not supposed to say things like that. But He is, cause He'd got it in for Eagle. Me mam says that God'll get me dad when He gets round to it. She says He's got a lot on his plate, what with all them husbands leaving their wives.

It made her smile, like she was dead pleased.

– 'ow?

– You'll see.

She didn't know. She just hoped. Sometimes when you hope, things do happen. I know. I hoped bad things about Eagle, and they happened.

# *Eagle's dead*

Slug talked about God when he prayed in assembly. We did dead legs and farted. He told our class to go into a room at the back of the stage. He brought this massive bible.

– I want to know who took the fire extinguisher from the back of the stage and let it off in the hallway of the old people's home on Harvey Road.

It was Eagle. Everyone knew it was Eagle cause he bragged about it. He was wearing a balaclava he nicked at the match.

Slug made us go in a line and put our hands on the bible one by one. He stood there as we walked past, watching our eyes cause you can tell from their eyes. Me dad says that it's the pathway to the soul.

– You swear on this bible that you didn't do this. You'll swear on your family.

Everybody swore on their families. It was hard not to laugh. We watched Eagle. He went up to the bible. He hovered his hand. Slug slammed it down.

– I swear on me family that I never took no fire extinguisher, and squirted it over the crusties.

You could see Slug watching him dead hard, looking at his eyes.

– I'm adopted, Eagle said afterwards. – It don't count if I swear on me family. I ain't got no family. Not that I know of. They should be dead anyway cause they left a baby.

I thought of me gran and granddad leaving Marion.

Billy Myers stood next to Eagle like he does cause he thinks it makes him look harder than he is.

– They must 'ave liked you, I said.

I was scared of Eagle. I don't know why I said it. I s'pose I wanted him to like me.

Eagle laughed. – I 'ate the fuckers. I wish they were dead. Me dad smacks me mam and me mam's stupid to let 'im do it.

I said, – They liked you cause you're decent.

I wish I hadn't said it. Billy Myers pushed me dead hard.

– You mean you don't think Eagle's decent.

– No. I said it's cause 'e's decent. Billy Myers is thick. He didn't understand. He wanted to start a fight.

Billy Myers looked at Eagle.

– No 'e didn't. 'e said 'e thinks yer not decent.

Eagle made this face. I knew he wanted to hit me. He knew I hadn't said it. I never would. Never ever. Dead honest. I knew Eagle was poor. His dad hit his mam, and he didn't wear pants or socks, even on the cold days.

Eagle started running at me. I legged it. He chased me across the playground.

– I'm going to kick yer fuckin' 'ead in outside the school gates, he shouted.

Billy Myers started shouting.

– Fight! Fight! Fight! He didn't know me dad'd gone. I didn't want to fight. I nearly stopped and let him kick me head in. I thought I deserved it. Your dad doesn't leave you for no reason. I didn't hate Eagle neither. You can't fight someone if you don't hate them. Now Eagle hated me, and there was nowt I could do about it.

Miss Crowe felt sorry for Eagle cause she could see that sometimes he didn't have socks. I don't think she knew about his pants. His jackets were too short as well cause they were his brother's from a different school, and his brother, Martin is shorter than Eagle.

In the end, Eagle never got me, cause he had to go. They

said he mugged an old lady on Harvey Road when he was bunking off school.

– I want you to write about getting ready for school, Miss Crowe said. – An account of the start of your day.

Everybody groaned. No one likes writing about stuff like that.

– All of it? Eagle said.

Miss Crowe went up to Eagle and stood right in front of his desk. She smiled at him.

– As much as you can. Make it up if you want. She said it in this dead soft voice. It was how she spoke to Eagle.

– I don't know what to put, he said.

– Well what do you do when you get up?

– I wash me face. Miss Crowe laughed.

– That's a good start. Then what do you do?

– I do me paper round. Then I light the fire if it's cold. Then I get me cornflakes and put the milk on, and then the water.

Miss Crowe looked at him dead funny.

– The water?

You could tell that she wished she hadn't asked, cause she suddenly realised why.

– Yeah, the water for the milk. To make it stretch.

Some people laughed. Eagle went dead red. He looked down at his book. I'd never seen Eagle go silent before. It was sad.

Miss Crow clapped her hands together.

– Right then.

She didn't say no more. She turned her back on us for ages and wrote a load of stuff on the board. Billy Myers started mucking around. When she turned round her eyes were red.

– Billy, just get on with it. Her voice was all croaky.

– It was Eagle, Billy said.

Miss Crowe looked at Eagle. He was writing dead hard with his tongue sticking out the corner of his mouth, like he does when he's concentrating. He knew I was looking at him. He looked at me.

– I'm still kicking yer fuckin''ead in after school.

Eagle thought I deserved it. He knew I didn't have to water the milk down for me cornflakes to make it stretch. Sometimes you get what you deserve.

After school, I ran away from Eagle. I saw him coming when we got outside after the bell. When I started running, I saw me dad. I hadn't seen him for ages. He just disappeared after he went. Me mam said he'd gone into hiding. He was coming across the school field with a pair of binoculars round his neck that me gran and granddad bought him one Christmas. I stopped. I didn't know what else to do. Me dad waved. Billy Myers caught me and grabbed me arm to stop me from running away. Eagle came up to me. He saw me dad.

– So yer old man's come to save you, Jackson.

– I didn't know 'e was there, I said.

– I'm still kicking yer 'ead in, Jackson.

Billy Myers shoved me. – Yeah. 'e's still kicking yer fuckin' 'ead in. You little twat.

– Why?

– For being a twat.

I knew then that Billy Myers couldn't even remember why. I do hate Billy Myers. That's a fact. If it had been Billy Myers instead of Eagle, I wouldn't have felt so bad.

Eagle punched me right in the side of the head. It made me ear ring like a bell.

Me dad started running straight at him. Eagle laughed. He stuck two fingers up at me dad.

– Look at that fat twat. 'e's goin to 'ave a fuckin''eart attack!

I'm glad 'e's not me fuckin' dad!

Eagle ran, and Billy Myers followed him. I wanted to say I wished he wasn't me dad neither, but I didn't. I wanted to die.

Me dad came up to me. His binoculars were swinging so hard they hit him on the side of the head. He bent down and put his hands on his knees. There were girls sniggering.

– You! me dad yelled.

Eagle turned round. He gave me dad the finger again. Then he ran off.

– Who the hell was that?

I watched Eagle go round the corner.

– No one. 'e's no one.

I thought me dad was going to chase him, but he didn't. I was glad.

– He hit you.

– It didn't 'urt.

– Your ear's all red.

I touched me ear. It was dead hot.

Me dad stood up and put his hands on me shoulders.

– You need to understand, Des. I had no choice.

Most of the kids had gone.

– Me mam can't cope. She's 'aving a nervous breakdown.

– Who told you that?

– Auntie Mavis. She called the doctor. 'e says she needs to see someone. Auntie Mavis says that when you 'ave a nervous breakdown, you go all stiff.

– What sort of Doctor?

– Someone that 'elps mad people.

Me dad shook me. He had that wild look in his eyes again.

– Your mam's unbalanced. It's everything that's happened. I couldn't stay.

– You left me with 'er. You can't leave me with 'er if she's mad.

– A boy's place is with his mam.

That's not true. It's a boy and his dad. Charlie does stuff with his dad. They've got a scalextric, and a car each.

– I saw you with Louise. In the field.

He let go of me.

– No you didn't.

– Yes I did. Charlie saw it too.

– It wasn't me.

– What wasn't?

– It wasn't me in the field. It was someone else.

– 'ow do you know if you weren't there?

– I just know because I wasn't there. He started raising his voice. – You were mistaken. Anyway, this isn't about someone in some bloody field, Des!

– But I saw you.

– Des, it wasn't me. Do you understand?

It was him. He was lying. Nobody tells the truth no more. He's a lying git.

– Do you understand?

– Yeah.

– It's yes.

– Yeah.

– I had to go. You have to understand. There's no question about it. Look, I've got two tickets for the match.

– Gaz Smedley's dead, I said. – 'is dog pulled him into the road. The bloke's gone to prison like the bloke in the bank did.

Me dad laughed. – Nobody's dead, Des.

– Yeah 'e is. 'e don't come to school no more.

– He's probably moved away.

– I'm telling you 'e's dead. That's why we didn't go to the match.

Me dad got these two tickets out of his curvy wallet cause he sits on it in the car. He gave me one.

– Here.

I looked at it. It was warm from the heat from me dad's arse. It said *Derby County versus West Ham.*

Me dad tapped the ticket.

– Geoff Hurst. He won us the World Cup. I'll meet you by the *Bridge Inn* at one o'clock. We need to get a good spot.

– What about me mam?

– She can't come.

– She'll go mad.

– She already is if you listen to that gobby cow, Mavis.

– No, she'll go mad if I go.

– No she won't. You need to be a man. Stand up for yourself. You need to give that lad who hit you in the ear, a good hiding.

Me dad thumped me on the shoulder dead hard. He put his hand in his pocket and gave me fifty pence. It was warm where it'd been next to his knackers.

I saw Miss Crowe coming up the driveway from the school. Me dad waved at her cause she's pretty. She's a million million times prettier than Louise Draper.

– She your teacher? He thumped me again.

– English.

– You're a lucky boy, he said.

I think he fancied his chances with Miss Crow. Me mam says he shouldn't be walking the streets.

He walked away, and I saw his car round the corner. I watched him go. I started walking across the field looking out for Eagle, but he wasn't there.

Eagle never came back. That day was his last day. I felt dead happy. I sang a little song in me head.

Eagle's chair was empty. Nobody said owt at first. Billy

Myers said he beat up an old lady for her dough, and split her head open. After that he did a Post Office, and nicked all the stamps.

– 'e's gone to this special school for mad twats on the other side of Nottingham.

We didn't believe him at first. Billy went soft. He started trying to be nice to people, but he still got duffed up now Eagle was gone. That's what happens to cowards in the end. No one talked about Eagle until McTavish went mad one day cause we brought mud into the changing rooms after footy.

– Jesus! he shouted. – There's shit all over the floor! You might trample mud all over your own carpets, that's if you've got bloody carpets, but this is my bloody changing room! Then he went dead quiet. – No back chat then? No smart Alec with a quip? No of course not. There's no Eagle. McTavish was dead angry. – And for those of you who don't know, our friend Eagle's not with us any more. Gone to meet his maker. Not that I imagine he would have got in. Not with his track record. You little yobs could learn a lot from that foolish laddie.

Nobody said owt. McTavish knew he'd said a bad thing, cause he got the mop and bucket. He threw the mop and it hit this kid in the eye. He was crazy mad. He started throwing boots all over the place. Then he went into his office and banged the door. We could hear him shouting for ages, and kicking things.

Billy Myers knew. He'd sworn on the bible he would tell no one. And he didn't. I sort of respect him for that. He was loyal to Eagle.

Everybody knew by dinner time that Eagle had taken some tablets with beer. They said he was sad cause they'd taken him away. He was in this place where they sort bad kids out.

Eagle was dead.

Miss Crowe didn't come into school for two weeks. We had this woman from another school who shouted all the time. When Miss Crowe came back she was thin like me mam, and her eyes were red. I knew then that she loved Eagle.

Slug never said owt in assembly neither. We just sang an hymn, Harris did his usual silent but deadly, and Charlie gave me a friendly dead leg. I nearly collapsed with the pain. Even though we all hated Eagle really, we knew Slug should've said something about him. It was only right. Except for Miss Crowe, everybody was glad Eagle was gone. Nobody said it though. Nobody speaks the truth.

# The ghost of Gary Smedley

It was raining at lunch break. I was on me own in the library cause McTavish had made Charlie and Billy Myers go and put the corner posts in for the footy. Miss Crowe came into the library. She went behind this shelf where I could still see her. She went right along to the end of the shelf where the S's are. I know cause there's a full set of EB in the library, and that's where the S is. I saw Miss Crowe take out a book. She opened it and walked over to the windowsill. She got out this pen and wrote something, and put it straight back.

I pretended to write with me head down. She walked straight passed and left the library.

I waited for ages until no one was looking. I went over to the shelf. I'd seen which book it was, cause I remembered the cover. There was this quill on it with Shakespeare's head. It was the Shakespeare book we'd done in class: *A History of William Shakespeare*. It sprung out cause it had been covered with sticky-backed plastic with the book open. I went through the pages and didn't see owt at first. It was on the inside cover. I remembered Eagle had written this stuff about Shakespeare cause he couldn't spell proper. He was left-handed and his writing was all on a slant. There was this other bit at the bottom. It was Miss Crowe's writing under Eagle's. She wrote

## *Eagle 1960–1972 RIP.*

I don't think I really believed it before. Eagle really was dead.

I sat down on the floor with the book, and thought about it for ages 'til the bell went. I thought about me granddad and how he was old and that that's okay. But Eagle was twelve, like Gaz Smedley was, and that ain't okay. That means they'll always be twelve, even when I'm an old man, which I don't want to be. Eagle'll still be twelve cause he can't get old like Peter Pan can't. I knew then that it was God. God had got Eagle. He'd been dealing with all them other things. Now He was catching up. I wondered if I was next on His list. I hoped it might be me dad. I didn't think kids were supposed to die. I don't know why God does that.

One Saturday, Charlie and me went past Gaz Smedley's house on our bikes.

– I don't think 'e's dead, Charlie said.

– Cause 'e's dead. We'd 'ave gone to the footy if 'e ain't dead.

– 'is dad got this money.

– What money?

– Gaz said it was from winning a competition in the *Reader's Digest*. He said that 'e gets twenty grand a year for doin' nowt.

– That's bollocks.

We stopped outside the Smedleys' drive.

– It's bloody well empty, Charlie said, pointing. There was this *for sale* sign outside that had been blown over by the wind. The windows had this sort of cream on the inside like they do in shops when they close. The grass was ten feet tall.

– I'll give you ten pence if you go round the back, Charlie said to me.

– Fifty pence.

– Fuck off. I'd do it for fifty pence.

Charlie got off his bike and dropped it in the hedge.

– Come on, he said.

We ducked under the windows and went right round the back into the garden. They'd left the swings. The windows didn't have the creamy stuff on round the back. They didn't think nosey bastards like Charlie and me would go round.

– I bet 'e's in there, Charlie said.

– Who?

– Gaz.

– Like a ghost?

– Yeah. 'e won't have gone yet. They always come back 'ome first. Make sure it's okay. Then they go to 'eaven after they've done a bit of 'aunting.

– That's bollocks.

– Me gran came back. Charlie said.

– 'ow'd you know?

– Cause me granddad never did the washing up. 'e came down one morning and it was all done and put away.

– Ghosts don't wash up. They scare the shit out of people.

Charlie didn't say no more.

Charlie went to the kitchen window and pressed his face onto the glass. Then he jumped back.

– Fuckin' 'ell! he yelled.

– What!

– 'e's there! I saw 'im. I saw him. Bloody Gaz! 'e's standing there, looking. 'is face's all mushed like a mouldy spud, covered in blood! He put his head in his hands. – Oh God! Oh God!

I went to the window and looked in. The kitchen was empty. There wasn't even a cooker. I could hear Charlie laughing.

– I got yer, I got yer!

I pushed him over. He landed on his arse on the grass.

– You twat! You could've given me an 'eart attack. I mean that'd kill an old bag. I 'ope yer sitting in dog shit.

– But yer not an old bag, yer a young twat. He got up. – Anyway, did you tell yer mam about yer dad in the field?

– 'e said it wasn't 'im.

– Course it was fuckin' 'im. Jesus man! Don't yer know yer own dad. You could see his belly bouncing up and down like 'e was up the duff.

– 'e said it wasn't 'im. 'e said 'e was somewhere else. It was someone else.

– Then 'ow would 'e know that if 'e wasn't there? I didn't say owt. I knew he was right. Me dad thinks I'm stupid.

– 'e's got me a ticket for West 'am. I showed it to Charlie He looked at it dead hard. I could tell he was dead jealous.

– You jammy git. 'ow'd 'e get that?

– Dunno. Geoff 'urst. 'e won the World Cup.

– Not on 'is own 'e didn't. Anyway, 'e's dead.

– No 'e ain't. Is 'e?

– Course 'e ain't. Not every bugger's dead. – They reckon Eagle's dead, – but 'e's not. Rob Willis said 'e saw 'im down the *Main Centre* nicking *Doc Martens*. 'e's another one of them ghosts like Gaz and me gran.

– Charlie, Eagle's dead.

– You don't know that. Just cause 'e 'asn't kicked yer 'ead in don't mean 'e's dead. 'e's lying low. 'e's a fugitive, like the bloke on the telly.

– Yes I do know.

– Prove it, he said.

I knew I could.

On Monday, first thing, before the register, I took Charlie up to the library. He don't go in it very often. McTavish says the library's a mystery to kids like Charlie.

I showed Charlie the book that Miss Crowe wrote in.

– Don't prove owt.

– I'm telling you, Crowe wrote this.

– Bollocks.

– It's 'er writing.

– They say Eagle fucked 'er in the stock cupboard.

– Who the fuck's they.

– You know; they.

– You mean slaggy Scott and 'er merry band of prossers.

– No, I don't. It's they. Everyone who knows. They're like the *KGB*.

– So what you mean is that you know fuck all then.

– Des, these are the facts. 'e was down the *Main Centre*.

– She loved 'im.

– Who loved 'im?

– Crowe. She loved Eagle.

– That's bollocks. She was old enough to be 'is mam!

– I'm telling you, she loved 'im. I think she wanted to be 'is mam.

– Why would a teacher love some snivelling little twat like Eagle?

– She loved 'im cause 'e had no socks, and 'e wore the end of is mam's tights in the winter. 'e put water on 'is corn flakes, and 'e wrote about cowboys and Indians when we were trying to be clever bastards cause we're supposed to be. It's cause we've got socks and you've got *Doc Martens*, and those spazzy plastic gloves with the black and white squares on the knuckles. They're driving gloves and you 'aven't even got a fuckin' car!

Charlie was staring at the book. I could tell he thought it was true.

– You don't know owt of this.

– Charlie, look, it's 'er writing. It's Eagle's writing as well.
Charlie read the words.

– That's dead funny. It's too clever to be Eagle.

– But 'e said it in class. She gave 'im three 'ouse points. It was when you were telling that stupid story about yer dad being dead. And she said 'e was clever. 'e just acted like a twat.

– Well 'e was. You don't know she did this.

– Yes I do.

– 'ow?

– Cause I saw 'er do it.

– Yer lying.

– I'm not.

– You lied about yer dad.

I just looked at him and I didn't say owt. Charlie went red cause he knew it was me dad. He knew I was telling the truth cause he started to tell one of his stupid jokes. He did it cause he felt bad about the things he said about Eagle. We all did. We didn't know he was going to die. If we'd known he was going to die, we wouldn't have said them in the first place.

– There was this coloured bloke from Jamaica.

– Where's Jamaica?

– Jesus, you thicko. It's somewhere in Italy.

– There aren't any coloured people in Italy.

– Look, it don't matter. 'e was a coloured bloke and he talked funny. You know *dis and dat*, like they do.

Charlie's jokes go on for ever.

– Anyway, this coloured bloke was sitting there with 'is dick in a bowl of custard, and this other bloke came along and said – *what you doing?* And the coloured bloke says – *I'm fucking dis custard.*

Charlie started laughing so hard he couldn't get his breath back. Then he stopped cause he thought he was going to have an asthma attack. – Do you get it?

– Course I get it.

– Okay, he said. He held up his hand and made a circle. – What's this then?

– I dunno.

– It's wanker's cramp. Do you get this then?

– Yeah, I get it. He starts laughing again and coughing like he's been smoking *Capstans*.

– I've got another one about Jamaica.

We had to go cause the bell went.

– I'll save it 'til break, Charlie said.

Charlie says that one day he's going to be a comedian like Bernard Manning.

– You'll 'ave to eat a lot of pies, I said.

Charlie pulled one of his faces like he does.

– Being fat don't make you funny.

I didn't say owt after that. Charlie says all he wants to do is make me laugh. I don't need him to make me laugh. His mam, Eileen's as fat as a bastard, and she ain't funny. Not one bit.

## Apple bobbing, the flood, and facing the SS

After me mam had had her cup of tea with Auntie Mavis, she packed a bag.

– It's scouts, I said.

Me mam looked at me like I was stupid.

– Is that all you think about? You? You? You? Your father's left you, and you don't want to stand up and fight, go round and stand up to him, tell him what a coward he is for sneaking off into the night.

– But it's apple bobbing and toffees in flour and *British Bulldog*. We get prizes.

Me mam started to cry.

– Prizes! Prizes! Is that all you can think about; toffee apples!

Auntie Mavis got me head and pressed it against her. I got this gob full of sheep fur.

– It's all right Derek. You go to scouts and do your bobbing and what not, and then come to me and Uncle Bob's after.

Auntie Mavis took us to her house so I could get me bike. Uncle Bob was standing in the kitchen looking at two chicken legs like he was wondering where the rest of the chicken had gone.

– For God's sake man! There's no use staring at them. They're not going to walk to the bloody oven on their own! Auntie Mavis shouted. Even me mam laughed a bit. – We'll need another leg for Mary.

– Hello prince, Uncle Bob said. – We don't have a three legged chicken Mavis.

Auntie Mavis looked like she wanted to smack him one in

the chops.

Uncle Bob kissed me mam on the cheek.

– Sorry to hear it, Mary. Me mam sniffed. – It'll look better in the morning.

That's what they say; adults, that it'll all look better in the morning. Then they have a cup of tea.

I went to scouts and we did the bobbing and the flour and Andy White was sick, cause he swallowed some. Then we smoked the *pipe of peace* in the back of the hut and drank some *Toby Light*.

Charlie wasn't himself. He'd got to have a tooth out on Monday, and he was shit scared. He couldn't think about owt else. I told him about me granddad in the field with the horse bloke and how he didn't have no gas or owt.

– But yer granddad's dead.

– So.

– So 'e can't feel owt no more.

– Yeah, but 'e wasn't dead when 'e 'ad is tooth out.

But Charlie wasn't listening.

I stopped for some scratchings at the chip shop, but the old bag said she'd put them in the bin cause they weren't hygienic.

– You lot can start paying in future, she said. – Times is hard for all of us, what with the job cuts at Royce's and the *carriage-side*.

I didn't know what that had got to do with chips. But she wouldn't give me any scratchings, even if she had got any, which I know she had cause I could see them in this little box by the fryer.

Auntie Mavis was waiting for me when I got to her house.

– Your mam's in bed asleep. I've given her one of my tablets. I've got the camp bed out in the front room.

She left me and when it was dead quiet, I turned on the

colour telly. It was only the test card with the girl and her teddy and the blackboard and everything, but it was colour. I watched it for ages. It was still on in the morning making this ringing sound.

We stayed at Auntie Mavis's for yonks. I went to school from her house.

– You can't come to my 'ouse, I said to Charlie, cause sometimes he does after school.

– Why not.

– Cause you can't.

– That's stupid.

– We got a burst water pipe. The whole 'ouse is flooded. It went right up the stairs. We're staying at Auntie Mavis's 'til it's fixed.

Charlie looked at me dead hard. I thought he was going to ask me a question, but he didn't.

– You get everything new, he said.

– S'pose.

– They might give you a colour telly. People do that. They set fire to their old telly, then they get a colour one cause they say it was colour.

We didn't go home for three weeks. Me mam couldn't stand it. So we had to get more clothes and go back. When we got home, Charlie came round.

– It's all the same, he said.

– They dried it out.

Me mam came into the kitchen.

Charlie looked at me mam. Her face was all white like she'd had the blood sucked out of it.

– Des says you 'ad a flood.

I wanted to smack him one. Me mam looked at me.

– That's right, Charles. We did. Me mam just told a black

lie. Just like that. It was as easy as falling off a log, as me gran says. – They did a good job and dried it all out. Everything's as good as new.

Charlie looked at the lino where the cracks are by the door. He knew me mam was telling the truth. She's a grown-up.

Charlie's mam knew about me dad cause Auntie Mavis had told everybody in the hairdressers. She goes every week. Me mam says she gives them her life story.

– You give information and you get information, Auntie Mavis says. – It's what makes the world go round.

When I went to Charlie's, Mrs Shaw got out this tin of biscuits and she gave us some pop.

– Sit down, Derek, she said. – We've not seen you for a while.

Mrs Shaw's got fat hands. The rest of her's fat as well, but I ain't ever seen no one with dead fat hands. I don't know how you get fat hands. You'd never play the piano.

– It's not been that long, I said. It was when we saw me dad in the field with that slag. But I wasn't going to tell Mrs Shaw.

Nobody ever says owt, but they cart Mrs Shaw off to *Pastures* sometimes cause she goes bonkers and starts screaming at everybody. She thinks they're robots who've come to take over the planet. Me dad says not even aliens would take on Eileen Shaw. It's cause she's highly strung. They stick these electrode things on her head and put a million volts through her brain, and she's a zombie for ages.

– Oh it's been at least three weeks, she said. – But you've had a lot going on. What with the flood. I've not seen your dad around lately. She smiled, and cause her face's so fat her eyes disappear into these groves. She looks Chinese.

– No, I said. – 'e ain't been around.

– Why's that then?

Charlie pulled at me arm. – Come on. Let's go.

Charlie's mam whacked him on the side of his head with the back of her hand.

– What d'you do that for?

– I'm talking to Derek. She looked at me again with her piggy little eyes. – Mr Shaw normally sees him in that yellow car of his going to work. Obviously he goes later now he's gone over to the white collar side. But what with Mr Shaw coming home from the night shift, he sees him.

– 'e's on a course.

Me mam told me to say it cause we're ashamed.

– It seems a long time to be on a course.

– It's a big course.

– Have another biscuit.

– No thank you.

She had four chocolate ones just while we was sitting there.

– What sort of a course is it?

Me mam hadn't told me what sort of a course it was. I didn't even know what a course was.

– I don't know. It wasn't a lie.

– Well you must know something. I mean if he's away at the weekends as well. Is he away at the weekends?

– No. I didn't know what else to say.

– We haven't seen him.

– 'e's busy. We 'ad a flood. 'e's been painting.

Mr Shaw came in with his little briefcase. He put it on the table. There was this red mark on his face.

– Someone closed the door too fast. He laughed.

He picked up the biscuit tin and put it back in the cupboard.

– I thought we were trying, Eileen, he said.

What he means is she's a fat pig.

– I only had two little ones. Didn't I Derek?

She's a greedy fat bastard and she'd had seven cause I counted.

Mr Shaw looked at me and winked. – Is that true, Derek?

I looked at Mrs Shaw's fat face. There was this dribble down the line next to her chin.

– Dunno. I lost count. I didn't mean to be rude. It just came out.

– Derek was just telling me about his dad and how he's on this massive course, and that's why we haven't seen him, Mrs Shaw said.

Mr Shaw picked up his briefcase.

– That sounds good, Derek. Explains why I haven't seen him on his way to work. I like your dad. He always waves even though I'm blue collar. That's nice. I like that. Now you and Charlie go and play.

I got out me chair, and out the kitchen as fast as I could. I heard Mr Shaw shout at Mrs Shaw.

– He's a kid, he said. – Just a kid. How old is he? Twelve. You've been interrogating him like the *SS*. You're like your mother; got to know everything about other people's business. You won't let go. You're like a bleedin' dog with a bone!

I know who the *SS* is. They're Germans. I didn't know Mrs Shaw was a German. But I do know that all German people are fat and that you can't trust them as they'll drop a bomb on you as fast as you can say fuck a duck. That's what Uncle Bob says. Well not fuck a duck. He never says that cause of his mam looking down from the sky and everything. She wouldn't like it.

## Tinned tomato soup, and three coins in a fountain

I went to meet me dad at the *Bridge Inn* for the footy. I didn't want to go. I hate the footy now. I hate the noise and the *boot boys* in the *pop side* where they go with their *Doc Martens* to kick heads in. I used to love footy, but it's not the same. I'll never see George Best now cause he ran away and nobody knows where he is. It's what people do when they're famous, like Howard Hughes in me EB.

– I'm cooking tea for when you get back, me mam said. – Steak and kidney pie, roast potatoes and peas with bread and butter pudding for afters. I've made some soup. She gave me this flask. – It's tomato. It'll keep you warm. She put me Derby County hat on me head. She grabbed hold of me.

– I'm not doin' it. I can't make 'im, I said.

She shoved me away.

– Tell him he needs to come. You can make him come. You know you can. He'll listen to you.

It was nearly one o'clock. I had to go.

I could see me dad's car outside the *Bridge Inn*. It was parked round the side with the nose just sticking out. Me dad got out and came over.

-- Hello, Des. He looked like he was going to cry. He hadn't had a shave and I could smell the beer on his breath. – We'll show them the way home today, he said.

He always says *we'll show them the way home*.

We sat in the car. He looked at me for ages like he didn't know who I was.

– How are you? he said.

– Charlie's mam keeps asking me where you are. I don't know what to say.

– She's a nosey old bag. Tell her to mind her own business. That woman's eating herself into an early grave. Happy people don't look like Eileen Shaw. Happy people are thin.

– Me mam's thin. She's not 'appy. Annie Gray's mam's thin too, and she's not 'appy.

– You have to remember that those two women are insane. Des, this is nobody else's business. You hear that?

I gave him the flask.

– It's tomato. Me mam made it.

He took the lid off the flask and sniffed it.

– It's out of a tin. Tomatoes only grow in the summer. You can't make tomato soup in the winter. It's *Heinz*.

It wasn't *Heinz* neither. It was from *Fine Fare*. I didn't tell him. Me mam never buys *Heinz*. She says it's just a name and that the bosses just go off on their yachts to the Caribbean. She says it's like the bosses at *Qualcast* where they make the lawn mowers.

– While everybody else is working their fingers to the bone, they're off living the *life of Riley*, Auntie Mavis says. Whoever Riley is.

Me dad poured some tomato soup in one of the cups. He gave it to me. It was dead hot. I love tomato soup.

– Of course it is possible to make tomato soup in the winter, he said.

– 'ow then?

– What do you think Scott did?

– Dunno.

– Powdered soup. It's the future Des. One day you'll carry your dinner round in a tablet. They won't have shops; they'll have machines where you can get whatever you want in a tablet. You take it and you're not hungry any more.

Me dad drank his soup dead quick, like he's got an asbestos gob.

– Me mam wants you to come back for tea.

Me dad looked at me and he went this funny colour. He got out the car and went round to the bonnet. He puked this red stuff all over the floor. It looked like blood. Then he spat and got back in.

– There's something wrong with that, he said, tapping the flask. – Your mam put something in it?

– No. I watched her. She opened the tin, put it in the pan and made it 'ot then she put it in the flask.

He pointed at me. – See, he said. – I told you it was out of a tin.

I felt sick.

– Me mam wants you to come 'ome for tea. I know he heard me. – Will you?

He put his hand on me leg. It's not right for a bloke to put his hand on another bloke's leg.

– So you admit she got it out of a tin.

He had this wild look in his eyes.

– Me mam thinks you've gone mental.

Me dad laughed. I could see all his fillings. It's cause they had no toothbrushes when he was a boy.

– What do you think, Des?

– Dunno. She wants you to come 'ome for tea.

– We'll see, he said.

It meant no. It always means no.

We beat West Ham five one. Geoff Hurst never turned up. It's cause he's too old and he can't walk properly nowadays cause his knees are knackered. Hector scored three and I got me hat nicked. There was this kid behind me. I know he saw what happened. Nobody said owt. They were West Ham fans anyway. They deserved to get thrashed.

It was dark when we got to *The Bridge Inn*. Me dad stopped the car, but he didn't turn the engine off. I wanted to get out.

– Are you coming then? I asked him.

He looked at me for ages. I didn't want him to come, not really, but I didn't want me mam to go mad either.

– One day you'll understand, Des. I had to do this. I had to get away. It was killing me. I'm sorry you're involved. You just have to get on with what you're doing and you'll be all right. Get a good job, do the right things and stay out of the dirt and grime.

– So will you come 'ome for your tea then?

He looked out the window. It started to piss it down. I hadn't got me coat. It pisses it down all the time in Derby. There was steam coming off the bonnet.

– I can't.

– Me mam said I'd got to make you come. She needs you to come.

– Not today.

– What do you mean not today?

– Maybe another day.

I had to tell me mam something.

– What day then?

– I'll be in touch. There's Aston Villa. It's away. We've never been to an away match.

– So you're not coming then?

He gave me fifty pence.

– Don't tell your mam. Get one of those matchbox cars you collect.

– I don't want no matchbox cars. I need you to come. She'll

go mad. She'll kill me. I can't go back there. I didn't bring the knives with me.

– The knives. What knives?

– The knives in the kitchen. I take 'em so she don't do owt stupid.

Me dad just shook his head.

– Your mam's not that type. She's too selfish.

I was thinking it, but then I said it. – I could come with you. Stay with you.

Me dad didn't look at me. He just stared out the window and kept turning the wipers on and off.

– Look, Des. It's not possible. You're better off with your mam. Boys need their mams. I'm doing this for the best. You do understand don't you?

– S'pose so. I didn't know what he was talking about. – So you're not coming then.

– No.

– She'll go mad.

– Your mam's always mad about something. Chucking things about, yelling. It's the yelling that does it. All that yelling. She never knows when to stop.

– She ain't got no money. She says she wants the car; that it's 'alf 'ers.

He laughed like it was some dead stupid joke.

-- She's not the one who lies under it week after week to keep it going. It's not easy Des. This is an old car. Done thousands of miles. I can't afford a new car. Anyway, you need to go.

– It's raining.

– Dodge the raindrops, Des. Float like a butterfly!

– Butterflies die in the rain.

– Don't try and be clever, Derek.

I got out the car. I was going to ask him again, but he closed the door and he drove off dead quick. I stood in the rain. One of his back lights didn't work, which would never have happened before.

When I got back I could hear me mam in the kitchen. There was steam coming out the windows. She was singing this song about *Three Coins in a Fountain*, which me dad used to sing when he went to the bog. It was cause I knew she thought I'd bring him back.

The back door was open. There were pans bubbling on the cooker. I could smell the steak and kidney pie. Me mam's a good cook like me gran.

– Mam.

She walked straight past me and went and looked out at the road. She stood there for ages in her apron in the rain. It was making her hair flat. Then she came back in and slammed the door dead hard. It moved in the frame where this crack was.

– Where the hell is he then?

– 'e didn't want to come.

– What do you mean, he didn't want to come?

– 'e said 'e'd come some other time.

Me mam pointed at the cooker with her foot.

– What do you think I've been doing all afternoon while you've been watching football? What do you think all this is for? This is wasted food. He's gone off to some seedy little place God knows where. All this damned waste. Why didn't you get him to come?

– Mam, 'e wouldn't come. 'e just wouldn't. I couldn't make 'im.

– I don't know what the hell we're going to do.

– It'll be all right. I know it will.

She turned the cooker off.

– That's the trouble. You think it'll be alright. He's left you. He doesn't want you. He's made that as clear as the nose on your face. All you can say is it'll be alright'. I only asked you to bring him home. How hard is that? I ask you, how hard is that?

– 'e wouldn't come. What can I do?

– You could have tried harder. You could have told him. You could have told him what he's doing to us, that this is the cruellest thing anyone's ever done.

It wasn't true. There was Hitler who killed all them Jews and Mr Shaw who wants to shoot every bugger that moves. Me dad wasn't that bad.

– I did me best.

– Well your best wasn't good enough, Derek.

How can your best not be good enough?

– 'e's taking me again. It's away to Aston Villa.

– And you think you're going?

– Dunno.

– You go and you don't come back. Do you hear me?

I didn't say owt. I knew she didn't mean it. I knew she was sad and mad and all those things. She went out the kitchen. I followed her.

– I'm sorry mam. 'e just wouldn't come.

I heard her go up the stairs and the bedroom door slam.

Me mam slept. I had some of the steak and kidney pie, which wasn't cooked properly in the middle. I ate it anyway cause I was hungry, and me dad wouldn't buy one of them pies at the *Baseball Ground*.

– All those people. He pointed at the *Pop Side*. – I bet those yobs over there have eaten half a horse between them. They'll be sick as dogs.

– I thought they used 'orses for dog meat.

– There you are then. Those pies are full of dog meat.

I didn't think they were. But me dad's never wrong, like Auntie Mavis. She reckons she had some French cheese and it gave her the shits for two months. She had to have a blood transfusion and everything. There was this shop in Derby and when Auntie Mavis saw it, she thought it said *French Fish* cause she's as blind as a bat.

– Look! she said. – They're bloody everywhere. They come here whenever they like without a bye or a leave, with their bloody stinking garlic.

Uncle Bob gave Auntie Mavis her glasses. It said *fresh fish*.

– You're right Mavis, it's not very clear.

It was as clear as *the nose on your face*, as me mam said.

With the size of Auntie Mavis's nose you couldn't bleedin' miss it!

## *Mecca, and women on the loose*

Me mam used to make me go to church on Sundays so that me sins were cleansed. I used to go with Charlie, but he sat on the rec, so I did the same 'til the vicar told me mam and she went mad.

– I'm not going to church no more, Charlie said. – I'm a Muslim like all them people in Moretonside. They don't go to church cause they're in their shops all the time, flogging dirty mags and fags and stuff. They 'ave to pray five times a day to the west, but they can do it wherever they are.

– They 'ave to pray five times!

– Yeah. They 'ave these mats and everything. They lie down and groan like they've got belly ache. I've seen 'em. There was this bloke doing it in 'is shop.

– To the west?

– To the west.

– To Edmeston?

– No you twat! To Mecca.

– That's a shop.

– I know.

– What they praying to a shop for?

– I dunno. It was in the *Derby Evening Telegraph*. I read it on me round. These blokes went beating 'em Pakistan people up cause they 'ate 'em cause they take their jobs. It'll be bloody Billy Myers's dad. 'e's a lazy bastard when he ain't in the clink. He bloody well deserves to lose 'is job.

– I bet yer dad still thinks they should all be shot.

– No 'e don't. 'e says they're all God's children. Anyway 'e buys 'is dirty mags in Moretonside. Mind you, e'd have 'em shot if they came and lived next door. We were laughing dead loud when the vicar saw us.

– Fuck! That's it, I said. Then he told me mam. So, now none of us go to church on Sunday.

Me mam and me went to Risley the day after me dad wouldn't come for his tea. Risley's dead posh except for the council houses, which are painted all different colours so people know they're not private. Jim and Brenda's is *Caribbean Blue*.

– They haven't got a phone, me mam said. – We're just going to turn up.

– Why?

– Jim knows your dad. He'll talk to him. Make him get some help. He's mentally ill. This isn't your dad, this is someone else. This isn't the man I married.

– So who is 'e then?

– This is another person. He looks the same, but it's not him in there.

It was pissing it down. I drew this face in the mist on the bus window.

– What person?

– You know exactly what I mean, Derek. Don't try and be clever.

I knew what she meant exactly. She was saying me dad wasn't me dad cause he was doing things she didn't like. Me dad goes with Louise in the fields and in the car down lanes cause I've seen them. Me mam says she knows nowt cause she don't want to see me dad the way he is. It's what grown ups do. There's this bloke and woman who have their dinner in the *Co op* on Saturday. They never say owt to each other. She just looks at her dinner, and he looks at the waitress's knockers. One day they brought a cake out cause someone had said it was their wedding anniversary. They'd come every Saturday for twenty five years. They asked the bloke to say something.

– She hates me.

I think he said it as a joke. His wife said it was true. He looked dead upset. It was like he never knew. They'd sat there hating each other, and neither of them said. They should have done what me dad says. They should have faced the facts. They wasted their whole lives hating each other.

We got off the bus. Someone had slashed some of the seats with a knife. The stuffing was hanging out. Me mam got out this umbrella with flowers on it.

– I'm not walking under that thing, I said.

It stopped raining. We walked the rest of the way to Jim and Brenda's house. It's got stone cladding to make it look like it's right out in the country. It ain't cause there's a *Fine Fare* on the corner. There ain't no *Fine Fare* in the country cause there's no people to buy owt.

Jim was wiping the rain off his car. He's a salesman in the Rover garage, so he's got one. Me dad says they're the best cars in the world. He says, if you've got a Rover then you've made it.

Jim saw me and me mam. He looked dead pleased. He likes me mam. He stopped wiping the car and came out onto the road and trod in some dog shit.

– Buggers!

He waved his fist at his next door neighbour who he hates cause they don't cut their grass.

– Mary! This is a surprise.

Jim kept looking back at the house. He kissed me mam. Me mam grabbed him. She started crying on his shoulder. We were out in the street. It was dead embarrassing.

– Jim. I don't know what to do.

– Mavis told us. It's a terrible thing, he said. – What with the lad and everything.

– He's lost his mind, me mam said.

Jim winked at me. It's all the blokes do. They don't know what to say to kids cause the women do it. It's nature. It says in me EB that it's the *hunters and the gatherers*.

– What do you think to the new car, Des? It's the new model. Three litres. Runs like a dream.

It looked the same as all the others to me.

– It's nice, I said.

It was a lie. It's an old bloke's car.

– Colin's taken the car, me mam said.

Jim grabbed her arm. – He's been to see me, Mary. You need to know that.

– Where?

– At the showroom

– When?

– It was last week.

– Thank God. What did he say? Did you talk to him? You know- man to man.

– I gave him a test drive in the new model. Said he was thinking of one. He seemed fine to me.

Me mam looked like she wanted to smack Jim one in the gob. It wasn't what she wanted to hear.

– He wanted a bloody car!

Me mam was shouting. It was a good job she wasn't near no doors to slam.

Jim kept looking back at the house. I saw Brenda at the window. She banged on it dead hard. It vibrated. She was saying something, but we couldn't hear her cause they've got this new double-glazing.

– He wanted a part chop, Jim said.

– The old car!

– He wanted finance. He seemed dead keen.

Brenda opened the door. She yelled. She's got a voice like a fog horn.

– Jim!

Jim grabbed me mam's arm.

– This is difficult, Mary. You know what Brenda's like.

Jim looked scared.

– We can't stand on the pavement, me mam said. – We need to talk about this inside.

Me mam started walking up the path. Jim chased after her.

– Mary stop, please.

Brenda was walking down the crazy paving. She waddles like a duck cause she's short and fat. Halfway down, she tripped over the crazy paving, and nearly went arse over tit. Her face was all red. She looked like a snorting bull. She went right up to me mam cause she's short, she was looking at me mam's neck.

– I'm sorry Mary, you're not welcome here. Not after all that's happened, Brenda said to me mam's neck.

Me mam looked at me. I looked at Jim. He started wiping his car again as if he hadn't heard.

– Brenda, me mam said. – Jim's seen Colin.

– I know he has. I'm acquainted with all the facts. Jim told me. Jim tells me everything. We've got no secrets you see. We've got a strong marriage. Haven't we Jim.

Jim turned round and looked at me mam.

– Yes, we have. Very strong. It's very strong.

Jim was nodding like another one of them dogs you see in the backs of cars.

Me mam went over to Jim.

Brenda snatched Jim's rag out his hand and pushed him.

Jim's dead skinny. Brenda could break him in half. Jim staggered back against the wing of the car. It's a good job it wasn't Brenda. She'd crush the front end.

– Get inside, Jim. I'll deal with this, Brenda said.

Me mam got hold of me hand dead hard and squeezed it.

– We've come to see you. Colin's gone again. We don't know what to do. I need to talk to someone who can get through to him. Someone he trusts.

Jim was creeping away up the crazy paving.

Brenda pointed at me mam with a fat finger. It looked like a sausage.

– We know he's gone, Mary. We know all about it. He said he couldn't go on. He was at his wits end.

Jim was standing in the front doorway. Brenda waved at him.

– I said, inside, Jim. Now!

Brenda stood dead close to me mam. She had this dress on that looked like a flowery tent. Her ankles were all swollen. Her toe nails looked like massive sheep's horns. She pointed her finger right in me mam's face. It nearly touched her nose. That's what adults do when they want to make a point. It's dead rude.

– I'm only telling you this once, Mary. I'm not beating round the bush. I don't want you round here. Neither does Jim.

Jim was standing at the window now. He was shaking his head at me. Me mam's mouth was open. She's always telling me when me mouth's open that I'm catching flies.

– Do you understand me, Mary?

– Brenda, I don't know what you're saying. We've been friends for how long? I can't remember.

– Twenty years, Mary and not a crossed word. And now

this. It beggars belief.

– Yes, twenty years, Brenda. Look we've been through thick and thin. Think of Elsie and Stan and all the heartache that caused.

Brenda let out this noise that sounded like a fart, but it came out of her gob.

– You leave my family out of this. Elsie and Stan are happy now, which is more than I can say for you and Colin. He keeps leaving! Happy men don't leave happy homes. You've got to feed a marriage, Mary.

I don't think Brenda feeds Jim. He looks more like one of them prisoners of war that had to build that railway for them Japs.

Elsie's Brenda's sister. They went to live in New Zealand cause Stan lost his job. He did drawing at Royce's, but me dad said, what with the lay-offs, they ain't got nowt to draw no more. They went on this boat for six weeks, which was full of bananas and spiders. They swapped husbands and wives with these people they knew, and then they came home. Me mam said that Brenda had a nervous breakdown cause of the kids and everything, and the worry.

Me mam tried to grab Brenda's fat arm, but she pulled it away. I thought she was going to fall in their shitty little pond, which is full of green slime and dead fish cause some kids put bleach in it. Brenda's cheeks started to wobble like jelly.

– I came to see Jim, me mam said.

– I know you did. Do you think I don't know what's going on in your scheming little mind! You're not seeing him.

Jim was still watching us from the window.

– I thought he would talk to Colin and make him see sense.

Brenda held her hand up like the policemen do when they're stopping the traffic.

– He's talked to him and that's the end of it.

– Please, Brenda.

I wanted to go home. I tapped me mam on the shoulder.

– Mam.

She pushed me away.

– We need to sort this out, Brenda, me mam said.

I thought they were going to have a fight.

Brenda folded her arms.

– There's nowt to sort out, Mary. You lose one husband and I'm not having you coming here sniffing about my Jim like a bitch on heat. I know that's what you're up to.

Me mam looked at me. Then she started to cry.

– And that's no good, Mary. The crocodile tears don't touch me. You might soften witless little blokes like Jim and Mavis's Bob. Yes Mary, and she'd better watch out now you're on the loose, because he's away with the fairies, mad as a bag of frogs, talking to his mam and all that palaver. He's vulnerable. He's like a child, not right in the head since the death. He wouldn't stand a chance against a determined woman. Me mam started waving at Jim. Brenda grabbed her arm. – They're weak, Mary. You know that. But my Jim's never looked at another woman.

Me mam did this evil laugh.

– There must be something wrong with his bloody eyes then!

– Ha, Brenda said. – People in glass houses don't throw stones, Mary. You need to think on.

– I just want to talk to Jim.

– He's in the house, and that's where he's staying. He's not talking to no one, especially not you, Mary!

– 'e's at the window, I said. – 'e's waving.

Brenda looked at him. She shouted dead loud.

– Get away from the window! Go into the kitchen and put

the kettle on!

There was this bloke with his dog crapping on the pavement right at the end of the street. Even he could hear her.

– Mam, I said. – Let's go. Brenda looked at me.

– I feel sorry for you, Des. Caught up in all this filth. But your mam's not coming in here. Women on the loose, they're a threat to decent living people. Remember that boy before you think about getting involved. Look at their past. Women are stronger than men. Your dad'll have found some tart in Moretonside or Willow fields. It won't last. He'll come crawling back with his tail between his legs. Your mam needs to cut his what nots off, put them on a stick and read him the riot act.

Brenda went back up the crazy paving, and stopped at the top. She was out of breath.

– I'm lucky with my Jim. Solid gold. His mam had his dad in a firm grasp. You let Colin go, Mary. You let him go. You were too soft. You can't be too soft with men, or they'll lead you up the garden path.

She went inside the house and slammed the door. Me and me mam were still standing on the pavement. It started to rain. We had to wait ages for a bus.

*Keep going while the going's good*
*Merry Christmas with The Golden Hind*

When we got home me mam went mad. She started opening all the cupboards and slamming them like me dad was still there.

– Mam, I said.

– Leave me alone!

She was doing it for yonks and yonks. I tried to play solitaire, but I couldn't do better than five. Me mam came into the back room. She put something in her shopping bag. I didn't see what.

– Tea? Yorkshire pud and onion gravy? She looked dead happy, just for a minute. It's cause she'd had what she thought was this dead good idea.

Me mam used to make the best onion gravy in the whole wide world. I waited until I heard her in the kitchen. I opened her bag. They were on top of her gloves. I didn't touch them cause they can get fingerprints, and the cops have got you forever and ever amen. I knew then why me mam was so happy. She'd found the spare keys to me dad's car.

I went up to me bedroom and I listened to *Radio Derby*. They played *School's Out* by Alice Cooper who's a bloke that wears make up and everything. After that they played *I'd like to teach the world to sing*, so I turned it off.

When it's Christmas we have to walk to the church from school in a line. They'd made me and Charlie read out the bible about the shepherds and the holy birth, and how they went to Bethlehem and everything. Billy Myers was mucking about, kicking arses and nicking caps while we walked along.

– Eagle should've kicked yer 'ead in, Jackson, he said. – I think I'll do it in 'is memory. His two new mates grunted and grinned.

I saw me dad crawling along the road in his yellow car. I felt this pain in me belly like it was a knife. Charlie saw him too.

– It's yer dad! he said.

He was driving dead slow. He was looking at the kids. Some of them where sticking two fingers up at him. Some girls shouted at him.

– Yer dirty old bastard!

They thought he was looking at them like old blokes do.

I knew he was looking for me.

– Let me go on the inside, I said to Charlie. I wanted to hide.

– It's yer dad. 'e won't see you if yer on the inside.

– I know, you dozy twat! I don't want 'im to see me.

Me dad was dead close, but he was going to miss me. Then Billy Myers shouted. Me dad's car window was open.

– 'e's 'ere!

Me dad drove down the road. I thought he was going, but he stopped the car. He got out and started walking back. It was like the conveyer belt with the circular saw in *Batman* that's going to cut him in half. Then it stops, and you don't find out 'til next week if he gets out. I was going to find out right now if me dad was going to get to me.

I wanted to jump over a wall. I wanted to die, or knock meself out so I didn't have to see. He found me cause Billy Myers was pointing and dancing round. Me dad came right up to me.

– Hello Charlie, he said.

– 'ello Mr Jackson.

Me dad pulled me by the arm. I thought he was going to cry cause his eyes were all wet. I said this incy wincy little prayer, but God didn't come and strike me dad down with a bolt of lightening. He never comes. You can say a million prayers and the bastard never comes. Me gran said that God came to get me granddad when he called for Him. But it ain't true. Me granddad had just got too many pies in his blood!

Me dad just looked at me and everybody started walking round me and rubber-necking.

– Des, he said.

Billy Myers started laughing.

– Oh Des! Daddy's 'ere.

Me dad pushed him on the shoulder as he went past.

– You! he said, – shut your mouth!

Billy Myers spat on the floor near me dad's foot.

– Me dad'll kick yer fuckin' 'ead in.

I grabbed me dad's arm. I wondered if his jacket arm was going to drop off like all the others.

– We're going to church, I said. – I 'ave to go.

He was holding these presents all wrapped up and everything. He gave me this big parcel. It had cars on the paper.

– It's the *Golden Hind*, he said. He told me what it was! – I've painted the hull. Just to get you going.

What's the point in giving somebody an *Airfix* model if you've half done it? I wanted to give it back.

He gave me the other present. It was titchy.

– This is for your mam.

It had a card on it. It said *from Colin*.

I tried to give him them back.

– I can't take 'em. I'm going to church.

– I'm going away in a couple of days.

– Where?

Billy Myers was hanging about by the wall.

– Me dad'll kick yer 'ead in when 'e get's out, he said to me dad.

I think me dad looked scared.

– Out of where?

– Clink, Billy said. – 'e killed a teacher.

I could see McTavish looking at us.

– It'll be a while then, me dad said.

– It'll be a while then! Billy Myers said in this voice.

– So where're you going? I asked him.

He tapped his nose. – Mission. North, where it's cold.

I think he was having me on. Then he kissed me on the cheek and he whispered, – Rochdale.

– Where's that?

– Just north. I love you, Des. You know that.

I was a dead boy. Me dad kissed me on the cheek on Laxton Lane in front of everybody.

– Fuckin' 'omos! Somebody shouted. Tina the slag pot Scott joined in.

– Fuckin' 'omos', fuckin' 'omos', dirty little bastards!

Me dad waved at them, then he just got in his car and drove off. He left me on the edge of the pavement holding the presents.

– What's going on here? McTavish shouted right in me ear. Then he looked at me presents.

– It was me dad, sir, I said.

– What's wrong with Christmas Day laddie?

– He's going north. McTavish just looked at me.

– North? What do you mean north?

I thought about telling him about Scott, but I knew it sounded stupid. It said nowt about Rochdale in *South with*

*Scott* cause it was north.

– 'e's on a course, sir. 'e won't be here for Christmas Day.

– On a course on Christmas Day! What's he training for? The Next Santa!

Everybody laughed. I wanted to cry. Me eyes went dead sore. I had to hold me breath to stop the tears coming out.

Charlie came back down the line. Everybody stopped. I looked at Charlie, cause I knew he knew. He looked away at a Christmas tree in this window with lights on and everything. This bloke who was looking out at us had seen Billy Myers piss on his hedge. He stuck two fingers up at us. He turned round, dropped his trousers and showed us his arse, which was white and covered in spots.

Me mam didn't believe me; not about the bloke and his arse, but about me dad and the presents on Laxton Lane on the way to church.

– You're saying he came up to you when you were walking to the church!

– Yeah. 'e did. Dead 'onest.

– Derek, I don't believe you.

– It's dead true. I got the presents. They're in the garden under the bush.

I didn't bring them in cause I knew she'd go mad.

– Get them!

I went out to get them. It was raining and the paper was a bit soggy. I could see the picture of the *Golden Hind* on the front of the box with all its rigging and everything. Me mam looked at them. She prodded the boxes like she does with the fruit at the market.

When she prodded the boxes, she did this face where her jaw goes stiff, then she went mad. She grabbed the one with the label on that said *MARY* in big letters. There weren't no kisses or owt. Then she just stared at me. I knew it was coming.

– Why didn't you tackle him?

– I was in a line. I can't tackle me dad. 'e was on the road. It was dangerous.

She put her present on the table and looked at it. She poked it again and kept walking round and coming back. She banged it with her fist.

– You know what this is! You know what this is!

She started waving her present in the air.

– I think it's a box of *Quality Street*, I said.

– This is blackmail!

– You mean *Black Magic*. They're deffo *Quality Street*. You can tell from the shape of the box.

– Don't try and be clever. You took this, Derek. Now he's off like a thief in the night.

– 'e said 'e's going in a couple of days.

She took me parcel out of me hands.

– Can't I open it?

She prodded me dead hard in the shoulder. It hurt cause her fingers are like a skeleton's.

– Is that all you do? Is that all you do; think about yourself all the time when he's swanning about wherever he likes!

She opened her present. I was right; it was a box of *Quality Street*. It was flat in the middle where she'd hit it with her fist. Some of the chocolates were flat as well. She threw it at the wall dead hard. It burst open and all the chocolates fell out on the floor. After that she went out and slammed the door. I waited until I couldn't hear her no more. I picked them up and stuffed the purple ones with the caramel and the hazelnuts in me pockets. I knew she'd never notice. Me gran says you've got to make hay while the sun shines. She also says you've got to go while the going's good, which is what me dad did I suppose. He's a dead man if he doesn't keep going. When I go I'm just going to keep going.

# The car thief and the hostage

It was nearly Christmas. That fat twat, Jimmy Osmond was in the charts with *Long-Haired Homo from Liverpool*. Charlie's mam bought it, cause she's a fat pig and fat pigs stick together in the sty going snort, snort.

It was snowing just a bit, but slush on the roads.

– Four inches by tomorrow, Charlie said.

– That's bollocks.

– The weather man said.

– They don't know what they're talking about.

– Yes they do. They've got maps and everything. They've got these machines that measure the wind: Anemometers.

– 'ow'd you know that? It's the sort of thing Charlie knows.

– 'cause I do.

It ain't going to snow.

He knew I was right. It never snows at Christmas no more; not if Jimmy Osmond's singing! Charlie's dad says the dog starts howling when he's singing cause it gives him the belly ache.

– Don't forget to bring a game for the last day, Charlie shouted. He was already running away. – I'm bringing *Mousetrap*. Don't go bringing one of them five zillion piece jigsaws of some mountain or I'll burn it.

I was going to take me chess set.

Like I said; I nearly died. I know things. I can see them before they happen. I didn't want to go home, cause I knew. I knew it'd be there, standing outside the house. I stopped on the corner and hid in the bush. It was raining and running down the back of me neck. The arm was coming off me coat again. Me gran says once an arm comes off, you can't sew it back on proper. She says it's just one of those facts of life, like babies being born bald.

It's not supposed to rain at Christmas. I've never seen no Christmas cards with rain on. It's always snow and peace on earth and good will to all men and turkeys, poor people, and children in homes, old people that ain't got nowhere to go, and sit in their own piss.

Me dad's car was there, parked in the space in front of the house. It was dirty. Me dad's car's never dirty. I could feel the hammer in me heart banging dead loud. One day it's going to burst out.

I knew me dad didn't want to be there. I could see it in his face. He looked like he was in pain.

– Des! he said.

He hugged me. Me mam was grinning cause she'd got the car back and me dad as well; like two for the price of one at *Fine Fare*. I knew he didn't want to be there cause it was obvious. He was there cause me mam had nicked his car.

Auntie Mavis told me what happened cause she can't keep her gob shut. She didn't think me mam did the right thing. Me mam turned up in the car park outside me dad's office and waited 'til someone came to the window. When they did, she shook the keys at them. After that she got in the car and started it. She revved the engine dead loud until there was all this smoke and everything, which drives me dad mad cause he says it damages the piston rings and the valves. Me dad came to the window. He says if you can't understand what happens under the bonnet, then you shouldn't be driving it. I know he went back into the office to talk to Louise who he was probably having sex with on the desk cause that's what people like that do. All the time.

Me dad came down the steps dead fast. He ran out into the car park. Louise was probably watching him behind the blinds. I don't know how Auntie Mavis knew all this. She must have given a lot of info to get a lot of info.

– I'm taking it! me mam shouted.

Me dad ran up to her and tried to grab the keys. Me mam wouldn't get out the car. She just kept revving and revving.

– I'm taking the car! she shouted.

– You can't. It's my job. Don't be stupid, Mary. It's my life, my job.

– Then come back. If you need your bloody car so much.

– I can't.

– Why?

– You know exactly why.

– Then explain it.

– I can't.

Auntie Mavis said me dad tried to drag me mam out the car. It was *an ugly situation.*

Me mam slammed the door and nearly snapped me dad's fingers off. He got in the other side to try and talk to her. She started driving, so he couldn't do owt about it. Everybody was watching from me dad's office window. I bet Louise was screaming and screaming.

Auntie Mavis didn't say no more. Me dad came home cause he loves the car more than owt else. He probably loves it more than Louise, but she don't know that yet. He's bound to, cause she's got a face like the back of a bus. Nobody loves anybody that ugly. It's not right. It alters *the order of things*, as it says in me EB.

I was counting me conkers. Me dad came into me bedroom.

– Conkers, he said.

– I've got two 'undred and twenty three.

He just stared at the conkers like they might change into something.

– I thought we could get the boat out. Put it back on the river. You know. Make sure it's buoyant.

I didn't want to do the boat. I knew he didn't mean it. They were just words. Me dad uses a lot of words that no other bugger understands. It's cause he's white collar.

I looked at him dead hard, in the eyes. They were all red and he had drink on his breath.

– Will you go again?

He had this conker in his hand. He squeezed it dead hard and it split, like he can do with an apple.

– Now I've only got two 'undred and twenty-two.

– Don't you think it's enough?

– S'pose.

– You working hard at school?

– S'pose.

You've got to just get on with it, Des. Remember.

He went over to the window.

– The dirt and grime. It sucks you in and then it spits you out. Me dad looked like he was finished.

The siren went off for the night shift. You can hear this little buzz, like a bee and it gets louder as they come down Moor Lane, even though there's no Moor. You can see them if you're on the London Road, which goes for one hundred and twelve miles all the way to London. It's where the posh people live like the Queen and the Mayor with his stinky cat.

Me heart was banging dead hard. I needed to know. Your word's all you've got. I needed to get his word.

– So will you go again?

– When you're an adult you'll understand. I had to get away.

– But will you go again?

– No, he said. I had his word.

– Do you promise? It'd kill me mam. She'll go like Annie Gray's mam.

– She's not right in the head.

– What, me mam?

– Mrs Gray.

– Me mam said it was cause 'er husband left 'er and went off with this woman to live in Moretonside. 'e never came back.

– He couldn't come back, Des. Clive Gray's dead.

I laughed. I was nervous like Charlie gets.

– It's not very funny, Des. The man's dead. He was driven into an early grave. That's what it was.

– Did 'e kill 'imself?

Me dad just looked at the floor. I looked at it as well. This little beetle crawled across it. It took it ages just to go a few inches. A carpet is like a desert to a beetle.

– He dropped an electric fire into the bath, me dad said.

– Why did 'e do that?

– He wanted to kill himself.

– Was 'e boiled?

– Yes, I suppose he was in a way.

– Like a potato?

– Just like a potato.

– Did it fall off the wall?

– No, Des! He dropped it in on purpose.

– Is that what you'll do?

– I've felt like it at times.

– So you won't drop a fire in the bath?

– No.

– Do you promise?

Me dad looked at the window. It was nearly dark.

– The grass needs a cut, he said.

– Do you promise?

– I promise, he said. He didn't look at me.

Me granddad used to say that you've got to see the whites of their eyes. I couldn't see the whites of his eyes. I remembered what me granddad said about the Japs not looking at you. I didn't trust me dad neither. I was beginning to wonder if he was shifty.

Auntie Mavis, Uncle Bob and me gran came for Christmas. It was shit. It didn't snow, and me mam and dad pretended that Father Christmas was real. Everybody was living a lie.

– He's been, me mam said.

– Who's been?

– Father Christmas.

– 'e don't exist.

– Des, you don't believe that.

– I'm twelve. Nobody who's twelve believes In Father Christmas.

– Well that's a real pity. All the magic's gone out of everything.

It didn't take a brain surgeon to work that out.

Charlie got a *Raleigh Chopper*. He came round on it. It's got this little wheel on the front and a big one on the back. He did a wheelie and went right off the seat and banged his head on the concrete. He cried like a big baby. There was this lump on the back of his head like a gob stopper. It's got this gear stick like a car. It's dead ace. I got a *Scalextric*. But me dad just sat there in his paper hat, drinking beer and watching telly. He looked stupid and miserable.

– You need to get Colin to the doctor's, me gran said to me mam when we were in the kitchen. – He doesn't look right. Look at those eyes.

We all looked at his eyes.

– What you looking at? me dad said to me when he caught me looking at his eyes.

– Nothing.

He knew I was lying.

Auntie Mavis made me go out to the kitchen. I listened through the crack. I've listened to lots of people talking through cracks in doors. I'm getting dead good at it.

– It'll be drugs, Auntie Mavis said.

Me mam was shaking her head.

– He's not the man I married.

I could see me dad, and I could see the photo of their wedding in front of the church and everything. It was definitely him. Except he's got this belly now.

– Bob'll talk to him.

I could see Uncle Bob through the crack. He looked up at his mam or whoever it was he was talking to, and he said something. I think whoever it is, spoke to him, cause he shook his head. I think they told him to stay out of it. I wish I had someone in the sky I could talk to.

– Man to man, Mavis said.

Me mam and gran were looking at Uncle Bob. Me gran thinks Uncle Bob's only half a man cause he was in the home guard and he never stabbed no one. Not like me granddad who stabbed loads of blokes. I wondered why Uncle Bob didn't tell them about his shrapnel. He started rubbing his leg and pulling this face. He always rubs his leg when Auntie Mavis asks him to do owt.

I went in to see me dad later. He was putting the rigging onto the masts of the *Golden Hind*.

– She's almost sea-worthy, he said.

I saw it out the back. Me dad had moved the boat into the middle of the grass, and taken the cover off. You could see this crack in the hull.

– We can fix it, he said.

It ain't big enough for owt but the river.

He held up the *Golden Hind*.

– There, he said.

It had glue dripping off the masts. Me dad would never have glue dripping off the mast. His hand was shaking.

– These galleons were tiny. That boat out there is not much smaller. This boat, he said, holding it up, – went round the world.

I looked outside. It was raining.

– Auntie Mavis's going to get Uncle Bob to talk to you.

– What about? Cloud spotting?

– They think you're mentally ill.

– They think I'm mentally ill do they. They're twisted, Des. That's what they are. Twisted. What's he going to talk to me about? God? His mam, floating about on a bloody cloud? The war? Swanage?

– 'e's got shrapnel in is leg. It moves about. It was a Messerschmitt. 'alf is mates died.

Me dad just laughed.

– He's no more got shrapnel in his leg than I've got a plate in my head. The worst thing that ever happened to Bob was marrying Mavis. It's a life sentence. You get less for killing a man. If he'd killed Mavis early on he'd be out now with some bit of stuff from Nottingham.

Me dad gave me the *Golden Hind*.

– This is a present from Auntie Louise. Don't tell your mam. You know what she's like.

I knew what me mam was like. I knew she'd either go mad or pretend it wasn't happening.

# Pizza and Gravel

I was wondering what had happened to God, cause nothing bad had happened to me yet. Maybe He was having a rest after getting all the others. I counted them up. The list was getting longer. He'd got me granddad and Gaz Smedley, Eagle, Annie Gray's dad, and loads of other people. It don't make no sense to me that with all them people up there, why they can't do owt about all the problems. I mean, He's got a full team. I said a prayer. I prayed for Louise to get killed.

– You can't kill nobody, Charlie said. – You'll go to clink for yonks and you'll be an old bloke when you come out and 'ave to wear a nappy.

Charlie's granddad had to wear a nappy before he died. His mam said he became a baby again.

– That's what happens, Mrs Shaw said. – Once a grown up, twice a child.

Sounds okay to me if you get two lots of presents.

I knew where Louise lived, cause I followed me dad one day on me bike. It was when he was going to fix her car. I never saw him do owt to the car. He was always inside.

Louise lives with her mam and dad cause she can't get no bloke of her own; except for the bloke who was killed in the car. Me mam said Louise made it up cause she's a desperate woman. Now she's got me dad.

– I'm going to 'ave a ton of gravel tipped outside her drive, I said to Charlie. – Eagle did it with Slug. They don't ask for no money or owt till you get the gravel. Then they send you a bill.

We went to this phone box in Moretonside. This woman with a posh voice answered the phone.

I gave the phone to Charlie.

– You do it, I said. – She don't know you.

– Fuck off!

– But, they don't know you.

– They don't know you neither, you daft idiot.

They said they'd deliver the gravel tomorrow. It was dead easy. You can order gravel for anybody at any time.

– What's your name? the woman asked. I did it dead deep.

– Charles Shaw.

Charlie nearly pissed his pants. He was bricking himself all day cause he thought his dad would get a bill.

– They don't know where you live, I said to Charlie.

– They 'ave ways.

– They don't 'ave ways. They're a gravel company, not the bloody *Secret Service*.

They delivered the gravel cause me and Charlie went past on our bikes in the dark. Louise's car was in the drive. She couldn't get it out. Me dad was shovelling it out the way with this old bloke who looked like he was going to have a heart attack.

– It's yer dad, Charlie said.

I stopped and jumped off me bike and went into the bush. Charlie rode past, but me dad didn't recognise him. I was shaking. I didn't know what to do. I nearly went out and told him it was me. But I didn't.

When he'd gone in for sex, I slashed her tyres with me penknife that Dave Noakes gave me. I wished I hadn't. It was a bad thing to do. I know if they knew it was me, then they'd send me away like they did Eagle. I'd have to kill meself. I knew Miss Crowe wouldn't write in a book for me like she did Eagle, cause I've got socks and stuff.

I rode me bike as fast I could. I went the long way round,

right down to Findern and past the power station. I went by *Pastures*. I could hear them jumping up and down to make their brains vibrate. It was like thunder. It started to rain. They did that.

Me granddad said that if all the Japs stood on chairs and jumped off at the same time it'd crack the world into two pieces.

– The Japs could do that, he said. – They're brainwashed to do what they're told.

I could still hear the nutters jumping. Lightening flashed. I could see everything. There were these horrible faces pressed against the windows of the loony bin, with goggly eyes and horrible grey tongues. They were coming. I knew they were coming. The nutters were taking over!

# Dead Dog Floating

Even though I knew Miss Crowe loved Eagle, I still kept trying. Me gran said you should never give up. So I didn't. I really wanted her to like me.

It was nearly the end of the summer term. It was dead hot outside. Charlie had got hay fever, and was sending snot flying all over the classroom.

– I want you to write a poem, Miss Crowe said.

Everybody did this groan, cause we all hate writing poems. It's what puffs do for their boyfriends. There was this bloke called *Oscar Wilde* and they sent him to prison for bumming.

Billy Myers put his hand up.

– Miss, it's nearly the 'olidays. I don't know no poetry. They don't do poetry at the *carriage-side*.

– You won't be going to the bloody *carriage-side*, slaggy Scott said. – You'll be going to borstal where Eagle went.

She knew she'd said a bad thing cause she went like a beetroot.

– Then think of some, Billy. Miss Crowe said. – It doesn't have to rhyme. You know that. I've taught you how to do it. It's a story. It just needs to flow like a gentle stream. I want you to write something that means a lot to you; something that's been important. It could be a memorable day.

Miss Crowe was wearing this dead thin top. When she stood next to the window, the light shone through and you could see her knockers. We were all looking, even though they weren't very big.

Charlie asked me; – small or large knocker man?

He does that sort of thing. – big piss, little piss? – big knob, little knob? He's really into measuring things. One day he wants to be a scientist as well as a detective and arrest Mr West and his son.

Miss Crowe read this poem out. It was about a tree and the leaves and how they fell off in the winter and how the tree went to sleep.

– Best efforts, she said.

She sat down at her desk and started marking books. I could see her putting red lines across the pages.

– But Miss! Billy Myers kept saying.

– Just get on with it, Billy!

He started sniggering. Slaggy Scott prodded him.

– It just needs to flow like a gentle stream, Billy.

Miss Crowe let us go when we finished. She read Billy's and some of the others as they handed them in. She didn't even look at mine. I knew she wouldn't.

The next day she handed them back. I didn't look at mine for ages. I just left it upside down. When I turned it over I could see that she'd given me a gold star, three house points and a big red tick. I couldn't believe it.

– Good, she said. – Some of you could have tried a lot harder. But there's one person who put heart and soul into their poem. I want that person to come and read it to the class.

We all looked at Billy Myers.

– Derek, Miss Crowe said.

I was still looking at Billy. I didn't think she meant me, even though she'd said me name.

– Come on, Derek. Let's hear it from the horse's mouth.

– Me?

– Yes, you!

I knew I was going to get me head kicked in for this. It's only right you get your head kicked in for reading a poem out in the front of the class. It's what puffs do or Walter in *Dennis the Menace* or that Oscar Wilde.

– Do I have to, Miss?

– Go on Jackson, Billy Myers said. – Let's 'ear yer poem that flows like a gentle stream.

Miss Crowe pointed at him.

– Lip Billy! Actually, Derek's poem is about water.

I stood there and me hand was shaking. I did try dead hard. Now I wish I hadn't wrote what I did.

Miss Crowe turned me so I faced the class.

– So tell us what it's called, Derek.

I looked at them all. They were watching me, waiting.

– It's called *Dead Dog Floating*, Miss.

– And Derek has also drawn a beautiful picture.

Miss Crowe held it up for everybody to see.

by Derek Jackson 2C

## DEAD DOG FLOATING:

Dad and me went for a walk,
Down to the canal near by.
The lock gates have fallen into the water,
And they've stayed just where they lie.
It was hot and the water was smelly,
Dad said he was building a boat.
He said he was going to the South Pole,
And we needed to keep it afloat.
With a hull made of steel,
So that it cut through the ice.
Captain Scott took dogs and he paid the price.
But out of the reeds came this terrible thing,
We stood by the canal dead still.
It drifted out with flies on its skin.
Dad prodded it with his stick.
And it burst like a punctured balloon.
The smell made us feel dead sick.
It was green and it flew right into the sky,
And my dad stopped talking about his boat.
The green stuff it landed,
Right on my dad's coat.
And he shouted at the dead dog,
And he shouted at me.
But he still built the boat and he called it 'Hay fever'
But it never ever went on the sea.
And the dog was gone.
I looked all over the place,
But all I could see in the water,
Was my face.
I can still see it now even though everything's gone.

That dead dog floating,
That dead dog floating.

I finished it. No one said owt for ages. I just stood there. I
looked at Miss Crowe. She was just looking at me. I didn't
know why. Not right then.

— Derek, that is wonderful. Her voice was all shaky. I didn't
know what to say. — Is it a true story, Derek?
    — Yeah it's dead true. Dead 'onest.
She laughed and I thought she was taking the piss.
    — Dead honest! she said.
    — Yeah, dead 'onest!
Then she ruffled me hair and I knew; I knew she liked me.
It's the best thing that happened to me this year. I know other
things too. I know she was sad for Eagle; dead sad cause she
couldn't help him. Me dad says that people like that can't be
helped. I don't believe that no more. You can help people. Eagle
was angry cause his mam was killed on the zebra crossing. He
was angry cause his dad beat her, then she died. I'm angry. Not
as angry as Eagle. But I know what it feels like. Knowing that
Miss Crowe liked me, is the best feeling in the world. Then
Tina Scott started clapping. I thought she was taking the piss.
But she wasn't. It's cause Miss Crow said it was good, and
that was all right. I think Tina Scott knew other stuff too, but
she never said. I feel bad for calling her a slag. I quite like her
really. She'd never like me.
    — Sit down, Derek, Miss Crowe said. — You never know, you
might become a writer one day.
    Everybody laughed.
    I could never be a writer. Not in a million million years.
Amen.

I followed Miss Crowe one night. It was dark. I think she saw me cause I fell out the bush I was sitting in. This bloke came up to her. I was going to run at him and save her cause I wanted to be a hero. It was so she'd like me even more. She held his hand and he snogged her. They were at it for ages at the bus stop. I ran off. I felt stupid. I wish I hadn't seen it. But you can't un-see something. It's like you can't un-know something once it's happened.

## The bribe and the Matchbox cars

Me dad didn't really talk to me mam; not proper anyway after he came back. Me mam told everybody how happy they were. The phone still rang when me mam was out, and it went quiet when I answered it. When I gave the phone to me dad, he started talking to this bloke who'd got the wrong number. He thought I was stupid. He still does. In the end, the phone calls stopped. Louise Draper got what she wanted.

It was the summer holidays and it was dead hot. Me dad had taken the day off work. He was sorting his stuff out, like he did. I was cleaning me bike. He cooked dinner.

– You should go out on your bike Des or you'll rub it away. You'll make the metal so thin you'll wear it out.

– Can that really 'appen?

– Course it can. There was this rider in the *Tour de France* who polished his wheels so hard, they collapsed just before the finish line.

It was one of his stories. It was bollocks.

– We could get the boat out, I said.

I knew he wasn't interested cause he'd put it away again without fixing the crack.

– I'm sorting stuff out, he said. – I never get time. You go for a ride on your bike. It'll do you good. Blow the cobwebs away.

– I ain't got no cobwebs.

– You know what I mean. Don't be clever.

We had dinner and I helped me dad do the dishes.

– You should go on your bike, Des. I've got a lot to do. Come back later.

He kept going on and on.

He was packing things in boxes and putting them back in the shed. He kept looking at me.

– Order, Des. Order's the thing. If you don't have order then you have chaos. If you have chaos you have no control. That's the trouble; people don't have control.

He just carried on doing what he was doing. I sat on me bike and I watched him. He looked like he was a very long way away. When he came up to me, he looked like one of them people with a shrunken head.

– You need to do something, Des. Look, go for a ride. Get some sweets or something. Find Charlie.

– He's gone to Tenby.

– Tenby.

– It's in Wales.

– I know where it is.

– We could go to Tenby.

Me mam kept going on about going on holiday.

– We could go to Tenby. You're right. Maybe we will.

– When then?

– We'll see.

It meant no. It always meant no. We weren't going to Tenby. We weren't going nowhere.

– I ain't got no money.

– If you carry on talking like that, you never will have. They earn ten quid a week in the dirt and grime; if they're lucky.

He took out his bent wallet from his back trouser pocket. He got out a five quid note.

– Do you still collect those matchbox toys?

– Yeah.

He gave me the five quid note.

– Go out and get a couple.

I laughed and held it out.
– It's five quid!
– I know.
– But it's massive.
He hugged me, and kissed the top of me head.
– Then spend it wisely.
He said things like that.
– Cor, thanks! You sure?
– Sure as eggs is eggs.
I got on me bike and sprinted up the hill. Me bike shone dead bright in the sun. I stopped at the top of the hill. I saw me dad wave. I waved back.

I did this massive circuit, down these winding lanes where I pretended I was Barry Sheene on his *Suzuki*. I ended up on the A6. There was this kid on a motorbike killed on the A6. He missed the corner and lay dead in the woods for ages until some tramp found him. He stank like Charlie's socks. So did the tramp.

I went right round into Edmeston where Auntie Mavis says that evil roams the streets, and where all the criminals live. I went along Harvey Road and past the chippy. I could smell the chips. They have these massive fish that Charlie reckons they inject to make bigger. Sometimes they have two heads!

I parked me bike outside the toy shop and went in. They always look at you dead suspicious, cause they've had a lot of nicking from kids. When the bloke behind the counter saw I was on me own, he didn't follow me like he usually does.

On one wall it's covered with matchbox cars and things. They're in alphabetic order so you can find the one you want. I saw it straight away. The bloke came over.

– Don't touch the stack, duck. You'll have the lot down. It took me two days to do it. Are you thinking of buying something?

– Yeah, I am.

– Most of the kids want to take them out, poke them and put them back. These are collectors items, these are. They're not for messing about with. He looked at me for ages. – Do you get me?

I showed him the five quid.

– That's five pounds.

– I know.

– Where'd you get five pounds?

– Me dad gave it to me.

– It's a lot of money.

– I know.

– You sure your dad gave it to you?

– Dead 'onest. I saw the *Porsche Carrera*. – Can I 'ave a look at that one as well?

– What do we say?

I had the cash.

– Please.

He got it down. I followed him to the counter. He got them out and held them like they were diamonds.

– Can I have an 'old?

– Let's see your hands, he said. I held them out. – Grease makes them rust. He gave them to me.

The *Volkswagen* was white and the *Porsche* was gold. It was hard to decide, so I bought both of them. They cost one quid. I could have bought eight more.

The bloke put them in a massive brown paper bag and gave me me change.

– Remember to give the rest back to your dad.

– It's mine, I said.

– Do you want me to ring him?

– If you want. 'e's in.

– Then maybe I will.

He didn't have me phone number, and I didn't give it to him. He never rang me dad.

I stood outside the shop with me bag. It was dead hot. I thought about Charlie in the sea at Tenby. I got out the Volkswagen. It was just like *Herbie* from the *Love Bug*, which I never saw cause me mam said it was rude. She says anything with love in is rude. 'specially now, since me dad went. She says that we get to see everything now and there's nowt left to the imagination. We went to see *The Railway Children* for me birthday cause it wasn't rude like *Steptoe and Son*. When their dad comes out the mist at the end, I could see that me mam was crying with tears, and all me mates were there. She thought it was me dad coming out the mist. I could tell her he ain't coming out of no mist. Not ever.

– Stop! I said.

She kept on crying, so we sat there in the pictures till me mam could wipe her face. I'll never ever watch *The Railway Children* again. Amen.

I held the car up to the sky. I could see right inside to the seats with the stripes on and the steering wheel. I know they're only plastic really, but they look dead real. When you open the door, you can even see the gear stick.

I was looking through the car. I could see the shops on the other side of the road. I saw Annie Gray's mam walking dead fast with her bag. She had the dress with the big flowers on and this dead grim look on her face. I think she was crying. I moved the car, so I could see the rest of the road. Then I saw him. I saw me dad's car. It was at the traffic lights up the road opposite the *Crest of the Wave*. The traffic lights went from red to green. He started moving dead slow like he does. I put me car back in the bag. I went to the edge of the road. I waved when he went past. I know he looked, but he didn't stop. I knew then what he'd done. I knew it was all me fault. Me heart was in me mouth.

Me legs were like jelly on the way home. I hid the cars in the shed and I went into the house. You know when something's wrong. You just do. They say that houses can keep secrets like a real person. When something happens inside, you can tell. I could tell that something had happened.

I went up to me mam and dad's bedroom. I looked in me dad's wardrobe. It was empty, except for some old books and the coat hangers. I looked for a note, like people leave when they go. I couldn't find one. I knew then he was never coming back. He'd had enough with explaining. He'd even taken *South with Scott*.

I didn't know what to do. I ran round the house. I don't know why. It was Friday. Me mam always used to go to the hairdressers on a Friday. She don't go no more cause she say's it reminds her of the day. It makes her want to scream. She cuts it herself now. It makes her look like one of them people from *Pastures*. It's cause they're jumping up and down all the time, and it's dead hard to cut their hair straight. Me mam don't care no more. Just like Annie Gray's mam. They might be best friends one day. They'll probably set up a club for skeleton people.

I sat down in me mam's chair. I didn't cry. I've stopped crying. There's no point. You just get sore eyes.

# The bloody little idiot, the social ladder, and the Freemasons

I rang Auntie Mavis.

– What do you mean he's gone again?

– 'e's gone.

– When?

– Today. 'e went this af'. I saw 'im go.

– He's probably gone into town.

– Not with all is clothes 'e ain't.

– All his clothes?

– Even 'is pants!

– I'm on my way.

I looked at the kitchen clock, which is seven minutes fast so we're never late. It was half-past four.

Auntie Mavis had the dog with her and Uncle Bob.

– Hello, prince, he said. – Grim business.

Auntie Mavis gave him one of her looks. She went up the stairs and started slamming doors just like me mam does.

– He's right, she said, when she came downstairs. – The bugger's gone. Thief in the night.

– 'e went this af', I said.

Uncle Bob looked up at his mam. The dog farted and filled the kitchen with deadly gas. Auntie Mavis opened the back door to let it out cause me mam's sellotaped all the windows.

– It's all the meat, Uncle Bob said.

– Take him into the garden, Bob. I need to talk to Derek.

Bob took Bob into the garden.

– Bob's got a twisted bowel, Derek. We might lose him,

Auntie Mavis said.

– Uncle Bob?

I knew there was something really wrong with him. It wasn't just the shrapnel.

– Not Uncle Bob. The dog! It's not the meat. He's rotting on the inside. Uncle Bob's pretending it's not happening. He loves that dog.

That's bollocks. I see him kick it. He hates that dog as much as he hates Auntie Mavis. Uncle Bob wants to go back to Swanage with a bit of stuff from Nottingham.

– Look, she said. – This'll definitely kill your mam. She can't take any more. But me and Bob are going out. We can't stay. She put her mouth dead close to me ear so that it tickled when she breathed. – You can't tell anyone, but it's a *Masonic Dinner*. Bob's been invited to become a *Freemason*. It's because we're on the social ladder, and we have to go. We've got to be there. We have to be seen. It's a jacket and tie job. He's getting his trowel and apron and everything in a few weeks. Then they go to these secret meetings and do favours for each other. Harry Pickard's one. They're the one's with the Formica everywhere. That'll be us soon. She held up her finger right next to me nose. – Don't tell anyone.

– That Uncle Bob's a *Freemason*?

– That's right, Derek. There's a good boy.

– He lays bricks?

– Don't be clever, Derek. Everyone knows about the Masons. It's for the top people.

– On the ladder?

– Yes, Derek, on the ladder.

– But who's going to tell me mam.

– She knows, Auntie Mavis said.

– Does she?

– Of course she does.

– When d'you tell her.

– Months ago.

It didn't make any sense.

– He only left this af'.

Auntie Mavis looked at me dead funny.

– What?

– You can't 'ave told 'er months ago.

– Not about your dad. About Bob and the Masons. Bob was going to recommend Colin. But not now. Never. It's not possible. Or for you, Derek, sadly. These things follow you through life. You're marked. It's like a disease. Your dad's landed you all in it. They throw people like your dad out of the Masons onto the streets. They never work again. Not in this country anyway. Some coloured bloke will get his job.

– Who's gonna to tell me mam that me dad's gone?

Uncle Bob came back into the kitchen.

– Bob's been sick again. I've put him in the car.

– So I've got to tell me mam that me dad's gone?

– I'm sorry, prince, Uncle Bob said.

Me dad was right; Uncle Bob's a waste of space. He looked up at his mam and said something. He smiled like she'd told him to get the hell out of there, while the going was good.

Then they went. Auntie Mavis revved the Austin Maxi and the dog slid around in the back. It was sick on the window.

I rode round on me bike for ages until it was nearly half-past six. It was scouts, but Charlie wasn't coming cause he was in Tenby with his dad and his fat mam. It was cooking at scouts; sausages on the open fire in the woods and then outdoor games.

Me mam walked round the corner. Her hair looked like a brillo pad on the top of her head. She looked like *Dennis the*

*Menace*. She knew as soon as she saw me, cause she stopped dead and dropped her bag on the ground. She put her hand up to her gob. I ran out and picked up her bag. I didn't want to stop in the street.

– Come on, Mam, I said.

She didn't move. I wondered if she'd have one of them nervous breakdowns. I thought I might have to lean her up against the wall.

– Tell me he's not gone, she said.

– 'e's not gone.

– He's gone hasn't he?

– 'e's gone.

We could have been there all day. I pulled her arm, and she started walking across the road.

– I was out, I said. – I went for a ride on me bike.

She stopped dead.

– Why? She was starting to shout.

– 'e didn't want to be 'ere, in this 'ouse. 'e wanted to be somewhere else. 'e wanted to go to the South Pole, but 'e's probably gone to Moretonside. Like you said; it's where they all go.

She looked like she was going to laugh, but she made this noise like a creaking door. She just stared at me with her eyes dead wide.

– You bloody little idiot, she shouted. – You bloody little fool!

She picked her bag up and threw it down the drive.

– What do you mean? I said.

– What do I mean! What the hell do I mean!

She was yelling now. All the neighbours would be listening. I didn't care.

– I don't know what you mean.

– You let him go!

– I didn't let 'im go. I went out on me bike.

– Why? Why did you go out on your bike?

– 'e gave me five quid. I went to buy *matchbox cars*.

Her mouth was open, but she didn't say owt at all. She looked like me dead goldfish.

– I bought a *Volkswagen Beetle* and a *Porsche Carrera*.

I don't know why I said it, cause it was a stupid thing to say. I was glad I'd hid them. She was shouting dead loud now. Just shouting the same thing over and over again. I couldn't listen to it no more. She started fading into the distance. All I could see was her mouth moving like Brenda's Jim, behind the double glazing. I think I closed me eyes. I was in this garden. The sun was shining. I was sitting under this massive rhubarb plant, eating it and dipping the end in this white sugar. There was lemonade, and it was cold and fizzy. That all disappeared, and I was in this field. There were daisies and buttercups. I was on a hill. I could see the sea. I couldn't hear me mam at all cause she wasn't there. I think it might have been Tenby even though I've never been. Then I heard her. She was shaking me. I came back. We were still in the drive. She was still shouting.

– So he gave you five pounds!

– Yeah.

– You took it!

– 'e gave it to me.

– He bribed you.

– What does that mean?

– He paid you off to get out of the way while he sneaked off like a thief in the night.

– That's what Auntie Mavis said.

She pointed at me and her finger was shaking. We were still standing in the drive. A woman called Mrs Shirley walked up the hill on the other side of the street dead slow, rubber-necking me mam and me. Mrs Shirley shook her head. I think she was thinking what me mam thought about the Gowers with all their door slamming. She was yelling in the street, which is much worse. It was bound to affect the house prices.

– Mavis knows!

– I rang 'er. I didn't know what else to do. She came over, but she 'ad to go cause Uncle Bob's a Mason. They've got this dinner. If they don't go they'll kick 'im out. She said me dad wouldn't ever be a Mason cause of what 'e's done.

Me mam made this noise again. I think she wanted me dad to be a Mason, so she could go to the dinners. – The dog's got a twisted bowel, I said.

Me mam made this snorting noise.

– What's the bloody dog got to do with it?

– It puked up the window in their car.

– So Mavis knows.

– I s'pose so.

– My God! The whole world will know by tomorrow.

Me mam opened the back door. I wheeled me bike down the drive.

She stood in the doorway.

– Bloody blood money. He paid you off Derek. You took it!

It was a good job me dad wasn't there cause she slammed the back door dead hard and the frame actually cracked. It was bound to happen sometime. It's not been fixed. Me mam says it reminds her of how bad things can get.

I went to get me *matchbox cars* from the shed. I stroked the Gowers' cat, but it scratched the back of me hand and made it bleed little beads of blood. I put the cars under an upside down plant pot. I think they're still there. I didn't want to see them no more. I went to scouts cause me mam didn't stop me, and we built this massive fire. After, we played hide and seek in the wood, but they never found me cause I hid dead high in this tree. When it went dark I went home. It's not the same without Charlie.

## *The colour telly as big as the flicks, Room to swing a cat, and the truth.*

After all that, me mam started on what me gran calls the slippery slope. I told me mam that I was going out to find me dad.

I rode me bike dead slow. The torch had broken and me back light was flickering cause the battery had leaked on the inside and it was rusting. I didn't know where I was going really, except I had this street name that Auntie Mavis heard in the hairdresser's. Me mam hardly speaks to her now after what happened. She's angry cause Auntie Mavis told loads of people so it made her own marriage look better than it is.

– Everybody knows the truth, me mam said. – There's nothing in that marriage. There hasn't been for years. The whole thing's an act.

I still go and see them. Me mam don't know. I like Auntie Mavis and Uncle Bob.

When she stopped shouting after me dad went, I told me mam about Louise and the field and the phone calls. Me mam rang her. Louise just lied like a pig. She said it was me imagination. Me mam heard what she wanted to hear cause grown ups are like that. It's just like the Emperor's story all the time.

On me way to find me dad, I went down this drain and fell off me bike. It buckled the wheel so that it wobbled, and I scraped me *Doc Martens* on the kerb. It started to rain. Me hands were freezing. I stopped at this garage and I went to the coloured bloke at the counter.

– I'm looking for Conner Street, I said.

The bloke looked at me and then at his watch.

– Why you want to be going there?

– I'm going to find me dad.

– Find him? He is lost?

– No 'e ain't lost. Me mam needs 'im back.

The bloke shook his head like I was mental. I wanted tell him it was everybody else and not me. He got this map out and put on his glasses. We found Conner Street, and he drew this map on the back of this piece of card he ripped off a crisp box. They were cheese and onion. It was in Moretonside. Me mam was right. It's where everybody goes when they piss off. I told me mam it was a map of Leicester. I told a lie.

I pedalled dead hard even though I didn't want to find him. When I got to Moretonside I could smell the curry, which me mam says is muck. It smelt dead nice. There were these bright shops with sparkly dresses. It's much nicer than *The Main Centre*.

I stopped under a street light and looked at the map. It was two streets away. I got off me bike and pushed it past the first one, and then to the end of the other. There was a sign that said *CONNER STREET*. I knew it was the one. Auntie Mavis knew it as well. I think she's probably even been to have a look. When it comes to trouble, Auntie Mavis never gets her facts wrong. She checks them out.

I didn't have a number, but I knew which one it was. I could feel this massive lump in me throat, and the hammer in me heart was banging like mad. They didn't have no gardens. I could see the floodlights from the *Baseball Ground* over the tops of the roofs. I stopped outside number fifteen. There was a light on inside and there were net curtains. I could see a can of *Double Diamond* on the windowsill. I knew it was me dad's place cause Louise's blue mini was parked up outside.

I waited for ages cause I felt sick. I took a big breath and knocked on the door. The curtains moved. I saw me dad at the window. He knew it was me. I could see the look on his face. It was shock.

The door had this window in it with swirly glass. It makes people look like they're under water with massive glasses on. I could see them both moving around. I heard footsteps on the stairs.

I waited for ages in the cold. I didn't think he was coming. I knocked again. Me dad opened the door.

– Des, he said. I was shaking all over. – I didn't expect this.

Me mam said I had to be mad with him.

– No. I know you didn't.

– How did you find me?

– Auntie Mavis, I said. – She 'eard it at the 'airdressers. Can I come in?

Me dad stood out the way.

– It's not much, Des.

Me hands were like blocks of ice.

– I'm freezing, I said.

He looked out into the street.

– You'll need to bring your bike in.

– What, in the 'ouse!

– It'll get pinched if you don't.

I got it and wheeled it inside. He had no carpets on the floor. There were two deck chairs in the middle of the room in front of this massive TV. I looked at the little sign on the front: *Philips Technicolor*.

– You've got a colour telly!

– It's only rented, Des.

– But it's still colour! Everybody rents 'em. They cost thousands to buy 'em new.

– It's only just colour. It's not a very good one.

– Still colour, I said. – You can't 'ave an only just colour telly.

– It's just a telly.

– We ain't got no colour telly. Me mam'll go mad if she knows you've got a colour telly.

– Then don't tell her.

I saw the massive speakers on bricks and the hi fi in the middle.

– You've got an 'i fi as well!

– It's borrowed, Des. From a friend.

– Who?

– You don't know them.

I was shaking like a leaf and I wanted to piss.

– I saw the car.

– The car?

– The car. I know whose car it is. The blue mini.

– Des, it's hired.

Me dad was lying like a pig. I was sweating dead hard.

– But yours is parked down the street.

Then I heard her cough. I hoped she choked on her own tongue, cause she was sitting on her fat arse upstairs waiting for me to go.

– I know she's 'ere.

– Who, Des? Who do you think is here?

He was talking to me like I was some dozy twat from the tech.

– Louise. We saw you in the field. I know it was her on the phone all those times when you said it was a wrong number.

– Some of them were. She needed someone to talk to.

– She can talk to 'er mam and dad.

One day when he was talking to these wrong numbers, I heard him say *soon your sun will shine* and I can't get it out of me head. Your sun will shine, your sun will shine. Your fucking sun will shine!!!!!!! I thought I was going mad like everybody else.

– I want you to get 'er down, I said dead loud so she could hear me.

– Des, don't do this.

– Get 'er down!

I didn't know what I was going to say, but I could hear me mam in me head. I was doing this for her. *Get her down! Get her down!* she kept saying.

Me dad went up the stairs. I could hear them talking. They were whispering like me dad used to do on the phone. I thought they might be planning to murder me. I tapped me jacket. I forgot to bring the knives.

They came down. Louise stood in the doorway. She was wearing a *Derby County* pompom hat. She looked like a bloody tea pot.

– I'm just going, she said. – I only called to see your dad. She was grinning.

I pointed at her.

– No. Me mam's dying. She's like a stick. She looks like Annie Gray's mam who walks up and down London Road in 'er summer dress.

Louise laughed. She's got this laugh like *Pinky and Perky* and they're pigs too!

– Derek, what on earth are you talking about? Who's Annie Gray?

– She's this girl at our school. She ran away to Blackpool and everything and 'er mam's gone mad…

Me dad grabbed me arm.

– Des, it's okay.

I pulled me arm away.

I pointed at the colour telly.

– I'm talking about this. You've got a colour telly. We ain't got no colour telly or an 'i fi or owt like that. I've got to do something about this.

Louise looked at me dad, then she looked at me.

– What are you going to do about it, Derek?

I couldn't think of anything.

– No more gravel or pizzas, I hope.

– I'm going to call the Police.

Me dad went into his kitchen. I followed him. It was dead small. I didn't want to be in the same room as her.

– You couldn't swing a cat in here, Des. You can see how I live.

Then it happened. I could see me dad swinging this black cat round and round and round and round 'til it hit its head on the corner of one of the cupboards, and its brains came flirting out its ears.

Me dad took a can out of a box.

– Here, he said.

It was a can of *Double Diamond*.

– It's beer, I said, as if he hadn't noticed.

– Time you had one, Des.

– I'm only twelve.

He opened it and poured it into a glass and gave it to me. When I got back into the room Louise was gone. She'd made her escape like the coward she is.

– I don't drink beer any more, me dad said. He went to the window and picked up the can of *Double Diamond*. – Been there for weeks. I'm in training, getting fit. I'm thinking of joining a club. Should have done it years ago.

The beer felt warm in me belly. It was dead nice.

– Me mam wants you to come 'ome. I came cause she can't cope.

– We'll see.

– You always say that. It means no.

– No it doesn't. We'll see means we'll see.

– It does. You always say it when you mean no. I can't tell 'er yer not coming 'ome.

Then he said it. I ain't ever heard him say it before.

– I'm not coming home, Des. Think how hard it is for me.

The *Double Diamond* was making me feel nice. He filled me glass again. I drank it dead quick cause I wanted the pictures to come. I didn't want to talk to him no more about owt. Me dad's voice started getting quieter 'til he sounded like this little bloke, miles away. I was on this cliff with this massive ice cream with a flake. I could see the sea. There were these seagulls flapping round and one came down and sat next to me. I was sitting in its nest. I could smell the sea and the sand like you can, and it made me feel dead happy. Then me dad came back.

– Finish your beer, Des.

I couldn't drink it all so I left the rest on the table.

– You've got big speakers, I said.

– Next time you come, you can bring an LP and we can listen to it.

– I ain't got no LP.

– Well you can listen to one of mine. There's Glen Miller and Harry James and Mantovani and James Last.

I ain't heard of any of them.

He opened the front door. It was dead cold. I wheeled me bike out and I felt dizzy.

– It'll be okay, Des. You'll see. Don't let go of your dreams.

– What about the South Pole?

I knew the answer. It was a stupid question for a little kid who knows his dad has swapped him for an ugly cow called Louise Draper.

– I'm there, he said. He tapped the side of his head. – In my head I'm there.

I knew what he meant. The places in your head are better than the real ones. I knew then that I couldn't ever go with him.

I rode me bike dead slow. I didn't want to go back home. I didn't know what to say. I didn't believe anything me dad said no more. I put me bike in the shed. I did think about one thing me dad used to say. He said *face the facts, Des*. He always said *face the facts*. So I did.

# *Once we practice to deceive*

## Back on the landing, right now

I'm staying at the bottom of the bed. I don't want to sit next to me mam.
– Well? she says.
– Mam.
– Yes.
She's expecting me to say something.
– I've got to tell you, I say.
I can hear her breathing. I can see her thin arms and her spindly fingers. It's not me fault I keep thinking. It's not me fault. Then I think it is; it's me fault I didn't bring him back. It's me fault that I didn't make her listen about me dad and that slag in the field. I've told a lot of lies. I think about *Jack the Ripper*. When you've killed one person it can't make no difference if you kill another and another and another.
– I looked all over the place. I rode me bike and me torch broke and it got cold. Auntie Mavis got it wrong. It wasn't the place she said. It's the 'air dryers; they make a load of noise. You can't 'ear owt; not really. You can't 'ear yerself think.
– You're saying you didn't find him then?
That's all she says. She's not angry or owt. She says it dead quiet. I don't know if I'm protecting the innocent, or I'm going to kill her. I don't know if I care.
– No Mam, I didn't find 'im.
She just lies back down and puts her face in her pillow.
I leave her and go to me room. I get into bed without cleaning me teeth. I can hear me mam making this noise. It

goes quiet.

I close me eyes and the sea comes with the sunshine shining on it. I'm sitting in the field with the buttercups all on me own. I know that me dad's right, cause I'm there too, in me head. I can't leave me mam; not yet. One day though, I'll find that field. I'll do things I say I'm going to do cause I know me dad's never going to the South Pole, not with Louise in her fuckin' *Derby County* pom pom hat! That's for deffo.

I know I told a lie. The truth is; I didn't tell it to protect the innocent like me mam says. I ain't telling no more, cause as Eagle said *after we done it for quite a bit we get dead good at it.*

Night night.

# Acknowledgements

*Dead Dog Floating* has been my favourite book to write so far. Derek Jackson spoke to me and I told his story, which I hope is reflected with the love and affection intended. I know it's a bit different, but as far as I'm concerned that's what life's about, and should be celebrated.

I grew up in Derby and I hope the book embraces the spirit of the place in the 70's when we had the *Baseball Ground* and Brian Clough. Much I know has changed since, but I hope the humour and irony of my home town still remains embedded in its heart. I'm sure it does.

My thanks go to my agent Sonia Land at the Sheil Land Literary agency, and her wonderful and always helpful assistant, Gabrielle Hancock. This is a significant departure from my first book, so thank you for running with this one. It means a great deal to me.

I would like to thank my writing friends and colleagues at the inspiring Exeter Writers for their enthusiasm about this work, and especially to Margaret James and Sophie Duffy who told me in no uncertain terms to 'get this out there!', and to all my writing friends when I doubt it, who remind me that this is a good thing to do.

This writing malarkey can be a lonely affair, and without the support of the people dear to me, I wonder if I would have made it this far- on so many levels. Thank you to all of you who have stuck with me and my ramblings for so long. Finally to my family, Ann, Grace, Eve, Hana and Otto. You are my reason.

12703780R00167

Printed in Great Britain
by Amazon.co.uk, Ltd.,
Marston Gate.